P9-DOB-088

THE
DEVOTED

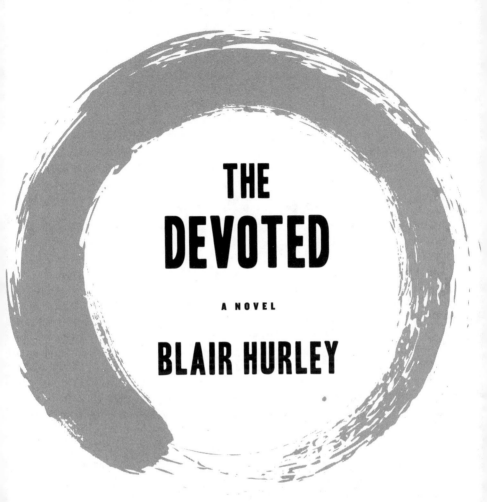

THE
DEVOTED

A NOVEL

BLAIR HURLEY

W. W. NORTON & COMPANY

INDEPENDENT PUBLISHERS SINCE 1923

NEW YORK | LONDON

For information about permission to reproduce selections from this book, write to
Permissions, W. W. Norton & Company, Inc., 500 Fifth Avenue, New York, NY 10110

For information about special discounts for bulk purchases, please contact
W. W. Norton Special Sales at specialsales@wwnorton.com or 800-233-4830

Manufacturing by LSC Communications, Harrisonburg
Book design by Fearn Cutler de Vicq
Production manager: Beth Steidle

ISBN 978-0-393-65159-1

W. W. Norton & Company, Inc., 500 Fifth Avenue, New York, N.Y. 10110
www.wwnorton.com

W. W. Norton & Company Ltd., 15 Carlisle Street, London W1D 3BS

1 2 3 4 5 6 7 8 9 0

For my mother

PROLOGUE

The Master wears the same navy robes that have been worn in Japan for eight hundred years; he pours the tea and rings the bell in the traditional manner, and says a prayer to the four directions, for the sake of all the sentient beings in all the known universes. Over the years he has grown accustomed to the kinds of people drawn to a Zen center in the surrounding neighborhoods of Boston: the determinedly healthy and the chronically ill, the spiritually restless, the sixties nostalgics, the Japanophiles, the addicts, the survivors, the bums. Zen, he tells the small crowd of regulars arranged in neat kneeling lines in the meditation room, offers no promises of redemption. If you are looking for absolution, go to a confessional; if you have bad dreams, go to a therapist; if you are seeking comfort, you will find no cozy visions of heaven here.

It is one of many Zendos in the Boston area, just one worn shop front among dozens of other sunny lofts and damp church basements, converted YMCAs and airless attic spaces. It's surprising, in this Catholic town, with a church on every corner, how many back rooms are filled with hopeful students in lotus pose, how many swinging signs with Buddha faces can welcome you in. It all depends on what you're looking for.

The Master decided long ago that he would not offer miracles. He's searching for excellence. The next student ready for his teaching. It's been a while since he's seen what he's looking for: something ineffable. Each week he chants and rings the bell, but he's secretly gazing out over the bent heads, studying form and technique the way a breeder studies horses in a paddock, weighing and evaluating.

There's the new girl. After a month or so of *zazen,* seated meditation, with her in attendance, he realizes he's started searching for her at the door before he begins the ritual chant. At first she came in a sweatshirt and jeans, her hair in a greasy ponytail, a wary scowl on her face, not sure whether to take all of it—the place, the people, him— seriously. A good quiet body. College-aged? She watched him when she was supposed to lower her head. He avoided her gaze when she sought it from the back of the room; he kept his eyes on the bell, the twisting motion of his hands as he chanted, like trying to hold water and slip it from palm to palm to palm. They were playing a game: she showing him she was not impressed, he showing her he wasn't, either.

He told the room, Nothing arises or ceases. Like you: You are everything you have ever been. You can't run away from yourself.

He could feel her burning attention. She was still and serious, weighing his words, testing the truth of them against her own life. Many people come to his Zendo to be soothed, but he does not think she is interested in a balm.

She has one foot she doesn't like to put her full weight on, and walks with a light deer step, hitching her hip to one side. Reddish hair and fine features, a large trembling mouth and a longing look. She's too thin but not underfed—merely that there is no one cooking for her at home, no reason to cook for herself. She's pretty in a half-formed way.

Like any good showman, he knows when he has people, when they are his.

What is he looking for? A willingness to learn; a heart-deep hunger.

One meditation session, he passes by close and murmurs in her ear, "With that sweatshirt on, I can't see your body. I can't correct your posture."

She flushes and straightens, and he sees the words take effect. The next week she wears a long black skirt and a white blouse. Church clothes. He can see her thin caving shoulders, her slumping shy girl's posture. He touches the small of her back, gently straightening her.

Now there is a line of current between them, he reciting at the front of the room, she listening at the back, her eyes never leaving his face until it is time to close them, to sink into the quiet surrender of meditation. His voice guides his students into various private corners of their lives. He tells them to put down the burdens of their sins. If it helps, to lay them at his feet. They come to him because they have the spiritual impulse, which is another way of saying they need someone to tell them they are good people.

As soon as the other practitioners get up, they are on their cell phones, reassuring children that they'll be home soon, telling husbands and wives what to put on the stove. But she has no one to call. She laces up her shoes in a thoughtful silence and walks home with her hands in the pockets of her coat, rain on her shoulders.

He invites her to assist him in the ceremony one day. She comes early to learn how to pour the tea into the ritual bowl, every movement careful, measured, a chant humming on the lips. He explains the symbolism: the careful stirring represents purity and harmony of the tea's ingredients. The offering of the cup, respect and compassion. The little silence that follows each sip, contemplation and tranquillity. It's complicated and arcane, but she nods gamely and jokes, "Very Catholic."

Then he tells her to forget the symbolism, because when you are pouring tea you are doing nothing but pouring tea. This is what makes the ceremony so difficult. She's scattered in a dozen directions, he can tell.

He asks casually, as if making conversation, "Who were you before your parents were born?"

"I was—" Her hand trembles as she tilts the cast iron pot. She's trying so hard to do it right. "I was nobody."

"Wrong."

"But what about—"

He shakes his head. "Tea. Just tea."

She bites her lip and tries again, and he watches the back of her neck, the hairs straggling down into her Peter Pan collar.

Then there's another day when she comes early, wet with rain, and confronts him in the back hallway of the Zendo. Practitioners are not supposed to be back here without his invitation but here she is, bowing deeply, her body rising and falling as she breathes. She must have run here. She must have felt an urgent need for something more than comfort. "I need to know some things—" She must be searching for a little grace.

"You'd better come in," he says, and holds open the door.

He likes her. He thought he was considering her, trying her out, but now he realizes the decision has already been made.

PART ONE

THE ESCAPE

Tuesday was Christmas, so Nicole's usual meeting at the Zendo had been moved to Christmas Eve. Her entire week revolved around the arrival of this day, her visit to the center, her meditation on the rubbery hand-me-down yoga mats, her Master passing by like a chill wind. The other practitioners sat kneeling or cross-legged around her, known by their breath and their bodies, strangers otherwise. Same laboring quest for quiet, same mixture of dread and delight. But this night Buffy had invited everyone to a holiday party in the city after class, and she was determined to be sociable. She came late and teetered on a high, precarious stoop after pushing the doorbell, not sure if this was the right house among the line of matching townhouses. Then Buffy's blond head bobbed into the window frame. "Nicole! What a surprise! I'm so glad you've come."

She left her coat in the foyer and followed Buffy through a smart black-and-white tiled hall to the living room. Space was dear in these Back Bay apartments, but the ceilings were high, the crown moldings and many-paned windows old and elegant. "Look who's joined us," Buffy said to the gathering in the living room, and Nicole waved, feeling their surprise. She remembered walking into cozy Christmas homes like this one as a child, her brother, Paul, too skinny for his suit, she itching at the toilet paper her mother had stuffed into the sleeves of her party dress. She remembered yanking up the crotch of the white tights that crept closer to her knees every year. Then, too, the adults had greeted her with a benevolent boredom before she found herself picking at the seam of a fancy couch in the corner, waiting for it all to be over.

Buffy poured her a glass of wine. "How is your work, Nicole? Remind me, what do you do?" Buffy was always kind in an absent-minded way. When they were all putting on their coats after a session, she asked the people around her, "How was that for you today? How was that for you?" She was a little bony for forty, spare as a marathoner, dressed now in a red skirt suit with large gold buttons, touching Nicole's elbow like an old friend.

"Oh, mainly I work in sales. For a shoe store," she added, naming the place but dropping the "Discount" from the title.

"Sounds like a hard place to stay Zen," someone else said, and Buffy inserted, "Try my house when the kids get home from school!"

The kids were there, actually, a girl and a boy fondling the presents under the Christmas tree. They didn't look up or seem bothered.

People lounged around the room or hovered in the doorway. They commiserated cheerfully about how hard it was to find time in the day to meditate. What is the thing that pops up in your mind?

Commercial jingles, several said. Television plots. Is that a freckle or a mole? The relentless urge to check one's phone for new messages. "The thought I have most often," said Nicole, "is me telling myself, 'Stop thinking.'" That made them laugh. She smiled in confusion, looking away. She knew she was an oddity, but she hadn't expected to be entertaining to George and Amy and Buffy, all of them watching her, imagining what her life might be like. She had been in the Zendo longer than any of them; she'd met her Master when her father died, ten years ago. She'd never missed a session since. Heads often turned to see her at the back of the room, chanting words in Japanese or Pali she knew better than Hail Marys now.

"I can't stop looking at the Master half the time," said Frances. She was in her thirties and appeared younger: something bubbly and teenaged about the lift of her shoulders, her ready blush. "He's not bad to look at!"

They debated whether the Master could be called handsome. He was like a surf instructor, ruddy and muscular. No, more like a man who'd spent years in the Himalayas: weathered and beaten up, but in a romantic way. He had a face with history, which men wore well.

"Wasn't he married before he became a monk?"

"He's not a monk," Helen said. She was a slim girl in a little black dress with spotted stockings and a high heel dangling from one raised foot. "He's a sensei, a teacher. He doesn't have to be celibate."

"But was he married?"

"He told me he'd lived a pretty wild life before his ordination. A bit like Siddhartha himself." A corner of Helen's mouth turned up. Nicole watched the spiked heel of her shoe jouncing on the end of her toe, threatening to fall. The others spoke on around them while they gazed at each other. She admired the lean smallness of Helen's body, couldn't help thinking about the way her own had softened and expanded these past few years, as though she had been left in water overnight.

"I'd agree he's not bad to look at. And the *gravitas* that comes from being so spiritually accomplished—"

"I'm not convinced he *is* that spiritually accomplished. I mean, don't get me wrong, I've advanced tremendously since I started working with him. But as for his own level of attainment . . ."

"In Japan, the priests can marry, you know."

"But not the nuns."

"Does he speak Japanese?"

"I thought you had to give all that up to be truly wise. Sex and love and all of it. I thought that was why we were all doomed."

The couples and groups shifted, forming and re-forming. Buffy slunk from person to person with a bottle, or waved them to the hors d'oeuvres. Nicole watched the conversation move from mouth to mouth, feeling full of her own self, the things she could say to surprise them if she were a little more reckless. Earlier that day, she'd told her Master about the party. "I know about it," he said. "I was invited. But it's not appropriate for me to attend."

She knew he wanted his students to think of him only in the specific context of the Zendo. He took pains not to be seen outside on the street or wearing civilian clothes. He stood in the front room or in the private meeting chamber; that was it.

"What if you came as my guest? If we came arm in arm?" she asked.

He almost smiled. Oh, she could make him smile from time to time. She held these moments close to herself, like a drawer of knives she could pull open and examine. "Nicole" was all he said.

She imagined telling her Master she was leaving. "This isn't helping my spiritual progress anymore," she'd say. "After we fuck, I'm in the wrong headspace all day."

Someone was passing around a joint, and it finally reached Buffy. "Jesus," she said. "Can I put the kids to bed first?"

She led the children away, and when she returned, she took the joint and pulled on it wearily. Amy patted her on the head. "Oh, to be a mother." Amy was in her sixties, thin and drawn and with coarse white waves of hair. Nicole remembered her announcing her reason for first coming to the Zendo: she had thyroid cancer and found meditation helped her with pain. Later the cancer came back and she joined the *sangha* officially, taking refuge with them, as the saying went. She wore heavy dark mascara that made her look striking and Goth, and helped to hide the sunkenness of her eyes. She seemed to have shrunk a little each time Nicole saw her, swaying on her mat by the window, but her look grew more fierce and militant. She burned with a clear and dangerous light.

"Nicole, you've been studying with our teacher for longer than any of us, I think," Buffy said. "Would you call him a true master?"

Now the eyes swung to her. Nicole leaned forward in the deep plush seat, pressing her hands between her stockinged thighs. They must think of me as a nun, she thought: a silent vessel, emptying herself year by year. "I would. I do."

That was the problem, really.

It was a strain, talking about meditation and the cold, clean promise of the Middle Path when they were by a warm fire drinking wine. The conversation shifted to traffic, then real estate; how real estate was affecting politics; how politics were affecting real estate. Nicole emptied her wine glass and set in on a refill when Buffy passed with the bottle. Now they were Bostonians again, not Zen students; snow was falling outside the window. They were abashed Christians and

7

lapsed Jews admiring the hand-knit stockings and the gently spinning ornaments on the tree. Now they could only talk the way you must when you are in a cable-knit sweater at a holiday party, passing a brass tray of cookies.

Presently she stepped out onto the stoop. She was not a smoker but she always enjoyed smokers' lonely company; after a night class in her community college days she'd sometimes lean on a wall with them and chat, looking at the world from its fringe. She had come back to Boston then, twenty-two and trying to return to a semblance of orderly life while the other night students, parents already with full-time jobs, laughed exhaustedly together.

George was out there, finishing a smoke; he smiled briefly. "Merry Christmas, Nicole." He stamped his cigarette into the snow and went back in.

It was cold enough to stop the breath in her lungs, but she did not go back in yet. If she'd gone back in, perhaps nothing would have changed for her that night. But she liked the stillness of the dark street, the shady promise of a few dim stars. In small wedges of the posher neighborhoods, Boston looked like a brick-lined alley in a Sherlock Holmes novel. The streetlamps were old and ornate, the stone steps worn and scooped in the middle. Christmas trees glowing in houses, snow gathered in the thick greeny pane of every window.

She went to close the door behind George and found Helen there, trembling with her cigarette to her lips. "How do you put up with people like that?" she asked.

Nicole crossed her arms, tried not to shiver. Helen always flustered her. "Buffy's a very kind person. Not everyone has to be the same as you. When you get older, you learn that."

"Blah, blah, blah." Helen laughed, low and throaty. "You know these people. Walking clichés, all of them. With their Christmas trees and their Buddha ornaments. But you're not one of them. I'll tell you where you're going next."

"Where?"

"My house. I'm having a few people over." Helen waved to the lit window. "Not any of them."

"It's late."

Helen went on as if she hadn't spoken. "I'm going to leave, and then a little later you're going to come." She was scribbling her address on a piece of paper, pressing her cold little hand into Nicole's. "I want my friends to meet you."

. . .

Now, wrapping her bronze Buddha head in bubble wrap, stuffing the space around it in the box with socks, she wondered why she'd agreed, why she'd obediently collected her coat and followed. Was it curiosity? A delusion that she was still twenty and not thirty-two? A grim determination to prove herself game?

When she was seventeen, she'd smoked pot even though it made her sick because her boyfriend's friends were watching, waiting to see whether she was cool enough to join their company. When she was twenty-two and a new Zen student, and her Master swept by in her third hour of meditation, she'd sit straighter, hide the tightening ropes of pain in her spine. There were these tests you had to pass to prove your worth; all your life you'd keep jumping through the hoops to show you could.

. . .

Helen's student housing was in one of the almost-derelict apartments near Boston University. The sidewalks were unshoveled and icy here, the building codes swept under the rug. Last summer a girl had died in the attic of one of these places, when the house burned down and there was no second door to escape through. When Nicole puffed up to the second floor and knocked, someone shouted, "Come in," and she pushed her way into a cramped little dorm-room space where four people were sitting at a kitchen table eating burritos. Helen was one of them, but they all stared at her as if they'd never seen her before.

"Am I early?" said Nicole.

"It's cool." Finally, Helen moved from her elaborate slouch. She took Nicole's coat and pushed out a chair. "We're just having dinner." They ate and talked around her about who was sleeping with whom while Nicole sat watching them, cold but sweating, like a sack of moist clay.

When the burritos were gone Helen stood up and went to the windowsill, where a few incense sticks were parked in what looked like a block of cheese. Mold was creeping up one side. "My little shrine," she said. "My American shrine. Let's bless the party. Nicole, give us a blessing."

The other three stared at Nicole humorlessly.

"You guys remember, I told you about Nicole," said Helen. "She's the best Zen student in my class. Master's pet." She smiled, but there was something mocking and dangerous in her eyes. "Come on, bless us." She bent her head.

Nicole put her hand on Helen's head to bless her. *"Namu Amida butsu,"* she said. "May this party rock."

The partygoers laughed.

Gradually other younger people began to arrive, dressed in ugly holiday sweaters festooned with knitted menorahs and red-nosed reindeer. The little room was soon packed and smoky, the in-jokes rampant, the relationships unclear. The sugary pop music from

Nicole's childhood was going through an ironic revival and so she knew the blasting songs, but no one danced; it seemed to be there simply to make it hard to hear anyone talking. When someone asked Helen where her Christmas sweater was, Helen went into the back room and emerged in a white sweatshirt with black patches taped on and an inflated latex glove tied to her waist. "I'm a Zen cow," she announced. "Get it? *Mu. Mu.*"

That was from the koan, the riddle that is every student's first foray into the frustrating puzzle of Zen. A monk asks a master if a dog has a Buddha nature and the enigmatic answer is *"Mu"*—nothing. How many people at the party knew the koan? Was it a private joke for her alone, some coded message? Helen's eyes searched for Nicole's over the crowd, latched on, and glimmered.

In a moment of chaotic sound, when the people began to dance, Helen pressed herself to Nicole. "I didn't think you'd come," she shouted.

"I was curious." Curious to see how young college students like Helen lived these days? How they navigated their foreign worlds?

They stared at each other. "He calls you his little *theri,*" Helen said, still in that shout so close to her ear. "He never calls me that." It was the Pali word for "nun."

Then Helen released her and slipped away, between two boys in matching reindeer sweaters, grinding briefly with them as she went. Nicole let the crowd pass her to a corner of the room, clutched her beer, drank it down.

A few swallows later, she reached the deck. It was about fifteen feet off the ground, rickety and swaying. The air was cold and quiet, compared to the roaring music inside. She leaned on the railing, drawing a deep breath.

"You're his best student," said Helen behind her. The Boston snow settled fairylike on her hair. "Everyone knows it. Are you training to be a master?"

She could feel the alcohol she'd had narrow her vision, eliminating the periphery, so that she had to swing her head to see things. With an effort she brought Helen into focus. She was angry now, or had been angry for hours, watching Helen dance around her, smiling that predatory smile. "I don't know," she said.

Helen slid to the railing beside her and lit a cigarette, cupping her hands around the lighter as though holding something precious.

"Why did you invite me here?"

"I wanted to see if you were a real person."

I'm real. She wanted to shout it; she wasn't a figure in a painting or a done-up doll; not a geisha or goddess, either. But she wasn't sure what she was. She wished she could see herself as Helen saw her: a threat. "Well? Am I?" she demanded.

"He knows everything about you, doesn't he? He's got you right where he wants you. You have to be more careful with who you're fucking. Do you ever think about what *you* mean to *him*?"

That was a question with no answer, the riddle she'd been trying to crack for ten years. She knew her Master needed her, the way a teacher with no student is no teacher at all. There were things they shared: intimacies that come from years of sleeping together, accepting each other's bodies again and again. They were an old married couple, childless perhaps, a fruitless, pointless union, but a union nevertheless. The cement of years sealing the cracks. "You don't understand," she said feebly.

Helen shook her head. "I know how to handle him, okay? He talks a lot, but I don't believe everything I hear. Maybe you should just get out of this. Before you get hurt." She was drunk, making her bid for ownership. *Leave him to me,* she was saying. Leaning heavily on the wooden railing, letting her chin fall to her chest.

Coldly, desperately, Nicole asked, "Why can't you leave us alone?"

Helen muttered something. It sounded like *"Mu."* Or maybe it was a curse. She lurched forward; Nicole shrank back. Then Helen was hanging over the railing, vomiting over it. Nicole grabbed her by the waist, trying to hold her steady so she wouldn't fall. Just walk away, some part of her said. Let this foolish girl go, this child who thinks she understands.

Shouts and laughter broke their silence; someone was calling Helen's name. She straightened, wiping her mouth, and stepped back inside. No one noticed when Nicole collected her coat and left.

. . .

It was well past eleven and the train was near its last run when she got on. She took the train toward the river, moving west to the outlying neighborhoods. For a while the engine cut out and they glided over the black Charles in silence, the carnival lights of the skyline retreating, the other skyline swallowing her up.

The sudden blast of heat made sweat run warmly down her arms. She could smell the sourness of her own body now, the accumulation of other smells, female fluids, shrill waxes, the bite of bile under a veneer of perfume. She was eighteen again and crammed in a car with two boys, one her friend, the other her boyfriend, and they were running away. It was inevitable, really, this stone that had been set rolling so long ago; with her good Catholic family, with her Master, she was always looking over her shoulder, figuring out how to escape.

It was all there, the sweet rot of herself.

. . .

"Mom wants you closer to me," her brother, Paul, had told her on the phone that week. He was six years older than her and had always been protective. "If you were in New York, I could keep an eye on you, and Mom wouldn't have to worry." From her beach community of the single, the elderly, and the insufferable in North Carolina, their mother directed family affairs.

"I told you to stop looking for apartments for me," she said. "I'm fine here. I'm okay."

"Don't you want to see your wonderful brother more?"

"My wonderful brother can visit anytime he likes. Bring the kids. Bring Marion. We'll video-chat with Mom and make it a party."

He called every week, full of breezy anecdotes about life and the kids (June's learning "Eight Days a Week" on the piano; Charlie's still into dinosaurs). They'd fallen off from their long phone calls when he was in college and she was still at home, when she'd complain about their parents and he'd listen, he'd always listen, the phone warming in her hand over time as though the heat of his sympathy could reach her. This time he sounded impatient. "Nic, there's a studio opening up near us in Murray Hill. It's small, but you don't need much, I know. The light is good. I could help you out with the deposit."

She started to explain that she was a New Englander, that she never did well when she left. She was best among all the people bundled in their coats half the year, minding their own business. But her old explanations had grown tired.

Maybe he'd gotten nervous at her thirty-second birthday, when she'd brought no friends to the family dinner; maybe she'd said too quickly that no, she had no romances on the horizon, when he'd asked. Maybe the change happened when he'd last visited and found her up at dawn, meditating silently on the patio of her apartment in her pajamas. To outsiders it looked severe, monastic. He'd seen the lone carton of milk in her fridge, the one plate in the drying rack. He was doing reconnaissance, she knew, for their mother. She'd caught him flipping through her address book. What did he think about the total absence of names except for his? She would never be free of his worry.

"What's keeping you there?" he demanded.

Once, when her Master had rolled off her and was retying his sash, she said, "That was good." He looked at her. Then she felt bad because they normally never said anything to acknowledge that they were fucking instead of sharing the sort of intimate spiritual space a master and student were supposed to share. She went home kicking herself and saying, "That was good! That was good!" and then hating herself more because she was a Zen student and lesson number one was not to anxiously inhabit the past.

She had no answer that her brother would understand.

. . .

On Christmas Eve, Boston was bright and black at once, the trees strung carelessly with lights, snow still pristine as fairy dust in the white uncharted paths of the Public Garden and the Common, in dark alleys and unlit secret passageways. Nicole was not yet home from Helen's, she might miss the last train, but she stepped off at Park Street, the Common beside her. At first she was alone, watching the puff of her breath seed the chill air; the last of the skaters on Frog Pond were gone now, no one spilling loud and drunk out of bars, no hockey fans yelling at each other in the crosswalks, no janitors and maids waiting at bus stops for the beginning of the night shift. Tomorrow, the city and its neighborhoods would be quiet. All of Boston, Christian and otherwise, hunkering down for the holiday. But gradually she found herself part of a line of laughing people, families in their nice long coats, girls slipping on the ice in their glossy Mary Janes. Their company seemed so cheerful, their direction so singular, that Nicole moved with them, following but not trailing behind, part of the crowds in their earmuffs and their Sunday best. Nicole was almost inside St. Paul's before she realized where she was: they were going to church, for the Midnight Mass.

She tried to step out of the current, but the crowd was jamming through the narrow doorway and she was blocking everyone. She went on instead to the little red velvet entry room, struggling past the cheerful removal of coats and counting of children's heads. She let the crowd carry her on into the church, and automatically crossed herself as she slid into a back pew. A boy in a white surplice handed her a candle with a white circle of cardboard to trap the dripping wax. She clutched it helplessly, looking for a way out, a door not blocked by the faithful.

The service began, with the crinkle and wheeze of an organ: children in white, gathered by the altar, caroling in sweet, high tones. For a moment, she let herself relax; "Silent Night" always had a hold on her, that call for stillness. Around her, churchgoers were passing a flame down their line of candles, tipping one to the next. Was it apostasy just to listen? The music filled the crowded space, soft and heavy, more lullaby than hymn. She closed her eyes. She was very tired.

When the song ended, a priest in white with a deep green stole shuffled up to the lectern. She wanted to slip away, but now she was not alone in her pew: a man was bent in what looked like earnest prayer, hands clasped to his forehead, head lowered. The Our Father began. This was no place for her, not now. She touched his shoulder.

He looked up quickly. He was square all around: square-jawed, square-shouldered, his chest broad, his legs wide and sturdy. His skin was gray and pebbled like a New England beach. "Excuse me," she whispered. He gazed at her, uncomprehending.

Then his eyes traveled downward, seemed to understand. Carefully, he tipped his candle to hers. Now both were lit, and he smiled, and she did too, not sure why this small gesture filled her with such unexpected happiness.

When everyone began filing up to the altar for Communion, she slipped away. But in the all-night ice cream parlor next door, where she was at the counter devouring a cone, he found her.

He waved through the window, and she waved back without recognizing him; then he came in and sat at the counter with her, and from the side she remembered his old-fashioned, triangular sideburns. She liked his sheepish smile.

His name was Sean. "I'm getting too old for Midnight Mass."

She laughed, roughly. "I don't normally—I was actually—"

"Me neither. But once in a while—you know. You get pulled back in." He nodded at her ice cream cone. "What did you get?"

"Moose Tracks." A decadent favorite, with swirls of fudge and peanut butter cups.

"Sounds good." He got up, asked for a sample, and came back with a tiny spoon, pulling it slowly from his mouth. She felt obscurely pleased. "What do you do?" she asked.

"Oh, I'm a buyer. I buy lawn equipment for a wholesale home improvement chain. And I buy antiques, kind of on the side, and sell them. As a hobby." She ate her ice cream quietly, a rare ease settling on her shoulders.

"Are you married?" she asked.

"Divorced. A year ago," he said, and put down the spoon, smacking his lips. "You?"

"Oh, I'm single. You know, unattached." She gave a short laugh. "Attachment" was one of those fraught words in Buddhism, like "pride" in Catholicism; it was something you were supposed to be fighting all the time. She was good at that. There was only the problem of her Master.

They kept talking until the roads outside were empty. Sean lived in Weston, a wooded neighborhood hugging Boston's outer rim. He talked about his ex-wife, married now, and his daughter. He showed her a picture: she was a high school kid, tall and blocky like her father, with the sure limbs of a rugby player. Sean told her about his wife's new husband, who was "some California guy," tan and wearing Ray-Bans and surfing at five every morning. "I can tell you're a born-and-bred New Englander," Sean said. "So you know what I'm talking about. I mean, who is this guy?"

She, too, had known immediately upon seeing him what kind of accent he would have, with its broad deep *o*'s ("Noath Shoa") and nasal *a*'s. It was something about the unhealthy pallor and roughness of his skin, the baseball cap exposing the red tips of his ears, the deeply scuffed parka that was stained with seasons of salt; she knew.

She smiled. "Yeah, it's another world." To New Englanders, there was always something disquieting about the West Coast. How did they get so tan? How much of all that blond hair was real? Did they really go around in bathing suits all the time? Bostonians were suspicious and prickly. Everything west of Worcester was Out There, irrelevant, and West Coast people were embarrassing, emotional, and false. No, you needed seasons to build character. Of course, Boston had its own problems. She had discovered only recently that the local term for chocolate sprinkles ("jimmies") stemmed from a racial slur for black people. Townies threw rocks at the integrated buses, got drunk at Sox games, changed lanes without signaling. Still, a dyed-in-the-wool Bostonian had no business leaving. You were Boston for life.

Sean reached under his cap to scratch his head. "You gotta go where you gotta go." It was the voice of her mailman, the guy who cashed checks for her at the bank, the cop who pulled alongside when she was sobbing in her parked car once and said, You got somewhere to go, hon? You're an Irishwoman, aren't ya?

Suddenly he was dear to her, in that way she sometimes felt bursts of love for Boston, for the sweet grubbiness of its people, for her own frumpy belonging, for the way even now the kids behind the counter were badmouthing the chain ice cream store next door. She felt a lump rising in her throat. He was looking at her intently. He knew her, too. He knew her story, or the parts that mattered. He brushed her hand with his own. "Listen—you got anybody to spend Christmas with? You want to grab a little dinner tomorrow?"

"Oh, I—" She wanted to. But she had to get home; she had to prepare herself for next Tuesday, and the next, and the next. "I don't know if I can tomorrow—"

Sean's face fell, just a little; he mastered the look well. "Sure, yeah."

"Rain check?" she said, apologetic.

"Yeah. Yeah, definitely."

He was getting up to go; he was taking the hint. But it took a long time to get suited up for winter, didn't it. He stood there, winding his scarf very slowly. She felt something like desperation. Don't go yet, she wanted to say. Don't you see, I didn't want to say no. You must see that. I can tell by the look of you that I'd want to feel your arms around me. It would feel like cuddling in an old armchair. Nubby and warm.

"I'll just go to the bathroom." He shifted off to the back of the store. He'd left his gloves on the counter. She grabbed her receipt and wrote. *Dear Sean, Please call me.* She left her number and stuffed the scrap into his glove. Then she was running out of the store before he could come back, running like a fool, her damp hair loose and freezing in the winter air, her coat flapping open.

. . .

On Christmas Day, her brother called. She listened to the happy crackle of wrapping paper in the background, tasteful choral songs trilling. Her niece, June, co-opted the phone, boisterous: "Why aren't you here, Aunt Nic?"

She explained that she hadn't been able to get off work. The day after Christmas was crazy for returns. "We're just stepping out to church," Paul said. "But that apartment, Nic. I've got to sign by New Year's, and you could be in it by February."

After she hung up, she opened a browser page and searched "Zen Boston." Maybe she could just join a new Zendo, erase her history with her Master and escape him. She wrote down a list of temples and carried it in her pocket. Now she had a week to try them out: you had to have a new bond before you could tear up an old covenant. Riding the T in the evenings to and from the Shambhala Zen Center, the Society of Compassionate Mind, or the Lotus of Universal Love, she imagined telling her Master she was leaving. *I'm going. Good-bye. So long. Sayonara.*

And then what would he do? She could creep up to the edge of the moment in her mind, but she couldn't see beyond it. It would be throwing away the art she'd been crafting for decades.

. . .

In Chinatown, there were Ch'an centers on the hot, linty second floors above the groceries. She rode the train there after work and wandered in and out of stores, taking things in. Here the grocery stores had their crates out on the sidewalk, offering thick smells of peanuts, roasted chestnuts, smoked ham hocks. There were plate-sized mushrooms, shaved blocks of coconut, and boxes of tiny fish glinting like dimes. She wanted to dip her hands in them. The prayer session she'd found online was due to begin at six, but still she lingered on the street, fingering the walnuts. She didn't know a word of Mandarin, which the services here would be conducted in. She could imagine the crush of bodies in the small, hot room, the directions in a language she did not know, the procedures of offering and incense and prostration she had not learned. People would stare. They'd wonder what she was doing there; they'd know she did not belong.

It was snowing, a slushy December mess that seeped up her jeans to the mid-thigh, and instead of going to the Ch'an center, she took cover in a gift shop. The space was tiny and crowded with porcelain, wall-eyed fortune cats that raised their paws in greeting. There were Buddhas too—Buddha postcards, Buddha cookie jars, Buddha Christmas tree ornaments, all shining, obese, laughing. The most common Chinese depictions were these frighteningly fat happiness Buddhas, naked and grinning, lucky when rubbed. They represented wealth and abundance and domestic bliss, but she found them alarming. She was a Catholic girl. Happiness in excess did not feel like religion.

The Tibetan art, too, was strangely frightening. The Buddhas and bodhisattvas in the murals and tapestries were blue and red and orange demons with the heads of bulls or tigers, steaming flame from their nostrils, waving dozens of arms and legs, brandishing necklaces of skulls, human penises erect and enormous. They were supposed to represent the fierce secret energies required for enlightenment. You could meditate and imagine them entering your body, filling you with power. She'd seen them hanging behind the heads of Tibetan lamas, rich and strange and dangerous. But they were too obscene for her.

Always the wood-carved Japanese Buddhas drew her in. They were slender and elongated, their hands carefully posed, the merest Mona Lisa smile curling their sorrowful lips. They seemed to say that suffering was only the beginning of something profound. They had something she didn't. What was it?

Grace, her mother would say.

The shopkeeper was in a tiny back room watching a K-drama on the security television, but he had spotted her looking at the Buddhas. "Do you like? This one is good for fertility," he said, displaying the pale female Quan Yin. "This one is for financial success. This one is for happiness in the home. Which one do you like? Which do you want?"

He held out Buddhas in bronze, in pewter, in plastic. When she backed away, he waved prayer cards. Finally she fled the store into the snow, hugging her cold flimsy jacket to her body, her heavy jeans dragging in the gray mush climbing in the streets.

. . .

Her Master's teaching lineage, threaded through with *roshis* from Japan, was handwritten on a scroll in his meeting room, looking like a pedigree chart for a prize stallion. It was a beautiful branching tree of Japanese characters, tracing all the way back to Bodhidharma, the mysterious monk who brought Buddhism to China. And at the end of this illustrious line, her Master had written his name in a schoolboy's careful cursive. The scroll was the only decoration in the bare room, besides a jade Buddha seated in the corner.

Her Master had one overlapping tooth that occasionally became visible in the corner of his mouth. It reminded her that he was a man, a man in need of orthodontia, not a spiritual being, and made her think she could leave, easily, that she didn't need him anymore. Then he would beat the side of a metal urn with a wooden staff—this traditional Japanese drum resounded with a great gong and made her heart beat slower with the thrill of it—and he would say, "When the wind roars, it is the universe that makes it roar. When I beat the drum, it is the universe that resounds! If your voice is loud or soft, it is the voice of the universe. Even silence has a voice!" It was a message for her, she was sure of it. When they were quietly meditating afterward, and his hand was on her shoulder, her body straightened and shivered and resonated with his touch. Then her proud, lonely plans to leave were useless.

. . .

The weekend pulled its afternoon silence across the sky. As the sun set on Friday and the house filled with a changed, somber light, she became watchful. There was something suspicious in how she could turn a light on in a room and find it still on an hour later, how the dishes stayed in the sink until she cleaned them, how if she left a book on the floor—just to test—it was still there in the morning. It was like having a stranger staying in the house who would not announce his presence, who was standing behind you every time you turned, who folded the towels and made the bed, burdensome in his sheer unobtrusiveness.

With snow heavy in the air, she sat on the deck in her parka, meditating. She sat so still that chipmunks and squirrels sometimes came to her knee. The cat, Kukai, sat nearby, drawn to her quietness, and sometimes jumped into her lap and sniffed up at her face to see if she was still alive.

Kukai was named after a Japanese monk who wandered the

country with his followers, handing out slips of wood with prayers on them. He was a scruffy tabby, a stray who'd appeared wet and thin on the hood of her car, balled up and bleeding from dog bites. Like other stray animals she and Paul had sometimes brought home when they were kids, he had strange habits. He stored food in hiding places, so that her feet crunched on kibble when she tried on her winter boots on the first day of the season. He yowled at birds and scratched and picked at himself until great patches of fur fell out. In the night she'd sometimes wake up, heart pounding, and find him staring at her, eyes shining in the dark. She thought he must have some trauma in his past and he was still sizing her up, trying to determine if she would betray him. She pulled him close and pressed her face into his fur, and he let her. Beneath the fur, his skin was rough and scabby, a network of scars. She thought, Somebody kicked you. Something bit you. You limped your way to my car. She thought, We can be strays together.

Now she sat on the porch with him and stared at the moon, waiting for the moment of transformation. Soon, soon, it would happen. You couldn't wait for it forever.

"Aren't you lonely, little *theri?*" her Master had asked her a week ago.

"No," she'd said.

"You were built for loneliness, weren't you. Some people are. Were you always this way?"

"I don't know."

"I think you are lonelier than you let on. Lonelier than you think." Her Master stroked her hair.

She thought, I have you. I have the stillness of afternoon light on snow. I have a cave in myself that I've carved out over many years. It's dark and close, with just enough room for me. Whenever I want, I just climb inside.

Loneliness had its routines. There was the part when you talked to the cat, bright and falsetto. Then there was the part when you talked to yourself, not liking it much but feeling the words arising anyway, the urge to speak like the need to pee. Then there was the part, worse, when you fell stonily into silence. Then words would not come, were gone, words were nowhere, until Sean's call roused them thickly from the mud.

"How about that rain check?" he asked.

. . .

Over the course of several days they went to a museum, a movie with Sean's hand on hers, and spent an evening in the city eating ice cream and cups of clam chowder, poking through the street stalls of Quincy Market. When had she last followed the red brick stripe of the Freedom Trail down winding, narrow seventeenth-century streets or sucked oysters out of her palm at an alehouse? In the post-Christmas doldrums, with snow piling in dirty slush heaps on every street corner, they had Boston to themselves. They shuffled along in their snow boots, looking at the Christmas lights on bare, scratchy trees, poking into the dark four-room houses of the Revolution. Every cruddy corner looked lovely. She held on to Sean's reassuring arm: heavy and solid, ballast to keep her from sweeping away across the ice.

She remembered a muddy spring when she was young, pressing into an angry crowd on the Common. Catholics rallying to a cause. Sean pointed out the Chapel of the Holy Spirit on Park Street, an old brick building, unassuming and square. "That's where I had my first Communion, would you believe it," he said. He rubbed his nose, shoved his hands in his pockets. She knew he was waiting for her to volunteer her story. "Where was yours?" he asked, when she did not.

"St. Augustine," she said. "It's one of the ones that closed."

"That's a shame. You could go to mine, if you like. It's a nice sermon."

She turned away, letting people slip by her on the narrow, snow-drifted sidewalk. She knew what he thought: he'd seen her in the Midnight Mass. And would it be that awful a lie? She smiled vaguely, and managed to trip into the gutter so he had to catch her, and she spoke brightly about an antique table she had seen at a garage sale (he loved antiques, his eyes glowed whenever he spoke of them), and they moved on.

. . .

She knew she couldn't tell him anything resembling the truth. No one would understand all of it, its scope and depth. Even Paul knew almost nothing. He asked her, sometimes, what she did all day, what the services were like in a Buddhist temple. Do you pray, he asked. Or do you make offerings to the god of Whatever?

The truth was, she had been under her Master's tutelage for nearly ten years. He had instructed her in the ways of a Zen student. He showed her how to clean the floors of the Zendo by pushing a wet rag while running, bent double; how to eat rice from a bowl, then drink tea from the bowl, then use a last splash of that tea to clean the bowl, each motion thoughtful, efficient, not a drop wasted; he showed her how to bow before a fellow student, before a respected teacher, how to prostrate oneself before a master.

First you press your hands together, then touch them to your heart, to your forehead, sites of compassion, of wisdom; then bend, press your palms to the ground, slide them until you are facedown, stretched flat, nose kissing the floorboards. Then get up and do it again. A pose of complete and perfect humility. Some monks in Nepal and Tibet considered this the holiest form of practice and went on thousand-mile pilgrimages through the foothills of the Himalayas, prostrating every step, until they had crossed into India and reached the Buddha's site of enlightenment. Every year, some died on these journeys. The ones who survived grew bone spurs on their wrists and wore the skin off their knees and hands. In serious Tibetan sects, you could not be considered a fully ordained monk until you had completed one hundred thousand prostrations. Her Master was merciful, though: only fifty prostrations a meeting, leaping up and down, sweating and straining and kissing the floor.

"See what a gentle Master I am?" he said, with a small, crooked smile.

Halfway through her prostrations, her brain entered some kind of shock, when the walls of the room faded, and around her was a brilliant white. She was frightened by this vertiginous blindness, but always her Master's voice, soothing and dark and warm, brought her home again.

She spent the first year of her studenthood in a dizzy excitement nearly all the time, full to bursting with a convert's zeal. There was so much to learn, and her Master guided her along gradually, reading her haiku while she sat with her eyes closed. *Now the swinging bridge / is quieted with creepers / Like our tendriled life.* She sat, absorbing the sound of the words, letting them sink line by beautiful line into her body. He taught her koans, beginning with the first and most fundamental, when a student asks a master if a dog has a Buddha nature and the enigmatic answer is only *"Mu." Mu* in Japanese means "no" or even more than no; it was a total negation, closer to "nothing." It didn't make sense, because the doctrine said that all sentient beings, from humans to oysters, had a Buddha nature. He told her to sit with the answer in her mind, ponder its refusal. He said, The koan teaches us about what religion can and can't give. We come humbly to the

Buddha, bowing and scraping, begging for enlightenment. We ask, and the answer is no. We ask and we ask, and still the answer is no. We plead for just a little awareness, just a little peace. But there is still something not right in us, and we are not asking the question correctly. And until it is right, the answer will always be no.

He told her to sit with the answer until it drove her insane. And just when she couldn't think about it anymore, on the other side of the wall of reason there would be a new awareness that enlightenment was within her own power, not the unanswered demand she had always put on one god or another.

She had not felt this way since she was nine years old and wanted to be a nun, felt meaning shining out of every windowpane or stranger's face, thought the world was a book written in a language you only had to learn to know its mysteries. The private room she visited each week came to be something more. It was a small, dark envelope of frozen time. A place where forgiveness, both by her and of her, was possible. All week she anticipated the return to it, the way an anxious lover awaits a letter in the mail. She realized now, that was it: she was in love.

And then what? When he first touched her knee, when he leaned close, when she felt his breath on her neck, when his hand traveled higher, when he asked so politely, wasn't this the intimate spiritual space they shared, hadn't she wanted this, the fruition of their bond?

And he showed her how to wrap her legs around his body and press him harder into her, a move that hadn't occurred to her with her teenage boyfriend Jules, and that made her groan with pleasure, and thank him for the privilege.

Once in a while they lay still on the straw mat afterward and breathed, and did not get up right away and adjust their clothes, and it felt good to be there, and she felt a little clearer, as though some cloudy toxin in the water of her brain had been filtered out. Her Master sometimes held on to her then, in a full-body embrace, accepting all of her, and told her he would be a home for her when she had no home. Then she knew she wouldn't be able to abandon him or the training, at least not yet. The years had slipped by her in this way, as she built toward her one hundred thousand prostrations, her calves growing whiplike, her hands shiny.

If she did her fifty prostrations every week, she calculated once, it would take her more than thirty-eight years to reach her goal.

. . .

When she wasn't practicing, she was in the back room of the shoe warehouse, digging for sizes. She floundered among fallen heaps of boxes, her hands closing on the bones of loose and scattered shoes. There was an element of the absurd in it, and the other saleswomen felt it, too. Instead of sorting and organizing, they just stood by, smoked an illegal cigarette or swiped long-fingered through their phones.

In the back room they joked about the customers, making up stories. That woman, insisting her feet hadn't grown two sizes since her third child. The man buying penny loafers to impress his future father-in-law: he was going to propose to his girlfriend. But you could just tell, from the sweaty-palmed way he gripped the shoes, that he'd be turned down.

In the back room, the saleswomen rubbed each other's aching feet. "You deserve a break, girl," they said, laughing. Outside the boss was waiting, the customers were tapping their bare feet, saying, "Where is that salesgirl?" But someone was always waiting for them. Their husbands, or kids, or boyfriends. Where's dinner, where's my catcher's mitt, where's size 10 of this sandal? They ran up to their lives saying, Sorry I'm late.

On their breaks, the saleswomen stood around in the parking lot and talked about their husbands and boyfriends and lovers. There was always something going wrong, something disappointing. Missed anniversaries or absent support payments. But while they had spent years at the store, the same way Nicole had, they had something to show for it: children and husbands and nest eggs. She sent out résumés for office jobs sometimes, but when an interview came through, she backed away, afraid the commitment would interfere with her training.

What did she have to show after ten years? A spine as straight as a flagpole. An ability to sit still. A GED and a bachelor's and a mental library of Zen poetry, so many verses of cherry blossoms and falling leaves. How could that be all, how could that be enough?

Today Nicole hovered on the outside of their circle and the women pulled her in. Hands were on her shoulders, warm, with their beautiful manicures. She hid her own bitten-off fingernails in her palms.

"You're always so quiet," said Jolene. "Tell us your story."

"Yeah, come on, tell us," the others chimed in.

She knew that in this circle of women, her story was who she was dating, the man she was screwing or wishing she were screwing or formerly screwed. She began, obediently, the way all the other stories began: "Well, there's this guy—"

"Does he love you?"

"I don't know."

"Do you love him?"

"I don't know."

The women murmured sympathetically. "We know what you mean. Exactly."

. . .

Paul was waiting for her decision; there were only a few days left. In the Prana Power Yoga Cooperative of Boston, she stretched in ways her body hadn't moved in years, her joints becoming musical in their unfamiliar activity. She couldn't do goddess stance or downward-facing dog right. Her stomach muscles screamed in boat pose. The women around her, in their matching Lycra, looked like the eerily serene members of a cult.

At the Dharma Insight Collective, the white-haired woman who'd founded the center gave a rambling speech about her massive dogs, who followed her everywhere, who she was convinced were husbands from her past lives. Now they had both found each other, and they would have to share her in this life. She spoke about lighting our inner candle and shutting off the Internet because it was draining all of our heart energy away. She spoke of the vision quests that everybody used to go on in the sixties, when she was young—people just picking up and going somewhere, anywhere. What had happened to that beautiful life? Above all, she seemed confused by the people around her, by the world she now found herself in. It was not the world she had prepared for.

. . .

She thought, Helen's costume, the Zen cow, the word she'd said: it was a secret code. A desperate communiqué from behind an enemy line. A message to her younger self: Don't stay here, get out while you still can. Part of a koan, a riddle to crack.

. . .

When she has been his student for only a year, barely the beginning of what would be her novicehood in Japan, the Master waits for her arrival each week in the back room for their private meeting. She has studied and worked and prayed with an intensity he hasn't seen since he was a student himself, struggling to keep up in a Japanese monastery hostile to foreign-

ers. *The monks there hated him, his encroachment on their ancient and sacred offices. His teachers slapped him, yelled, drenched him with buckets of ice water at four in the morning. This is the hard, rocky path to perfection. He tells her how merciful he is to her, how forgiving. They meditate side by side, and his breath is the metronome setting the rhythm for her to follow. He knows she's close to her first moment of* kensho: *a burst of insight, the tiniest glimpse of enlightenment. At first you get it only in a flash: the understanding that the universe is both empty and contingent, a cause and effect and cause. He can tell when he listens to the studied calm of her breathing. The rise and fall of her chest makes the skin on his neck tingle. He has the teacher's zeal: this visceral vicarious joy in her learning.*

Cause and effect and cause. Like this: her quick intake of breath, the excitement of her insight, gives rise to his hand on her knee. And her startled look gives rise to his lips on her lips. How many innumerable causes have given rise to her earlobes, her neck, her soft breathing presence in his room. He wants to teach her something more. To not touch her would deny her something profound. She's ready for his instruction.

THE MASTER

On New Year's Eve, she met Sean at an estate sale in a woody suburb.

It was a cold day for antique hunting. They were the only people in the dark, drafty garage, the sellers huddled at a table in their parkas. Sean moved patiently from one piece to the next, looking for makers' marks, the sign that someone had been there, had taken pride in their work. There were always cheap knockoffs of Tiffany lamps, somebody's amateur watercolors. But among the trash there was often treasure, and he had a knack for finding it. At three different estate sales she watched him pull an authentic Steiff bear out of a pile of Beanie Babies, an early Frisbie's Pies tin from a stack of seventies board games, a chair from the 1700s from a herd of particleboard imitations. He told her he sent the vintage toys and games to his daughter. She loved that stuff.

All those New England Puritans busily churning out card tables—she had always thought antiques were fussy and drab, but Sean explained how cleverly a join had been hidden or how the grain of wood had been followed in this knotwork, in that table with its straight, clean lines. "Think of how many cheap tables and chairs we go through now," he said. "And all the while, my grandfather's desk was in the attic, as good as the day it was made. I pulled it out recently and it's just beautiful—you can see the work and attention that went into it. You put love into something and it'll last."

They walked in silence alongside the reservoir while she thought about this, gazing at the blue-gray water. It had been lightly touched with snow but was unfrozen, the powdery layers shifting and sliding over each other. She wanted to ask him if what he'd said was always true. Simply because you loved someone or something, was that enough to hold it close, to keep it yours? But it would be cruel to press him: she knew he was missing his daughter. The hurt was still fresh.

She picked up a few split-open beechnuts, fondling the spiky bell shapes, and then scattered them back to the ground, but Sean scooped them up again. "I'm saving them," he insisted. "It's a memory."

"That's what all these antiques are for you, aren't they? But they're somebody else's memories."

"I guess. But when I touch a good piece, and I see all the work that went into it, it's like I can picture the craftsman working on it, and later the guy sitting at the desk with his bills out, worrying about his kids, and the kid writing there because now his father's gone. You can see all the lives that have touched this one piece of wood. You're connected to them all." He smiled, embarrassed at his own earnestness, but she was humbled and charmed.

"Let's eat dinner at my place," he said. "We're wicked close, yeah?" She laughed. "Yeah. Okay." It was getting dark.

She followed him in her car, and saw him turn his head frequently to his rearview mirror, as if afraid she had changed her mind. They cruised along a twisting, narrow road hemmed closely by trees. At one point they crossed a bridge over the marsh and she realized how far out they were, miles away from her home, slipping through the tall yellow cordgrass and the water deepening its blue. Much of Weston was proper forest, and now they were sliding into its darker corners. Sean led her to a tall, narrow house, an old-style up-and-down Victorian with crazy, thick little windows and a widow's walk. A house like this in Weston would cost a fortune normally, but this one was ramshackle and decaying, too close to the marsh, sure to have water damage.

"My wife's and my house," Sean said as she got out. "She was so eager to get to California that she let me have it. Left me all the furniture, too." He stopped, jingled his keys in his coat pocket, smiled. "It's nice to have some company. Better when it's someone as pretty as you."

"I'm glad for the company, too," she said. She felt a little shiver of exhilaration as she watched him fumble with his keys: this house lost in the marsh, this friendly stranger inviting her in. But he wasn't a stranger after all, was he? She knew his type so well.

Sean reached for the light switch. "My wife took a lot of furniture," he said. "I have her parents' and my parents' in the basement, and I keep meaning to bring it up." The living room was almost bare, equipped only with a college student's idea of furnishings: fuzzy futon, television, IKEA table in cafeteria white.

They ate noodles out of bowls on the futon, watching television. There was a Bruins game on and they yelled and cheered at the screen, swearing at the disappointing shots. Nicole could hear her

Boston accent rising to match Sean's. She and Paul had gone to private school and had learned to speak what people called proper English, but at home they sometimes tried it on for fun. It was like having a traditional garment hanging in the closet, a kimono or sari, that you could put on and take off with ease. At midnight they switched the channel and watched the ball drop for the new year. Sean put his arm over her shoulders and she shrugged warmly into his embrace, and they kissed, his lips scratchy and warm. He held her for a long, quiet moment. He was good at tenderness, something she hadn't experienced in a long time. The newscaster wished for a year more peaceful than the last.

"I'm glad I'm kissing a Sox fan," Sean said. And then, the unavoidable: "Guess it'd be a long shot if I asked if you were Catholic."

"Long shot in this town?" she joked. Then, with a quick swallow: "Lapsed."

"Me too! Got an Irish mother on your back, telling you you'll go to hell?" he laughed.

"Something like that," she said.

He touched her arm. His relief, filling the room. Times were hard for Catholics, these days. There was much to be ashamed of. But still, Catholic magic was strong. You could laugh about hell and damnation while still feeling the weight of it on your shoulders. If you grew up believing, the yoke fit for life. Oh, the stern joy of being a Catholic! God knew you, and he was shaking his head over you. "It's nice to know we have a shared experience," he said.

Refrain from lying or deception, she thought. It was one of the five moral precepts of Buddhism, like the Ten Commandments. She could hear her Master's voice reading them out, and her own quavering voice, vowing to adhere to them.

She gritted her teeth. "Can I see the furniture?"

He didn't want to show her the basement. "I've had a lot of time on my hands, so I've just been arranging it. It's a little nuts down there." But she wheedled a bit, and he relented.

Sean led the way down a narrow staircase. The two of them stumbled through the dark until he found a light bulb on a chain. They were in one of those vast subterranean rooms, as large as the house, and it was crammed with old furniture. There were sofas, tables, grandfather clocks, armoires, easy chairs, even glass-paneled cabinets containing little porcelain ladies and bulldogs, miniature crystal vases and lamps shaped like bouquets of flowers. There were vases filled with roses and lilies made from tissue paper, and bowls of granite peaches, and Siamese-cat bookends and silver tea sets and souvenir spoons. It was all in the same style as the things Nicole's parents had owned: the sofas tightly stuffed, shiny, with clawed dark feet, the side tables with fleur-de-lis handles. Even the turquoise of the fabric was that particular shade of blue that seemed to exist only in the homes of the elderly. The knickknacks (brass mallards, china sailors in pea coats, little Christmas-village cottages) were the same sorts of objects quietly waiting in the old family home in Waban for Nicole, now that her mother had moved to North Carolina. Sean had two of everything, and he had arranged all of it in little sitting room configurations, as if the basement were a display room. There was a dining area there, another one in the corner, and two dens, one on either side of the stairs. Nicole sat down on one sofa, feeling strangely shy. It was just like the couch she had spent much of her adolescence on, reading on her back and leaving pistachio shells between the cushions. Back then she'd been starting to shed her Catholicism. She remembered her childhood friend Kumiko, with her family shrine, and all those books she'd read: *Siddhartha* and *The Dharma Bums*. She'd spent a lot of time imagining the Buddha as a handsome prince, a well-brought-up young man who saw sickness, age, and death and demanded an answer for it. She used to picture him in his fasting period, skin and bone, his face grave and beautiful in its deprivation. In her mind he still looked like Jules, the only boy she had loved.

Sean sat down beside her. He started to kiss her, slowly, clumsily. She ran her hands up and down his legs, feeling a quick need overtaking her, flushing her face, her neck, her elbows. Sean was moving urgently now, too. He bunched up her skirt and slipped his hand under it. He would let her lead, she realized. It had been so long since sex had meant taking another body for hers, handling it, exploring as she liked. She unzipped his jeans, letting him work them down over his ass, and reached into his boxers. He was still soft, not an eighteen-year-old who would be automatically astounded by her breasts or hips. Neither of them had the desperation of adolescents, but she wanted it badly, that lovely frenzy of feeling. She let him touch her until he was hard and panting; then she pushed his hand away. She scrabbled on the sofa to get on top of him, almost slipping, then worked him hard, enjoying the silky firmness of his skin, the tinny blast of beer fumes as he gasped, the sweet forbidden feel of the satin couch. Once he came she let him reciprocate, only because he insisted. She lay back on the sofa, letting her eyes roam over the cluttered antique showroom, while he labored honestly at his job. Even as her feelings began to swell and flood, she knew that no harm would come to her. He couldn't really touch her. She didn't know where she was, but it wasn't here. Her Master's hand was on her shoulder in his little private room as he read the precepts. *Refrain from sexual misconduct. Refrain from intoxicants. Refrain from lying.* Beside her, Sean dozing off, falling sweetly, swiftly asleep. *Poor blind man,* her Master would say. *He thinks he has you. Come, little theri.* All he had to do was call. In her mind she jumped up at his word and flitted away. She could no more refuse than she could flow backward through time, become another self, another life. She lay in the dark in Sean's unknowing arms, too frightened to close her eyes. Better to be under her Master's spell than to be flooded with guilt, with worry, with grief for what she had done.

. . .

Tuesday.

The streets in central Waltham were crowded with corner convenience stores, cheap Indian restaurants, and psychic palm-reading boutiques. It was a long walk from Nicole's apartment, but she enjoyed the focused solitude of it, the gentle huff up and down the hills, the long wooded tracts and backyards piled with children's toys, the high, sagging fences. There was the occasional place where her path crossed the train line and she could look down a long secret channel through the trees. Somewhere down that road, her childhood home on its hill, the curtains drawn. At some point she stepped out of the woods and back into town, and she could prepare herself for the week's sermon.

The snow had melted, but the sidewalks were still gritty with tossed sand. At the doorway of the Peaceful Healing Zen Center she dropped her sneakers, rotted with winter salt, at the end of a line of flats and loafers. It was nothing more than a glass storefront, wedged in between a hardware store and a Mexican restaurant. The restaurant was called Iguana Cantina; a giant animatronic iguana waggled its head over the door.

She hovered in the doorway of the meditation room: the holiday party guests were all there. She fell into a half-lotus at the back of the room and kept her gaze focused downward, not wanting to meet anyone's eyes, until the Master swept in. He was tall and broad-shouldered, and his face glowed with a restless vitality. As he passed through the aisle of seated practitioners, his hand went down, touching the shoulders of some and not others. Each touched person sat a little straighter.

The Master pressed his long-fingered hands together. "We think there is a permanent essence to us, a soul that continues from moment to moment and that survives when we die," he said. "But nothing, not even the self, has a permanent essence. What we think of as the self is merely a series of conditions—thoughts, feelings, actions—that have originated from the moment before. Our lives are a long row of dominoes falling. What do we call this phenomenon?"

Nicole could feel a deep vibration in her feet, a boozy flush that shot upward through her body. "Dependent origination," she breathed, and several others whispered it, too: "Dependent origination."

The Master nodded. He pulled a book of matches out of a long sleeve and lit a candle waiting at the front of the room. "Rebirth is the passing of a flame from one candle to the next. We are being reborn every moment of our lives." He demonstrated, lighting a second candle with the first. "What has been passed on?"

The room was tense and silent, pregnant with the answer.

"Nothing! Nothing but the energy of the moment before." The Master licked his thumb and extinguished the candles. "Let us consider the relevant sermon, the Fire Sermon." He opened his book. Nicole studied the Master in his navy robe with its patterned obi, cornflower blue. The broad masculine outline and rugged jaw: a cowboy priest. She imagined the shape of him underneath the heavy cloth, his genitals deep within another underrobe and then another, safe and pendulous.

The Master read, "'The Blessed One addressed the priests:— All things, O priests, are on fire. And what, O priests, are all these things which are on fire? The eye, O priests, is on fire; forms are on fire; eye-consciousness is on fire; impressions received by the eye are on fire; and whatever sensation, pleasant, unpleasant, or indifferent, originates in dependence on impressions, that also is on fire. And with what are these on fire? With the fire of passion, say I, with the fire of hatred, with the fire of infatuation; with birth, old age, death, sorrow, lamentation, misery, grief, and despair are they on fire.'"

Why had he chosen to read the Fire Sermon today? she wondered. It was as if he knew she had transgressed.

"Imagine being on fire," said the Master. "Fire is an energetic force, but it also destroys, it consumes. Imagine your life burning up before you, your body crumbling to ash. Our desire, our attachment, is destroying us. It is eating us from the inside out."

He closed the book and gazed at all of them. "You must free yourself from desperate, clinging love. Or you'll burn up."

In the silent meditation that followed, Nicole settled on the Zen koan Helen had referenced, calming her breathing, relaxing her spine.

Monk: Does a dog have Buddha nature?

Joshu: Mu.

She half-closed her eyes. What does *mu* mean?

Sometimes meditation was like following a bouncing ball down a flight of stairs. It had its own thrilling momentum. It floated her down levels of thought, leading her toward something silent and immovable at the core of her, the space where time unclocked itself and she became a singular being. On good days her meditation was like flying through her own mind, her inner self a map of neural nodes. There was a place she could reach where she felt a great growing warmth for Paul, her mother. A place where she forgave her father for dying. And another one, farther down, where her own past released its hold on her. Where she could be seventeen again and could think about her father, or about Jules, without the crazy blindsiding of grief and regret.

Meditation was not passive, as many people thought. It was like feeling your way down a flight of stairs in the dark, your every nerve awake and listening. If you felt your way through one room and another, you might find a well whose water never stirred. You might feel the damp inside of a cave. You might be able to speak to people who were gone and ask them questions. But she could not find these things without her Master's hand on her shoulder, his voice inside: *You have found what is vast and empty, the unborn.*

In her private meeting with her Master afterward, she said, "I can reach deep levels. You know I can. But I can only do it when you guide me, when you walk me through my own mind. Without that, I stay right on the surface. I wait for something to happen, but nothing does."

Her Master's large, sunburned face was relaxed and grave, his watery gray eyes settled on something over her shoulder. He would not reward her with his gaze until she had done well. They were seated on tatami mats in his second room, cross-legged, Nicole trying to exude serenity in the posture of her spine and hands. Over time, sitting cross-legged always pressed on her bad ankle, but the Master looked as reliable as stone. "When you're monitoring your thoughts, what returns again and again?" he asked.

"Well—" Her eyes moved to the ceiling, then back to the broad exposed V of her Master's chest. She remembered him telling her of his wandering and searching, the questing that had ended in Zen. You're like me, he'd said. It's taken you a long time to find your way. But now you've found me. She'd begun to cry, out of relief.

"It's you," she said. "It's Paul. I keep thinking about people I love, and I think, How can I let go of them? Love is a good thing. Being bound to other people, because they love you"—she choked—"is a good thing."

"Don't try to cut ties with a knife," he said. "Don't shove things and people away from you. Remember instead that your attachment is real, while the apparent permanence of these feelings and people is not."

"The Buddha says to make all desires cease."

"You don't begin by denying it. You begin by saying, 'Yes, I have this desire.'" He reached out and rested his hand on her knee.

Nicole held still. She was always surprised when they reached this moment in their meetings. They were teacher and student, very old, accustomed friends; each time he let his hand travel up her skirt, the shock was fresh. It was only then that she noticed the dry, furry smell of his robe, the warmth of the straw mat on her knees, the strange vegetal whiffs of his green tea breath. He draped himself on top of her, yanking his robes aside. She followed the sound of her breath up and down her rib cage. *I am awake.* Sometimes it was more like a dream, like the arrival of the white bear in her favorite fairy tale, "East of the Sun, West of the Moon." An enchanted prince in disguise, visiting her in her sleep. She let him place her limbs where he wanted them, let his hand clasp the back of her neck and pull her close. She let him drive into her furiously, the sensation bright and hot and clear like an injection of burning liquid amber. "Oh," she said finally, once. The grinning jade Buddha watched them from the corner.

Then he eased off her and they began straightening themselves. There was no higher authority to be worried about, no law or punishment from tribunal, cleric, or priest, but Nicole felt tense after each encounter, no matter how eagerly she leaned into his grasp. She did not know if it was a sinful thing, something to be ashamed of, or if it was holy and right.

Afterward they lay back together and he read her poetry from the sutras. He read the parts about the beautiful daughters of the god Mara, sent to seduce the Buddha on his journey toward enlightenment. He described their long, flowing hair and the many jewels that adorned their virginal bodies. His fingers traced her navel in trailing circles.

"My brother wants me to move to New York," she said. "Maybe I should. Sometimes I think I'm stalled here." The words sounded potent and frightening as she spoke them.

"And throw away all the progress we've made?" he said. "Why?"

"What am I to you?" she asked. "Am I just a nun?" She thought of Helen's warning: You need to know what you mean to him.

He didn't answer her directly. He read from the sutras instead, quoting Mara the deceiver:

You are bound by every shackle
Whether human or divine;
The bonds that tie you down are strong
And you shall not escape me.

"You are my student, little *theri*," he said. "It's wonderful to be a student in Zen. It's the best thing there is. There is nothing more you need."

Yesterday, she'd been with Sean. It had been awkward and fumbling, but they'd laughed and she'd felt some semblance of normalcy.

Then her Master stroked her hair, and made the promises that lovers make: that he would always be there, that she would never be without him. Wasn't that enough?

. . .

At home, she shed her clothes laboriously, exhausted as she always was after the session. Kukai slunk between her legs and then retreated from her outreached hand. After a minute in a scalding shower, up to her ankles in soapy water, she turned off the faucet and squatted on the shower floor to unclog the drain.

There was a wet mass of something in there. It was her own hair. She drew it out slowly, a great red-brown ball of it.

She reached in deeper and pulled out a fat twisted rope, which connected to another glob of hair, glistening, clotted with soap scum. She thought she might gag but kept pulling slowly so as not to break the chain of it, loosening cluster after cluster, watching it adhere sluggishly to the tile. It seemed like it was all here, handfuls, ten years' worth. And if she kept pulling, it would get lighter and redder, back to the strawberry down, the color of her hair when she was twenty-two and said, *I want to learn from you* and *I will be your student, I will be yours for this life and all the next lives* and that was all she wanted.

Here was the sick thing worming through her, the gummy plaque of her own desperation. This was the thing that made her watch Helen with the greedy territorial gaze of an old alley cat. *He is mine, he chose me, he has no more willing pupil.* Here was ten years' worth of oleaginous submission.

Naked, wet, she picked up the cordless and dialed Paul's number one-handed, dripping on the kitchen floor. When she'd managed to burn every bridge, there was still Paul. She listened to the lonely digital ring, her only connection these days to a world outside her Master's damp cave.

She'd run away from home when she was seventeen with her boyfriend, Jules, and another friend, just driven out of her suburb one night and not returned for the better part of a year. Her mother and Paul had then fallen into a long habit of worry that never left. Not until now did she wonder what her family had thought during that time: She was in trouble. She was the culmination of a series of bad parenting choices. She was a mistake. She was dead. Month after month that your child is gone, you cannot picture where she is or if she needs you. Then, as now, she'd come close to the brink before she'd admit she needed help, needed to flee from the mess she'd made, needed someone's arms to run into.

When Paul picked up, she asked, "Are you still there?" as though it hadn't been days at all.

"Always," he said. It was sweet, really. She had to remember that he was sweet.

"All right," she said. "Sign the lease."

JOCELYN

Paul had come to Boston at January's end, and for one weekend they packed like college students on the last day of the term: savagely, stuffing things in garbage bags. She threw out more than she kept, feeling a rare glee as she tossed chipped mugs, shrunken T-shirts, blackened pots. Shedding material possessions was a question not of letting go but of waging a ceaseless and vigilant war; you had to fight not to accumulate. There was scarcely an armful of clothes to begin with: long skirts with flower prints, peasant blouses, whatever reminded her that she was a wanderer-outcast at heart. But in her bare closet there was always that navy dress hanging at the back, the good shoes, the panty-hose rolled in a ball, things you needed from time to time.

She picked up a strand of tattered Tibetan prayer flags that had been strung on her window for she didn't know how long. No: she did. These were the same flags she'd had with her when she ran away, for that long gone year. Her bare feet were up on the dash and the flags streamed out the window behind them, a thread of blue and gold. She looked at Paul and stuffed the flags in her pocket, a magic act in reverse. Disappearing the memory.

The Buddha told his monks they might have two robes, a water filter, and a begging bowl. At the end, staring at the full garbage bags, Nicole had moved one chosen at random from the pack pile to the trash pile.

The ringing woke her.

"Is this Nicole!" a fuzzy female voice shouted down her ear. She was in the new apartment in Curry Hill, still amid a riot of unopened bags, her mattress on the floor beside its new plastic-wrapped frame. Out her window she could see a Middle Eastern bookstore with Arabic script, and a young man with his feet up on the counter, reading a book. Photo spreads on a travel agency's glass storefront advertised packages for the hajj. In a slanting rain she gazed at sandy minarets, green flags, and white-robed pilgrims moving like sea foam to the oil-black Kaaba. It was beautiful, the way all religions she didn't know looked beautiful.

"Yes? Who's this?"

"Jocelyn. I'm Buffy's friend."

"Buffy?" It was too early in the morning. Buffy from the Zendo, of the Christmas party.

"You know, from your meditation class? Buffy said you'd know—"

"Oh yes, of course. I know who she is. But how—"

"I guess she found out that you had moved? Anyway, I live in Brooklyn. She was just wondering if you might like to meet. It's always nice to meet new people in a new city."

Of course, Buffy would be the one to make inquiries after Nicole missed a session. She was stable and reliable; she was a married Back Bay woman who kept track of where to send Christmas cards. "I thought you might want to meet somebody here," Jocelyn said. "New York can be a lonely place."

New York might be difficult; but in Boston it was nearly impossible to make new friends, with every face hidden behind a baseball cap or a coat collar. They were all so buttoned up, so tribal, and Nicole was too, wary of change or too much kindness. She made a private promise to herself: Meet people. Make friends. They chose a time for coffee in a bookstore in Union Square.

She packed onto a 4 train among twenty-somethings with matching earbuds. When a man with a cane got on and began a loud, determined monologue, she listened, then dropped a quarter in his Red Sox cap as he swayed by. "God bless you, young lady," he said, and she bowed, half-expecting the pressure of a priest's hand on her head as after Communion, the brief push and clasp of her skull.

She watched chess games in Union Square under umbrellas and the evening rush at Whole Foods, the streetlights in rain and newsagents in their flimsy stands, enthroned behind Aztec temples of gum. Paul was away at another conference; except for her new employers, she hadn't spoken to anyone in days. In a week's time she'd applied for and gotten a job in management at Nordstrom Rack, overseeing women's wear. Paul had helped with this too, having heard something about an opening from a friend in textiles; she was keeping track of all the ways he was greasing the wheels for her, helping her to slide into her new life. Maybe the job would lead to something higher up, a desk job with corporate, trips to China to buy silk. She occasionally imagined that for herself.

She'd been fingerprinted by the borough of Manhattan as part of her new-employee background check. She'd wanted to turn to the unsmiling woman rolling her thumb on an inkpad and tell her she was on the run, an escapee. (Was that what she was?) She'd seen her first crazy ranting person on the subway, her first handful of Hasidim unsmilingly handing out flyers on Talmudic law, her first cop toting an AK-47. The people of New York did not have time for her and her stories.

In the bookstore she followed the signs to the Religion/Spirituality section, on the third floor. There was a pleasing library hush up here, among the unpopular shelves. She traced a line of the books on Buddhism and her finger stopped on a translation of the Therigatha. It was a very old part of the original canon, a collection of poetry by Buddhist nuns. She opened it to a random page and read:

I gave up my house
and set out into homelessness.
I gave up desire and hate.
My ignorance was thrown out.
I pulled out craving
along with its root.
Now I am quenched and still.

She closed the book and pressed her forehead to its spine, suddenly overcome. Her heart beating wispily, her breath too short.

In her very last Tuesday session, Helen had been absent. In the private meeting that followed, she bowed formally before her Master, pressing her forehead to the mat. One more prostration. Then one more, to hide the trembling. Twenty-six thousand and one.

Her Master was speaking of the importance of achieving no-mind, an advanced concept they'd been working on. It was not the same thing as not thinking; it was returning to a time before conscious, verbal thought. She kept nodding, but he could tell there was something changed in the air between them.

"You're not listening to me," he said sharply.

She bowed again, to hide her face. "Master—what if I were needed in New York?"

Above her head, his voice seemed to come from every corner of the room. "It's important for you to stay close to me. You're at a delicate stage in your advancement. One wrong move"—he put his hand on her thigh, closed his fingers tight—"and you could slide back into a deluded state. When we near insight, we become afraid of the truths we might learn."

In the dense silence of the room, she waited.

After a long time, he said, "And I would miss you."

Something was tickling under her tongue, some new anger was there to make her speak. She looked up, said, "You have plenty of other students to keep you busy. Helen, she's bright. When she comes back—you could keep working on her."

"You know you are my best," he said simply.

"Are you sure you don't tell all your students that?"

He laughed, a sudden bark. She could surprise him; she had that talent. But he quickly grew stern again. "You've become impudent. I ought to whip you with the *keisaku* until you see sense." He was referring to the flat wooden stick used during meditation sessions. If a monk slouched or fell asleep, or showed any lapse in concentration, the *keisaku,* the teaching stick, would be cracked across his shoulders. In Japan, it was serious business. It could raise welts.

Nicole took a deep breath. Monks were supposed to welcome the beating as needed assistance, to bow and thank their masters for this gift of instruction. "I'm sorry, Master. I accept my punishment." She bowed low, closed her eyes.

The *keisaku* leaned against the far wall. She heard her Master get up and pad by her in his socks. He stroked her shoulder with it, he moved it up and down her back. Gently across her body, caressing her.

She was shaking as she walked away from the Zen center that day. The street was quiet, the storefronts going dark, the animatronic lizard gazing at her with its unlit eyes. He did not know this was the last time.

The Buddha said that when a man has a poisoned arrow in his chest, you don't stop to wonder who fired it, or what kind of wood it was made of, or what bird supplied the feathers. You don't argue about what poison is on the tip.

You yank it out.

"Are you Nicole?" A woman was standing sway-hipped in the aisle. She looked to be in her late thirties, slim and dressed in draped vintage clothing—a frilly dress with an old housewife print under a Castro jacket, strands of her long blond hair tangled in a few necklaces. Whenever Nicole saw footage of hippies like her on television, she felt both longing and embarrassment.

She shelved the book of poetry and grabbed at a biography of the Dalai Lama instead. "You must be Jocelyn. How do you know Buffy again?"

"We worked together, oh, years ago, when I lived in Boston." Jocelyn touched the spine of the Dalai Lama book. "Do you think he's happy?"

"The Dalai Lama? Oh—probably. He's always smiling."

"He always looks sad behind his smile. Like he's got the weight of the world on his shoulders."

"He's not Jesus," said Nicole. It came out sharper than she'd intended. But this woman sounded like the sort she was always being confused with: women who read Buddhist sutras and horoscopes with equal credulity, women who liked their spirituality lite. She put down the Dalai Lama book and stepped away.

Jocelyn laughed. "True, true." They were quiet. "Damn. So you're a Buddhist? Like, a real one? I meditate a little, but Vipassana-style—I think that's what Hindus do."

They sat down at the café in the store and drank shots of matcha green tea. Jocelyn wanted to know if Nicole had grown up in Boston and what that was like. Nicole answered warily. There was a certain sleepy amiability to Jocelyn's questions that kept Nicole talking, telling her about the move, her brother, even a quick acknowledgment—something she rarely elaborated on—that she had converted to Buddhism when she was seventeen.

Jocelyn nodded, eyes wide, swallowing the room, the walls of books, Nicole. "So how did it feel?"

No one had asked her that before. "It felt like—like saying goodbye to someone you love."

"Oh wow, that's really sad," Jocelyn said. Then she smiled again and pressed her hands together, in greeting or prayer. "Come out with me tonight. I'm having some drinks with friends. If you're new in town, you need to meet some people."

"Thanks, but—"

"But what? Come on." She grabbed Nicole's arm and shook it playfully.

. . .

The party started around sunset in a bar in the Village, a dark little polished-wood pub with loud music and baskets of steaming sweet potato fries. Jocelyn waved around the group: "This is Nicole the Buddhist. That's Simon the painter, Jenny does videography, and Harold has this performance art thing going on right now in the Village—you should check it out . . ."

The friends, as Nicole had expected, were familiar to her. She sat lightly at the edge of a booth, ready to flee, as they introduced themselves: youngish, dressed in nervous black or army surplus, explaining to her a variety of ordinary jobs (receptionist, Web designer, something in advertising) while qualifying them with a "but" and an explanation of what they really were, which was poets, artists, filmmakers. The fledgling novels or drying canvases hovered in the wings of their every conversation. They were proud and detached, funny and bored with themselves, with each other. Their political beliefs were declared in pin form on their bags. When one of them arrived straight from work, still in tie and shirtsleeves, he was razzed heavily. The women were easy with their body language, tugging on his tie, ruffling his too-gelled hair, draping their arms around each other to make space on the hard pewlike benches at their long table.

They pounced on her as a new source of life. "If you're a Buddhist, doesn't that mean you're a nihilist?" one of them asked.

"I'm kind of a Buddhist, too," said the poet. "I went on a meditation retreat once. It was insane. By the end I started hallucinating and having all these crazy sex dreams." He nodded, widening his eyes. "Crazy, tantric shit."

"Going on a retreat doesn't mean you're a Buddhist," said Jocelyn. "This girl's legit. She converted and everything." She pushed a beer at her, smiling encouragingly.

"I bet Mommy and Daddy weren't happy about that," said the artist.

"Crazy *Kama sutra* stuff." The poet forged determinedly ahead. "Doing it with cows. Somebody there was an expert at tantric sex.

He said you haven't screwed until you've screwed in a state of higher awareness. Do you do that Tantra stuff?"

"Is that a pickup line?" asked Nicole, which got a laugh around the table. She flushed but held her gaze steady. The questions continued.

"*Do* you convert to Buddhism? What's the ceremony like?"

Nicole aimed for the question that was easiest to answer. "It's very simple. You take refuge in the Three Jewels."

"The Three Jewels?"

"The Buddha, the dharma, and the *sangha*." She did not translate the words. She let them all stare at her.

"So you must have seen the Dalai Lama talk. He was in New York a few years ago."

"I heard he was sold out from day one, as soon as the tickets went on sale."

"Actually, I'm a Zen Buddhist. He's a Tibetan Buddhist," she tried to say, but the conversation moved away from her, which was a relief. Jocelyn heard her, though. She had an amused, thoughtful light to her eyes. "You must get this a lot," she said.

The party kept changing shape, gaining and losing heads, always shifting. More people joined them at the bar and others left, then all of them headed to another bar, louder and brighter, with black lights and shot glasses lined up on every table. From there they all ended up in someone's apartment in the Village, a tiny one-bedroom dense with Turkish rugs on the walls and floor. Jocelyn, laughing and asking questions, looking deeply into all of their eyes, was easy to become attached to. The others followed her from room to room, or tugged her arm insistently like children until she moved to a different group to talk. They wanted to know what she thought of everything, and she obliged them, warmly, lazily.

She and Jocelyn took the train to Brooklyn over the river, looking back to the skyline, which was not as bright as Nicole had expected. It was dark and enormous. At the top of one building she saw a plane signal light blinking blue, and its pair in the water, blue-black-blue. "This is the bad bridge," said Jocelyn, when they had been quiet for a while. "Bad memories. I once almost jumped off this bridge."

She thought the woman must be drunk, speaking so freely. But Jocelyn's eyes were bright and steady; she spoke easily, unafraid of the consequences. Nicole wondered if this was the sort of thing New York people shared; or if saying it casually diminished its power; or if there was something particular about herself, some whiff of empathy about her that made her safe.

She turned her face away, worked her bag nervously with her hands. The scales were too heavily weighted in one direction. She groped for some matching intimacy to even them, but there was nothing she had the courage to say.

They found another apartment with a party going on; Nicole drank another beer. She was not in Boston, not pushing and squabbling among the young girls of the Zendo. She was not her old self, not anyone else yet. These were the people her teenage friends might have become, or hoped to. For the first time in years she wondered what Holly and Colin were up to now, if they had vaulted easily into their next lives. And Eddie? Had he finally gotten where he wanted to go? And herself? If things had gone differently, would she have become this person of effortless cool, leaning on the balcony of an apartment in Park Slope, free to dream herself into whatever shape she chose? She watched Jocelyn do her slow-shuffling white-girl dance to a song on the radio, hands over her head, laughing beautifully.

Well, ten-year detour notwithstanding, she was here now. She gripped her bottle, tipping it back into her throat.

Presently she found herself talking to a friend of Jocelyn's named

Elliot, a man with high, thin eyebrows and an artful, appraising stare. He pressed himself close to her in the crowded apartment, touching the icy neck of his beer to her wrist to get her attention. "I've dabbled in that a little too, you know," said Elliot. "Bikram yoga. That sort of thing."

That sort of comment always pissed her off. "What else have you dabbled in? Judaism, say? Did you try out getting circumcised for a while and then decide it wasn't for you?"

"Whoa, whoa." He held up his hands in the 'don't shoot me' pose, one finger and thumb still clutching the neck of his beer. "I getcha, I getcha. Fuck the tourists, right?"

"That's right." She turned away; she was ready for the conversation to be over. Here was her new, angry self. It was exhilarating to slip away without another word, not an apology, not an ingratiating smile.

He liked that, though. He followed her out to the narrow balcony, came up behind her and clinked her beer with his own. "Hey, you didn't give me a chance to apologize."

"I'm not interested."

"Look at you," he said, mugging at her. "She be badass."

She tried to focus on the skyline, a crowded network of lights, jumbled buildings—internal, unknown Brooklyn. "Maybe." Somehow the exchange had gone from galling to fun. This was how confident men won you over, softened you up. He leaned on the railing beside her and told her a long story about the cereal café in Fort Greene that also sold designer sneakers, displayed under museum glass beside the Froot Loops. Millennial nostalgia and New York fashion all within one storefront. He said, Now you can have whatever you had as a kid twenty years ago. So Lite-Brites and fanny packs and those bracelets you slapped onto your wrists were back in. He displayed the shoes he'd gotten there: electric-green Air Jordans. He'd picked them out with Jocelyn and her husband.

"Wait, Jocelyn is married?" Nicole interrupted.

"Well, yeah," said Elliot. "Totally, a hundred percent. And he's this straitlaced, nine-to-five guy. A *doctor.*" He made a face. "If I had to go to school as long as doctors do, I'd kill myself." It was the third such threat she'd heard that night.

The anecdote he was telling had lots of ins and outs, names she didn't know, places in the city she'd never heard of. But all of them were accompanied with the confident assertion that soon she *would* know them, soon she would have her own stories to tell about that laundromat, that overpass, that pizza place with its grizzled, toothless third-generation cook sliding peels into a brick oven. The story implied that it would have no end, that it would continue. Familiar buildings and parties and stories. And if she couldn't grab hold, couldn't add her own laugh line, she'd fail to belong. She listened hard, trying to catch the thread.

They moved to the crowded kitchen, and Elliot opened the fridge. "Another?" He came up, handed her a beer. "So what about you? Conversion. What was that like?" Before she could answer, he went on: "It must be—something really intense. You don't hear people talk about the moment, the actual moment. Except for the assholes who want to tell you all about accepting Jesus as your personal Lord and Savior. You can't get *them* to shut up."

"It's a private experience," she said finally.

"Like coming out or something."

"Maybe."

"You say, 'Dad, I'm a Buddhist,' and he says, 'I didn't raise no Buddhist kid' and gets out his belt."

Her father had handled it as he handled all things: with a heartbreaking, Olympic attempt to pretend nothing had changed. "God, no."

"I guess you're not going to tell me."

"No." She wasn't going to tell this smug stranger. There was too much at stake. And there was the Communion on the Common, and priests and dead cats. All of Boston was wrapped up in her conversion. If she tried to tell, he might laugh.

"It's as secret as the moment you fall in love," said Elliot.

"Yes."

It was loud in the kitchen, and they couldn't hear well. "Come on," he said. He led her down a tiny hallway into the bedroom and they sat on the bed, drinking thirstily. In the bathroom, girls' voices rose high in laughter. "Doing a line, probably," said Elliot. "It's hot, actually, what you do. I couldn't do it. It takes dedication. It takes belief. I am unable to believe in anything." In the next room over, the wall began to thump rhythmically. It had become that kind of party.

"Want to have some fun?" Elliot asked. He put his arm around her, moving in slow. She thought fleetingly of Sean—but they were taking a break now, weren't they? Wasn't this the blank slate?—then kissed Elliot firmly. He reached a hand into her blouse, icy from the beer.

The door opened. "There you are," said Jocelyn. "Elliot, enough snogging. You can see her later." She held out her hand. Nicole rose quickly to it, surprised by her own relief.

"Hold on there, Joss," said Elliot. "Cock-block much?"

Jocelyn smiled; Nicole wondered if it was possible to offend her. "Maybe next time, Romeo. I'm going home, and I'm not leaving Nicole among such ill-intentioned strangers."

"I get it, I get it. Girl solidarity."

They walked back to Jocelyn's building, laughing and slow. On the threshold of her apartment, Jocelyn turned and put a finger to her lips; they tiptoed into a dark living room, and Jocelyn threw on the lights. "My husband's probably asleep."

"You didn't seem like you were married." Nicole swayed into Jocelyn's shoulder, just drunk enough to think her honesty was what everyone wanted. The cluttered mismatch of hipster relics she had expected was not here; the apartment was clean and modern, with wall-to-wall bookshelves and a rocking chair with a seahorse blanket draped on it.

Jocelyn just laughed. "People will surprise you." A sound came from another room, and Jocelyn left, then padded back with a baby on her hip, bumping it gently up and down. Nicole picked up a silver rattle—Tiffany?—and put it back down. "You *are* surprising."

Jocelyn raised a finger to her lips. "Ssh. Don't wake my husband—he flies to Stockholm tomorrow." She rocked slowly, patting the baby. She said quietly, "You're surprising, too. Sorry they all swarmed on you. Being a real Buddhist has some cachet."

"That's all right. Even Buddhists think they're pretty cool."

"Why is that?"

"Because Buddhists *are* cool. To be a Buddhist, all you have to do is look at the people you love and say, Bye. You have to say, Whatever you thought was permanent or lasting will fade. The universe will die. The lights will go out. So don't get too attached to things, because they're not going to last. You have to have an existential crisis to be any good at it."

"So does that make you cool? Did you convert to be cool?"

"Me? No. Never was cool, never will be cool." She could hear the teenage girls in her class, the pretty ones: *fucking weirdo.*

"How did you end up here? How do you live this life?" Nicole waved her hand, took in the tasteful apartment, the view of Manhattan, the baby nestled so naturally, already asleep. Landscape paintings on the walls, coffee cups lined like soldiers on the shelf.

Jocelyn studied her thoughtfully. "You really want to know?"

"Yeah. I do."

Jocelyn stared at the baby in her arms. "I shouldn't be here. I grew up in Wisconsin, and my dad left us when I was a kid. As soon as I was old enough to drive, I came to New York. You name it, I did it. I had a lot of fun, too. Most of it was fun. Wake up on the floor of some underground club, don't know what you did the night before, but it doesn't matter. How can anything hurt you if you're open to everything, if your only answer to every question is yes? I was perfect. Free and unattached.

"Of course, that only lasts so long. And you start to see the people you know crashing. The people you met tonight, they're the survivors, the ones who pulled their shit together and made it out. There were plenty of people from my twenties that I can't find now. Went homeless or went home. Some OD'd. I was usually the one who'd be sitting in the waiting room after bringing in some friend because I could look pretty sober and not get in too much trouble myself. There was this night-shift ER doctor at Deaconess that I'd see. He'd come out and ask if I was a relative and I'd say no, just a friend. And his eyes were always very sad, and together we'd figure out next of kin. We'd go through my friend's pants pockets looking for phone numbers. And I'd realize I barely even knew these people. I didn't even know their last names or where they came from. After a couple of times, it got to be this weird joke. Like I was a regular at some bar and he was the bartender come to top me up, and we'd both laugh."

Jocelyn turned her eyes down the hall, to the dark bedroom, where her husband slept.

"Each night you'd go out into this exciting darkness. It was warm and it smelled like candy and ash and Jack Daniel's. And you'd have fun there, but you couldn't stay or you would die. There was this one friend who didn't make it back. That was when I spent the night on the bridge, daring myself to jump because I was so scared of—I don't know. How empty I was. In the morning I walked home and I knew how lucky I was, that I was unscathed. But not really. Not at all. Then the ER doctor said, 'When will you get tired?' and I said, 'I don't know,' and he said, 'When you get tired, I'll be waiting.' And he was."

She smiled at Nicole. "That's my story. That's why I'm here. Eventually you get tired. You try to run and run, but whatever you're running from always catches you. And I don't know if it's a good or bad thing. I just know I'm here, and I'm alive. Is that Zen?"

Nicole patted Jocelyn on the shoulder. "Yes. You are very Zen."

"I tried Zen for a while," she said. "It was very—compelling. But I had to get out; it was taking over my life." Jocelyn smiled again and looked at Nicole, serious now. "So what's your story?"

She opened her mouth. It was too dry to swallow. Just when she was going to have to make something up or tell the truth, her cell phone rang. It was an unknown number with a Boston area code.

"I'm sorry, I have to take this," she said.

In the elevator, she watched her phone vibrate and chime: a new voice mail. Sean? She looked at it for a long time, and then she deleted it without listening.

· · ·

That weekend, Jocelyn arrived at her apartment with a shopping bag in one hand, her head tilted in her friendly, appraising way. "Well? Coming?"

"Where?"

"I told you, I'm going to make sure you see the right things in this city. You need a tour guide who's worth a damn."

Several times that week, they drank thick Turkish coffee at a café around the corner or pushed baby Emmeline's stroller through the narrow aisles of bodegas while Jocelyn picked up lychee nuts and cans of coconut milk and anything that took her fancy. Then they walked for hours, sometimes huddled under a shared umbrella. There was so much to see. Jocelyn took her to the Earth Room: a fourth-floor walk-up in Greenwich Village packed wall to wall with twenty-two inches of rich, dark topsoil. Then late-night bars hidden behind unmarked doors, where smoking cocktails named after famous authors or garden plants arrived in mason jars. And wet covered farmers' markets, where Jocelyn picked wild artichokes, making plans for meals with her artist friends.

Nicole had not told Jocelyn the reason she'd left Boston. Nobody really knew. But she figured you could read her unease on her face, in the hunted way she looked over her shoulder in dark streets or startled warily at every ring of the phone.

On the subway, she and Jocelyn huddled close to make room for Emmeline's stroller, their knees knocking together as if they were much younger girls, like best friends. She wondered if Jocelyn was the kind of person who fell into easy intimacies with her woman friends, who climbed into laps or played with hair, seeking a physical closeness and emotional attachment. There was that girlfriend she'd had at nine who'd insisted that Nicole go into the bathroom with her, who'd chatted away on the toilet and seemed disappointed when Nicole had turned her back, mortified. There was some kind of a test girls gave one another, and she had failed.

Meet people. Make friends.

What was she so afraid of, really?

They rode the subway to Jocelyn's place over that troublesome bridge, and Nicole thought of what had almost happened there. She knew what Jocelyn had meant when she'd announced, the day they met, that she had almost jumped. Almost. Like an accident of fate, a lucky break: that tree almost fell on me; the storm passed over our town. It was out of her hands.

"You're thinking about what I told you. About the bridge," Jocelyn said abruptly.

"What?"

"I can tell." Jocelyn shrugged. "It's all right. I told you because I could tell you were a very private person. You weren't going to blab it all over town." Then she leaned into Nicole. "When are you going to tell me what brought you here?"

"What do you mean?"

"Come on. It's not a job. Is it your brother?"

"Not really. I needed a change."

Nicole felt the warm glow of Jocelyn's attention, the comfort of it. "Who called you the other night? What's your story?"

This is how women made friends, Nicole thought, how they learned to trust people, by confiding their stories.

It was a secret that no one really understood. Sometimes when she was feeling poetic, she thought about it in terms of the stages of the Buddha's life. The Prince; the Runaway; the Mendicant; the Saint. There she was in her bedroom in Boston, dreaming child dreams, safely enveloped in love. And then there she was, a teenager, smelling of weed, wary as a cat, creeping out of her house and into a car, riding away into the early suburban dawn before the birds began to sing. And then she was eighteen, busking on a street corner in a city she no longer remembered.

· · ·

Just a few weeks ago, she'd stood shivering in the damp air on Sean's porch, looking out at the marsh, scanning for the rustle and blue-gray of a heron. You could usually see them this time of year; they would be nesting soon, bound to one spot, and the males would be standing guard.

Leaving took time. There was paperwork, a subletter to find, her car to sell. When you are a Boston girl trying to leave your hometown, you begin with guilt and end with Irish good-byes. As she was making plans, another week passed and she hadn't told Sean she was leaving. She spent the weekend at his house, playing poker and walking in the marsh and running her finger up and down his jawline, feeling for the stubble that wouldn't yet be there until later in the evening.

Waking up beside him. Listening to his explanations of cherry, maple, mahogany, the care and love that goes into the graceful curve of a chair's arms. Reading books with their legs entwined. Singing Boston songs in their cracked winter voices. *Oh, I love that dirty water . . .*

It wasn't until the end of February, with Paul coming to pack her up, that she had to tell him.

"You look so sad," he said when he opened the door.

"Well, I guess I am," she said. "I have to tell you something."

It was funny, hugging in a Boston winter. There were at least a few inches of puffy coat between them. "Can we go inside?" she asked.

"Well—" He hesitated. "It's a mess. But okay."

The living room was filling up. Furniture from the basement had migrated upstairs; two hat racks and a narrow armoire were in the foyer. The kitchen counters were crenellated with knickknacks, the living room, a showroom jumble. "I've been meaning to sort through all this," said Sean. "I figured I'd finally get to it. It'll look worse before it looks better."

Nicole sat on a couch she didn't remember having seen before and picked up, from the coffee table, a china dog with blue sideways-glancing eyes. "Do you have to keep all this old stuff?" It made her uneasy, the way the knickknacks and furniture had of pressing in. Shrinking the air and light of a space. It was hard to swing her elbows, to draw a deep breath. It reminded her of all that family furniture, her doomed inheritance, waiting for her in her childhood home.

She looked at papers in a stack threatening to topple: bills mixed with credit card offers. "Quite a mess here. Why do you keep these things?"

He said, "I like it, okay? Is there something wrong with liking things?"

Here now, was something: the beginning of a first fight. A nice, tidy reason to say good-bye. Something that would make this whole process easier. "This is excessive, don't you think?" She felt exhilarated by her own cruelty.

"No, not really." He took the china dog and stood there holding it tightly, as though afraid she might throw it across the room. But sometimes you had to push away what was toxic to you, didn't you? And wouldn't it be better for everyone—a quick, clean break?

He sat down beside her, moving aside a stack of newspapers. "So. Tell me what's up."

"Well." She looked into her hands. "There's a lot you don't know about me."

He laughed. "Ditto."

"Well—" And she stopped. She had planned to ignore the shaking in her hands and tell him everything. First, about the strict Catholic house she'd grown up in, and then the conversion. About how she ran away, and after, how her Master became the center her life, and how that center was eating her up.

But she could not say it. Sean would be surprised at first, and cover his disappointment. He would arch back away from her and try to smile. And then he would be ashamed of her, though he would be too kind to show it.

Better to have him think she had to leave. A job change. A restraining order. She flicked through the most acceptable lies. "It's my father," she said finally. "He's sick. It's been going on for a long time, but he's worse. My brother wants me to come to New York." It was not so far from the truth. It was just that her father had died ten years ago.

Sean bit his lip and nodded solemnly.

She added, "I'm sorry. I've had this feeling for a while—I have to get out of this place. It'd be better if you just forgot about me for a while."

"Oh. Like we'd never met."

Now she was angry. "We were just friends, weren't we? Just friends having a good time?"

"If that's what you want to call it."

"Are. We're still friends."

"Are. Okay."

"What do you want from me?" she demanded. "I don't understand you!"

"What am I supposed to say? I'm not doing any better understanding you!" He looked away. "What do you really want me to say? That I don't like you after all? That I'm some no-good piece-of-shit guy who just wants some tail? Would that make you feel better—to think of me as a douchebag?" He stood up. "All right. I'll do that for you. I'll do what you want. Bye, Nicole, I won't miss that saggy white Irish ass of yours. There's plenty more around this town."

"That's more like it."

They sat in silence for a while. "Now we're both sad," he said. "Why do we both smile when we're sad?"

"It's a Puritan thing," Nicole said.

"But we're Catholics."

"Boston Puritan Catholics."

He sighed, and held on to her arm. "When do you leave?"

"My brother comes—"

"Don't tell me. Stay with me until you go. Let's make it an Irish good-bye."

"I thought an Irish good-bye meant leaving without the other person knowing."

"Exactly. You'll stay with me, and then one day I'll wake up and you'll be gone. Haven't you ever wanted to just—slip away, so you don't cause another person pain?"

She laughed. And thought, *Yes. Yes, that's exactly what I've always wanted.*

. . .

"So what's your story?" Jocelyn asked.

Now she could feel the threat in Jocelyn's innocent question, in her wide-open eyes. She could feel herself slipping. She had not been able to tell Sean her story; he was too close. But to tell a stranger? Why not? To walk the story away from herself for a little while. "Well, there's my mother," she began, hopeful, as she always was, that this time, she'd understand it all.

. . .

When she was back in her empty apartment, pouring kibble for Kukai, her phone rang in her bag. She fumbled for it, wondering if it was Sean, needing it to be him. She pressed the phone urgently to her ear.

"Hello," said her Master. "It's me."

Dear Sean,

Siddhartha and his monks are gathered around the fire. The day's begging is done, the meal is eaten; the moist evening air clamors with insects. The monks are squatting in their yellow robes. Even in the heat, they press close to the dying fire, trying to gain some protection from the insects with its smoke. There are nuns among them, too, staring into the flames, though it's hard to distinguish them. They wear the same voluminous robes. Their heads are shaved and scabby. Their faces are deeply creased. It is mostly older women, the widows, the mothers who have lost children, who take refuge here, with the man with the long fingers and toes and earlobes. They watch him out of the corner of their eyes, wondering if he feels the hunger they feel after just one bowl of rice a day. They want to please him. He looks like all of the other monks, but the group has instinctively angled toward him, listening. They really, really want to please him.

Look at the fire. He points, and they all look.

Look at the way it burns. We're like that. We're all burning up. Someone's got to stop the burning.

He tells them they're on fire. He says, If you were in a burning house and didn't know it, I would tell you any lie just to get you to come out, to heed the danger. I would make promises I couldn't keep. I would say great gifts were waiting for you. I'd say anything to make you safe.

My master said, You're burning up, poor thing. I'll put you out.

THE LIVING LIGHT

She told Jocelyn about her bronchitis when she was eight; there was something romantic about being young and sickly, wandering the house in her nightgown like a character out of *Jane Eyre*. She had lost her sense of smell and taste. The air had a disconcerting blankness that year, as if the world, with all its fresh mulch, its burnt toast, had ceased to speak to her.

There was nothing romantic, though, about the panicky feeling of too much fluid in her lungs. In the middle of the night, she sometimes woke to find her mother on the edge of the bed with a warm, wet rag, ready to cover her face because she had been coughing in her sleep. She remembered her mother pressing the bridge of her nose, the other hand on the back of her neck, the blurry smothering of the towel on her face. "There now. Breathe in."

That was as good a place to begin as any.

. . .

She knew from a young age that her mother was beautiful. She was tall, freckled and slender, and wore high-waisted slacks and loose blouses of heavy silk. She was not like the other mothers, dumpy and cheerful, pushing cookies in pilled sweaters. She never wore jeans; she wore stockings and high heels to the grocery store. When the four of them were all stepping out to a restaurant, their father grinning sheepishly in his fat retro ties, still surprised that he had ended up with her, Nicole and Paul looked at each other approvingly, proud of their parents, the way they brought a European glamor to their woodsy, snowy suburb.

This was the early nineties in the suburbs of Boston, when the only adult woman Nicole knew who lived alone was their frizzy-haired neighbor who'd had her dead dog stuffed and mounted in the window. "It's sad," her mother said whenever they passed the house or saw her across the room at a party.

This was the early nineties, when Boston's Big Dig was beginning and already over budget, a construction project that even preschoolers knew was going to change Boston forever. Her mother and father often hosted dinners for their friends and they all argued loudly about the destruction of the old Central Artery, the miles of tunnels that would bury Boston's traffic, the changing landscape of the city. There was a lot of talk about "old Boston" and "new Boston," but no one knew what "new Boston" would be. She remembered sitting in the kitchen with Paul, playing with toys and listening to their parents' voices through the door more than the words, her father's growing hoarse and deep, his voice a bulldozer, her mother's a reedy flute. Sometimes her mother's voice fell silent, leaving the chorus of the other adults. Then she would come into the kitchen holding a wine bottle by the neck with two fingers, and sit with them and silently pour herself a glass and another, looking faraway. Eventually, she'd be missed. "Liza, where are you?" a friend would call, and she'd touch Paul's and Nicole's heads and rejoin the party. Later that night they'd hear fighting in the bedroom: her father's voice low and pleading this time, her mother's louder and louder. Sometimes Nicole sat on the stairs and listened, struggling to understand: it was about humiliation, how could you say that, every time they come over you take their side. She pressed her forehead to the cool spindle of the railing. Soon they would quiet; they always did. Then, in the silence of the dark house, she could sleep.

This was before the Catholic churches began to close down and before the candlelight vigils were held. The scandals were beginning to break, but they were isolated, hushed, fodder for off-color jokes. At one of those dinners someone would make a crack about altar boys and the room would fill with uncomfortable laughter and her mother would promise to explain the joke later but never did.

It was when the wooded roads were still stacked with cars on Sundays and the pancake houses filled for after-Mass brunch. From her window Nicole could see their church, St. Augustine, through the trees of their neighborhood of Waban. She liked the church, the largeness and darkness of the old Gothic structure overlooking the highway. She liked the polished pews, the places where cracks in the wood had been lacquered over so that you couldn't feel them with your fingers. She liked the sermons about fear and trembling, as though God was the hand grabbing her shoulder when she went down to the basement and all the bulbs were blown. It seemed right to be afraid of God, watching you in the dark and brooding over you, his motivations little understood.

Remembering church now, she still felt the same combination of affection and dread. The special hush, the dark, dusty recesses, the places her eyes wandered and could not find definition, the sweet, plaintive wording of the hymns. She liked everybody bundling up late at night on Christmas Eve and hurrying down the hill in their good shoes in time to sing. She liked having her forehead smudged with ash on Ash Wednesday, and wearing the ash to school, and nodding to other children with the same smear of black.

In the "children's time," as the priest called it, she and the other kids were called up around the altar and he would trot out the usual kid-friendly Bible tales and then ask them if they had been good this week, as if he were Santa. "What have you done to please Jesus, Nicole?"

She never had an answer. Why would Jesus, bleeding up there, nailed to his cross, his eyes rolling in despair toward heaven, care if she'd flossed her teeth or cleared the table? He wasn't her friend, and he wasn't supposed to be; he was mysterious. He was a secret key to the universe's code. The code was written in blood and incense, in stained glass and silk, in bread and wine.

Back then, she used to see a gaggle of nuns go down the street or one alone in an airport and wonder what their lives were like. She took books about nuns out of the library, pedaling on her bike alone so she wouldn't have to show her mother what she'd gotten. She looked at golden-hued paintings of Hildegard von Bingen, the medieval nun who had received ecstatic visions of the Lord, who'd called what she saw "the living light."

What was the living light? Was it like being blinded by the fiery globe of the sun? Was it the flare of spots in your eyes after a camera flash?

She tried to imagine what ecstasy felt like.

This mystical world was better, somehow, than the ordinary world in which she lived. In her room, she swept a long black scarf off a shelf and draped it over her head. She worked her mother's rosary between her fingers. It was strange and exciting, as if she were entering a mysterious adult world and not the bright, chattering, stressful world of school.

With the scarf over her head, she pressed her hands together, said an Our Father, rolled her eyes piously to heaven the way Mary did in paintings. That was when Paul walked by her bedroom door. "Hey, it's Sister Nicole," he said, laughing.

She tore the scarf off her head, but Paul wrestled it back on, holding her down. "It suits you!"

"Get off!" She struggled and squirmed and spat, but he had six years on her.

"Come see her, Mom," Paul crowed. "The little sister. The child bride of Christ."

Nicole finally snatched the scarf away as their mother appeared in the doorway. "Don't make fun of her, Paul. It's sweet."

"Forgive me, Sister Nicole," said Paul, and he made a sweeping bow. She punched him as hard as she could, and he laughed again. "Not very nunlike," he said.

Sometimes the bronchitis shifted from chronic to acute and she was allowed to stay home from school. On these sick days, Nicole discovered that after sending Paul off, her mother sometimes returned to bed and slept till ten or eleven, or on into the afternoon. The house was a different place when she was the only one awake in it, the only creature making noise and turning lights on and off. There were whole rooms visited only on holidays that she explored, playing with the crystal animals on the credenza, staring at the knickknacks and family photos. There were so many things to see: ceramic Chinese dragons and little chipped plaster statues of Saint Jude and creepy antique rag dolls in blackface with giant eyes and red-ringed lips. She felt safe because of the presence of her mother upstairs.

When her mother came down, fully dressed, her face composed, she tried out new recipes, teaching Nicole to crack garlic with the flat of the knife before peeling it, to wash the rice of starch, to detect the right shades of red and pink and gray that made up rare, medium rare, and medium steak. On these winter sick days, she made the hearty stews and cassoulets, teaching Nicole the words in French for each part of the dish, letting her stir great ceramic pots of spicy sausage and aged confit with white beans softened overnight in bowls of water. Then she sat down and wrote the story of each dish's creation for a small food column that ran bimonthly in a local magazine.

On some days she stirred the stews and mashed potatoes in silence. "Keep up," she snapped. "Use some elbow grease. If you can't do this, you'd better hope you marry someone rich."

Nicole pounded her bowl of dough or batter until it felt like her arm might catch on fire, and then her mother softened along with the mixture. "What a good job you're doing. My little goose." Her tenderness was always a gift, exciting and frightening all at once because you never knew when it might crack and fall to pieces. She and Paul both knew a certain tone of voice—a frail shimmer—and the fear of it was deeper than her fear of the dark or of her lungs filling completely when she was sick, deeper than the fear of a hand grabbing her on the basement stairs or the one corner of their street where the lamplight did not reach. She was eight years old. There was already so much to be afraid of.

Sometimes her mother did not come downstairs. Once, when the day had stretched on into the fading light of the afternoon without her mother's appearance, she tired of flipping through comic books and shuffling around the porcelain ladies. In the drifting shadows of the living room, the antique dolls seemed to stare at her, their white-ringed eyes leering.

She crept upstairs and slipped through the bedroom door. Her mother was sprawled in her bathrobe on top of the covers, one long, lovely leg hanging off the edge with a carelessness that she never seemed to have when awake. Her red hair was a frizzy mess around her face, one hand manicured with dark red polish, the other bare. She had laid out her clothes on the chair the way she often did before showering. Nicole crept closer. The skin under her nose tightened. A strange air hung in the room: a glass with a rime of golden liquid on the dresser, a staticky radio turned low, with an old Billie Holiday song playing that sounded like sobbing. *In my solitude . . .*

She shook her mother's shoulder, and her mother yanked her arm roughly back, snarling, "Get—the *fuck* away from me!"

She ran, flying downstairs, huddling behind the couch. Now the safety of the house seemed to throb with danger, and her mother's voice—no voice she knew—rushed like blood in her ears. The dolls on their shelf glared balefully at her, and she flung them into the hall.

She was still there when the kitchen door opened and Paul returned from school, calling cheerfully; she listened to the thump of his backpack on the floor, the rasp of his shoes on the mat, from far away. She saw him stop at the thrown dolls. Then he was standing over her. "Hey. You all right?"

She didn't answer. After a moment, he went upstairs and seemed to know what was happening, because when he came down again, he was holding out her coat. "Come on. Let's get out of here."

They didn't go far, she remembered; they just walked down the hill to the ice cream parlor, where he counted out whatever pocket change he had so they could get a cone. He held her hand when they crossed a street, even though she knew it must embarrass him to be seen this way, holding his little sister's hand. They walked back up the hill slowly, their steps getting slower the closer they got to home. She dared a look up at him and studied the clenched boyish line of his jaw. "Why is she like that?"

"She just is sometimes," he said.

"But why?"

He paused, huffing a little at the climb. "I don't know. She gets depressed. She told me once that she feels like she's wearing a heavy coat that she can't take off."

Nicole nodded, struggling to figure it out, to file this away for future understanding. Paul sat on a neighbor's brick garden wall, still not looking at her. "She's good at hiding it," he said. "For years. The last bad time was when you were little. You wouldn't remember." His jaw worked. "Just stay away from her when she's like that."

She nodded, sniffing a little, and he put his arm around her. "You'll be okay," he said. "I'll be here."

She felt a fierce swell of pride: Paul was already in high school, never around when kids pushed her in the schoolyard or strange dogs barked at her from behind fences. But he always wanted to protect her.

When they crept back into the house, Paul grabbed the antique dolls and shoved them under his coat. "I've always hated these things," he said. "Come on."

They snuck around the back, and with a garden trowel he dug a small hole behind the wild mint growing scraggly and untended at one end of the yard. They buried the dolls there, solemnly and with great ceremony. Paul said an Our Father, and she made a tremulous cross, and together they said, "Ashes to ashes, dust to dust," and covered the ugly things with dirt.

"You're home," her mother said to Paul, coming downstairs, her hair done, dressed and effortlessly stylish. "Help me put these sweaters in the cedar closet. I'm afraid the moths will get them." She patted Nicole on the head, stroking her hair in a tender, possessive way, as if to make up for deserting her, touching her too much, and together they went into the cellar.

Only now, telling Jocelyn, did Nicole wonder what Paul had seen that she had no knowledge of. Perhaps that was why he was so protective of her. How lonely it must have been, without someone to tell you that things would be all right.

On other days, when her mother did not come downstairs, she remembered the secret she and Paul shared, those unshriven dolls quietly crumbling to dust. They were like buried saints in the garden. They would protect her while she waited for her mother to be her mother again.

. . .

In the summer when she biked up and down the hills of her neighborhood, she sometimes went too far and reached the supermarket, where strangers stood around the parking lot for no apparent reason, smoking and drinking out of paper bags. They were old men—old to her, anyway. And if she passed them in the day it was all right, but if it got dark and she wheeled her bike past to get a drink from the fountain, her legs in their shorts stood out like white birches in the twilight and she felt them lean in.

She was going to be a nun, she decided. Then she would be safe in the living light. Like a drifting ghost or a graceful, flightless bird, free of the hungry gazes of strangers, free of worry about her mother.

She kept imagining herself as Hildegard, and having secret visions. She biked through her neighborhood with her sweatshirt hood up, imagining it was her veil, and looked for the light that was supposed to come shattering down out of the sky. She looked for the living light in the green summer branches of the trees, in the ripples of air on the black roads, in the gleam of the cars that whipped by her when she cycled alone on Commonwealth Ave. She rode alone; she pumped up hills and glided down them, loving the rush of air in her face. She searched everywhere she knew to look, but the living light refused to show itself to her.

She knew that when it came, it would sunder everything before it, that it would pierce her straight through with its beauty. She was even ready for it to hurt. For something that powerful and pure to touch you, well—she was sure it *would* hurt. She practiced for it, digging her fingernails into her palms so that she left angry red tracks in her skin.

Hildegard said that God had miraculous healing powers.

Nicole prayed, *Dear Lord, cure my bronchitis. Sincerely, Nicole.*

Hildegard said, We must also endure pain to experience divinity.

In church, the priest reminded the congregation that the best evidence we had that we were fallen was the pains women bear, as a result of childbirth, and the other, unnameable pains. Evidence, he repeated, is there. In biology.

Nicole prayed, *Dear Lord, it's all right if it hurts. Even if it hurts a lot. I still want to see the living light. Sincerely, Nicole.*

The summer she was ten, an old friend of her mother's arrived with a storm of boxes and suitcases and a giant black Angora rabbit that lived in a hutch on the porch, forever harassed by the cats. She was a tall, angular woman with clean lines, all bone from shoulder to collar and down her flat chest. But bony in the way flattered by low V-neck sweaters. She often stood smoking on the back porch, standing like a model with her back bowed, her hip jutting, one slim elbow resting on the crook of her pelvis. Nicole's mother told her she was going through a divorce. "It's a very difficult time for Mrs. Owens. Don't ask her about the divorce, and just let her alone." Nicole's mother had a tendency to treat a divorce as a cause for mourning. She spoke in hushed tones all that summer and moved warily through the house, preparing plates of food for Mrs. Owens to eat separately in the guest room when she "didn't feel up to socializing."

You couldn't just ignore her, though. Her laundry was in with your underwear that had the days of the week on them: black lacy things, not like your mother's sensible flesh-toned bras. Her boxes of things lined the upstairs hall, and you couldn't help pawing through them sometimes, when the door to the guest room was shut. Nicole found curving modern glass lamps wrapped in paper, dishes with naked impressionistic women on them, a yearbook with Mrs. Owens and Nicole's mother in long white dresses and floppy hair, laughing, nearly twins. With the yearbook were books like she'd never seen before: *A Short History of Sex. Oriental Erotica. The Female Orgasm.* She flipped through the books quickly, reading out of the corner of her eye. Only a glancing sin. Here, Japanese ink-wash paintings: women with high eyebrows and blackened teeth, in a tangle of patterned fabric. Men clambering on top of them like bronco riders. In other books, medical diagrams, a naked woman from the side. Her hands on the inside of her thighs, busy. A naked man standing nearby, his genitals two sketched parentheses, attending helpfully.

After dinner, Mrs. Owens came down and played backgammon with Nicole's mother until late. At the stairs, Nicole listened to them laughing, high and sharp, like teenagers. She wasn't invited; Mrs. Owens and her mother talked long past bedtime, long past when her father shut the bedroom door with a sigh. In the morning there would be an empty bottle of wine left on the table, a plate with crumbs of cheese and crackers, an envelope with the backgammon score, the tally of the money lost, in her mother's neat hand.

And sometimes she'd be bouncing a tennis ball in the driveway and the ball would find its way around to the back of the house, where Mrs. Owens stood in her model pose, the cigarette hanging from a hand. "Come here," Mrs. Owens said the first time she wandered near. "Pull up a chair." She was one of those adults who treated you like an adult; she acted like you were in on some secret together. "Don't tell your mother I'm smoking," she'd say. "I promised her one a day, but I'm on my fourth. So goes the revolution, ness pah?"

Nicole didn't have a sense of smell, anyway; the cigarette smoke blew right past her. Mrs. Owens liked to talk about the beautiful house she'd run away from, all the nice things, the clothes she'd left behind—my God, the clothes. All the big designer names. Dior, she loved Dior. One dress, she could kill herself for leaving behind— black and white. Slit up to here. Neckline down to there. Her husband loved her in that dress. Don't get her started about the shoes. All she'd thought to bring were her loafers.

"Why did you leave all that stuff behind?"

Mrs. Owens smoked like a movie star. She took a long pull, looked at the cigarette, exhaled softly, inhaled again. "I just had to leave. I couldn't not. I'll get them later, if he hasn't already given them to *her*."

Nicole understood not to ask about who *he* and *her* were. It was better to sit on the edge of the deck in her shorts, picking at bug bites and letting Mrs. Owens's conversation drift over them. "Don't ever get involved with a man, Nicki, who's going to tear your heart out ten years later," Mrs. Owens told her. "Just don't do it. Have your fun. Live it up." Then a harsh, barking laugh, too big to come out of such a slender shape. Big with sadness.

"But you will, won't you," she'd say later, when it was getting dark and they were at risk of being discovered by Nicole's parents coming home. "Nothing I say's going to stop you." And she'd look around to make sure they were alone. "Nothing your parents can say, either. You'll see." She'd tap her nose slyly. "You'll see."

Then she'd have to stub her cigarette out, fast like a guilty teenager, because Nicole's mother was home, calling for them.

Later, she left, taking her enormous rabbit, her dishes, her boxes of books with her—except for one. Nicole had tucked it—*A Short History of Sex*—into the back of her closet.

A week later, when they were seasoning the big cast iron pans, the ones she could lift only with two hands, she asked her mother where Mrs. Owens had gone. Had she found that apartment she'd wanted? Did she ever get those clothes? Her mother told her that Mrs. Owens had worked things out with her husband, that she'd gone back. The relief in her voice was unmistakable.

"I thought she wasn't happy," Nicole remembered saying.

Her mother threw a pan into the sink with a clatter that made their ears ring. "You have to understand. I want you to understand. Marriages take work. They aren't always fun. You don't always feel happy. Sometimes you have to say to yourself, 'I'm needed here. I have to stick this out.'" She began scrubbing the pan, her thin, freckled arms rasping at a calcified layer of grease. "When it stops being fun, still, you stay."

This was '96 or '97—it was a bit hazy now—the year of the April Fool's blizzard. Schools closed, trains stopped, and people skied down Comm Ave. In the suburbs, the trees' branches buckled and froze in the ice, trapped until spring. The only kid in Nicole's class who lived near her was a Japanese girl named Kumiko who had asked to be called Katie the first day she appeared in school. They fell into an easy, excitable friendship during the snow week, meeting on the corner to wander the neighborhood, throwing snowballs at cars, darting across backyards, making snow forts framed by the frozen arms of the trees.

One evening they trooped through the snow to Katie's house for dinner. They shed their wet jackets and boots and Katie's mother made them murky green tea and gave them tiny cookies with the faces of cats. It was a tall, grand house with high staircases and dark unopened rooms. They were playing with Katie's model horses on the stairs when Nicole noticed a strange little setup in the hall: a cabinet with a dark statue of a serene seated figure ringed with flower petals and flanked by sticks like long cigarettes.

"What's that?" she asked.

"A shrine. For Buddha." Katie sounded bored. She nudged Nicole's horse with her own and made it whinny and paw.

"What's Buddha?" It sounded like a holiday, maybe one of the many Jewish holidays her friends had off from school and they had learned about in assembly. During one, you blew into a curled horn. During another, you couldn't eat bread.

Katie sat up and preened a little. "Not what. Who. He's like a god, only not really. And he's a real person, like Jesus."

"What does he want you to do?" That was what Jesus was for, wasn't he—he wanted the best for you, and he was disappointed if you didn't live up to his exacting standard.

Katie shrugged. "He just wants you to be happy. He wants all suffering to cease." Then she tossed her head impatiently, like a horse. "You can't understand Buddha. You're not Asian."

"Kumiko!" Katie's mother was in the doorway, and spoke sharply in Japanese. Katie shrank back. "I mean, you have to be a Buddhist to know."

They moved to Katie's room to play. Katie was obsessed with babies, probably because she had a two-year-old brother. "Now you be the mom," she told Nicole. "You pant and scream a lot. I'll be the dad and I'll coach you."

They gave birth to stuffed animals again and again, pressing their legs together and forcing them between their thighs.

Katie had posters on her walls with Japanese writing; Nicole wanted to try writing her own words. Katie was reluctant but eventually showed her the characters for "star," "moon," and "I love you." "How do you write 'Buddha'?" Nicole demanded.

"Like this." Katie wrote the word 'Buddha' in English.

"No! How do you write it in characters?"

"Hmm." Katie's hand hovered over the page. She drew two characters: a tree with one branch leaning and a little house with a single window.

It was like a code.

After dinner, Nicole watched Katie's parents light the long sticks of incense and make quick bows to the Buddha. The candles trailed thin ribbons of smoke. Nicole's eyes and nose ran. The air was filled with a strange odor; it was like tasting a new spice, sweet and rotting, clovey and sharp. It was the first smell she had been able to experience in years: a tiny miracle. When Katie's parents turned away, she gave a small, secret bow to the statue.

After her playdate with Katie, she put the scarf and the veil away, as her mother had told her she would, saying that wanting to be a nun was just a phase, and she stopped searching for the living light. But her mother was wrong about other things.

Once Paul was planning to go on an outdoor-adventure camping trip run by another church, and their old family priest, the one who had married her parents, came to their house. He drank a cup of tea and ruffled Nicole's hair and talked about what a good, old Catholic family they were, and her mother beamed and bustled about, preparing a plate of cookies. He told her mother not to let Paul go on the camping trip.

"Why?"

He wouldn't say exactly. His eyes darted everywhere and especially to Nicole's; she was sitting with her legs up on the couch, only half-listening. He told her that the pastor taking kids on the trip was unconventional and had a reputation and he didn't want Paul mixed up in all of that. He was a good boy.

It had taken her this many years, she told Jocelyn, to realize what might have happened on that trip, and what had probably happened to other boys. Their priest had saved Paul.

But what about the other boys, the ones who were not good?

Paul's life then was filled with chem tests and choir practice and soccer after school. Midnight lock-ins when the older kids would sleep over in the church after vespers, tell ghost stories, play poker with the cool young priests, the ones who secretly smoked and wore black cowboy boots under their cassocks, who roared up to services on motorcycles. The cool priests would give him advice about girls, and he trusted them, didn't he? And sometimes boys were chosen to help the young father get the candles and the incense ready before services. Usually poor kids, kids with single mothers, kids with no one at home. He'd feel glad for them, that they were finally getting special treatment, for once in their lives. Off they'd go, the lucky ones, into the private rooms. And some people knew and some did not, but either way he never said anything, because what was there to say?

This was '96 or '97. Soon the lawyers bringing suits against the archdiocese of Boston would begin quietly building their cases, preparing to drain the accounts of Boston's Catholic churches. Soon the churches with their rose and amber light would begin to shutter themselves, like the long string of strip malls along Route 9 (Candlepins, the retro bowling alley, with its warped wooden floors and cardboard pizza; Feng Shui, the Eastern-style furniture and rug outlet; Hearth and Home, your local fireplace fixture specialist), spooling out of Boston and westward, brightening the long forest road with their floodlit empty parking lots, tokens of failed enterprise.

THE NEW *ROSHI*

"I thought I was rid of you," she told her Master on the phone.

The unperturbed silence on the other end made her sweat.

"You didn't really think that," he said.

It was late; she'd just come back from dinner with Jocelyn. Her little kitchenette in the corner of the studio was still piled with unshelved dishes and pans. She opened the fridge, pressed a can of soda to her forehead, trying to breathe calmly.

"You can't get rid of me," he said. "Didn't I tell you? Don't you remember?"

It was almost plaintive, this simple call. Of course she remembered all the times he had told her that the master-student bond couldn't be broken. How even across lifetimes, masters and students recognized each other in different bodies.

"How did you get my number?" she asked instead. They'd never spoken on the phone before. Theirs was the rare relationship that left almost no trace: no call histories or e-mails, only a scribbled number for the Zendo in her address book. But the traces were all over her anyway. Hearing his voice, she could feel the sound settling into the familiar grooves of her brain, turning round and round.

"If you are still dedicated to your education, then I can teach you for a while over the phone," he said evenly, as if she had said nothing at all. "Is that how we will continue?"

She stood and paced a few steps, an old anger rising. "I left you, not Buddhism."

"You didn't leave me. I'm right here. I know what you've learned, and I know what you still need."

"You don't know me." Now she sounded like a petulant child. But he didn't know how or why she had converted; he didn't know about Jules, or her mother. Those were her secrets. All she had that he hadn't touched.

A long pause: Was he clearing his throat? Did he feel some emotion at this moment? Did he need her? Did he say to himself, Yes, I have this need?

"I know what we've promised each other," he said. "I promised I would always be a home for you. Have you forgotten the vow you made? You promised your loyalty. Your service."

"I know. I remember." She did not say that she had already looked up the location of a new Zendo. She had spoken on the phone to a Japanese monk, who'd set up a meeting with her new *roshi*. The secret burned in her belly. If she closed her eyes—that was all it took—she'd be back in her Master's private room, listening to his instruction.

· · ·

In Zen, her Master tells her three years into her training, the wives of priests are called "tea ladies." They are there to serve the men in their spiritual work. This job, her Master assures her, is no less important than the work of puncturing the wall of illusion and discovering the secret dharma. So she sits up straight and whisks the bright green matcha. She pours the tea and offers the hot cup in her burning hands. He takes it and sips, and then she is permitted to sip, too.

She pictures those tea ladies through the ages, greeting visitors at the door and taking their coats. Generating good karma as they poured the tea and backed away, knees together, taking tiny shuffling steps. What virtues were they storing up, squirreling away for their next, luckier lives?

Any protest she might make would necessarily take the form of *I want*. And in Zen, you had to want nothing. So she tells herself, I shall not. You make yourself happy with what you have.

Sometimes the ceremony feels like a wedding. As he drinks from the cup, he looks her full in the face, and she finds herself trembling and wet-eyed, as though they have committed to something larger, the bond of a lifetime. She knows he feels it, too. Often they reach for each other as soon as their cups are empty, and this, too, feels like part of the sacred rite.

What's so wrong about what they do, anyway? Just sex? She's long gotten over her Catholic horror of it. Jules, all the silly funny needy things they did together, took care of that. He taught her that a person could feed you in more ways than one. What's so wrong with just feeling her Master's hand in her hair, of responding to the voice of someone who knows her on the most intimate levels? You want someone who has an interest in your soul, don't you?

· · ·

On her day off from work, she went babysitting. Paul's kids were June, eleven, and Charlie, eight. Nicole saw them only once every few months, but they loved her. She was strange and interesting to them, not yet a cliché as she was to adults. They liked to hear her stories: the one about the Indian prince who accidentally marries a snake. The old woman who was cruel to a pauper and was reborn as his donkey. The dragon who wanted to be human. Paul listened to the stories suspiciously, waiting for the moral.

Marion worked partly at home for a publishing imprint specializing in travel books. While she spoke on the phone in the kitchen, making plans for a business lunch, Nicole listened to June perform the latest German waltz she'd learned on the piano, lips pursed in concentration, her straight dark bangs hanging stylishly low over her eyes. Whenever Nicole came to her brother's townhouse, there were signs of performance; last Thanksgiving, she'd been amazed by the many courses and the long rows of silverware at each plate, the piano gleaming darkly, the homemade pastries, the children presented in stiff little outfits that reminded her so much of her own childhood skirts and stockings.

June wanted her to play something; she hadn't since middle school, when she and Paul would stumble through a minuet on a neighbor's upright. But her fingers still knew how, she was sure of it. She let them move over the keys, remembering their relationship. It was like meditating—quieting the mind, listening to the body.

Somewhere in the middle of "Für Elise" she became aware that Marion had entered the room and was standing behind June, a hand on her shoulder. "Your aunt plays very nicely for someone who hasn't played in years, doesn't she?" said Marion.

There was something lightly galling in the way her sister-in-law had asked. There was, in fact, nearly always something abrasive about her, always at least one comment or arch look that made Nicole chew over the encounter for hours.

She figured Paul must have gone over the highlights of his sister's life, the headaches she had caused, the roles she'd played: dropout, runaway. How she'd disappeared without a word for months. But had he told Marion what it was all about? Had he told her about the quest? Had he told her about the money he'd lent? And whether he was ashamed of her?

She thought, Someday I would like to sit down and tell you the whole story. I want you to understand what my life was like. Who I was trying to be.

"Where's Paul?" Nicole asked.

"He's back in Boston. Another medical sales convention. Well, I have to go. Have fun, everybody." She swept her children up in rough hugs, and then she was gone, and suddenly the day felt lighter, full of possibility.

They splashed in their rubber boots to get bacon cheeseburgers at Zip Burger, a cheerful hole in the wall, then took the subway to Central Park. By then the rain was clearing. June and Charlie knew all the trails, but they were amused by her disorientation and let her navigate, looping back, dead-ending into ponds or statues or stone-walled bridges. Finally they reached the Egyptian obelisk and stared at the hieroglyphics, trying to make out characters long obscured by city smog. Then June nudged Charlie, and they darted away through the trees; it would be a little light hazing for the new babysitter. They knew Central Park better than she did and wanted to see whether she would panic and call their mother. Was their tribe sacrosanct?

She was equal to that. She sat down on the steps and closed her eyes. *Namu Amida butsu.* Let her breathing take over.

She heard them returning before she had chanted three times. "You're so weird," said June. "How did you know we would come back?"

"I have my ways."

That made her seem mysterious and wise. They drew in closer. June was scowling; she had serious concerns, questions on her mind. "You told us in Buddhism, there's no soul," she said.

"That's right." Dear Lord, I've become one of those people who relate everything back to accepting Jesus in your heart, she thought. But they wanted to hear, didn't they? They had asked.

"But if you do something wrong, then whose sin is it?" June asked. "Shouldn't you still feel guilty?"

Oh, you good Catholic girl, Nicole thought. "Buddhism says the person you are today might be a little different, but she *depends* on the person you were before. You choose every moment who to be next. Your mistakes are your own."

June nodded, clenching and reclenching her fists. "But with no soul, who are you?"

She wanted to tell her, That part nearly broke me, too. There were the koans her Master had whispered to her over the years, challenging her to crack puzzles that had no answer, mazes with no entrance or exit. He told her the koan of the girl with two souls: a man fell in love with a girl against their parents' wishes and married her and took her away. When he returned much later, he was shocked to find the girl sleeping in her parents' house: she had been sleeping there as if enchanted all these years. Which is the real girl? her Master asked. Which one is you?

She and the children were standing above a great flight of stairs leading down to the rear of the Met. A strange feeling of vertigo overcame her, as if she might go flying down the steps. She said, "I'll tell you a Zen koan. They're like riddles with a lesson in them." She paraphrased: "Two monks were walking together down a very muddy road. It was raining, and the road was beginning to flood. Soon they met a pretty young girl in a kimono, unable to get across the road because of the water.

"'Come on, girl,' said the first monk. He picked her up and carried her across the road.

"The monks went on, but eventually the second monk said, 'We monks don't go near females, especially young and pretty ones. It's against the rules. Why did you do that?'

"'I left the girl there,' said the first monk. 'Are you still carrying her?'"

The children were silent, working it out. Nicole remembered her Master giving her this koan near the beginning of their relationship, when she'd been so afraid of what they were doing, how wrong it was. He sent her these coded messages in reply. What did the koan mean? That to regret was the true sin. Love is an act, so let's act.

She remembered the way his hands trailed over her body. The way time did not seem to pass in that windowless back room. It was like being insulated from time and memory.

Now that she was outside that space, the world seemed windy and dangerous.

They wandered down the stairs and looked at the artists selling paintings outside the Met, the canvases wrapped in plastic against the threat of rain. One table was offering little Indian statues, and she bought them each a bronze one, a female Buddha of wisdom, a male Buddha of compassion. As they climbed the stairs, taking the scenic route back through the park, Charlie and June started bickering. June said, "You never understand when I tell you things," and Charlie insisted that he did. Nicole watched June's face; she was carrying something heavy around with her today. Nicole wished she could help her with it, but could anyone, really? Had anyone been able to help when she was seventeen?

The next time she looked around, June pushed Charlie hard. He staggered, and one foot reached for purchase but missed. For a moment she saw that he was going to fall down the granite stairs. She lunged and caught his shirtsleeve, and he slammed to the ground, safely in her grip. June backed away, her face white.

Nicole crouched and hauled Charlie into her lap. He was crying; he had a scrape above his eyebrow. It was astonishing how much blood could pour from such a superficial wound. "You're all right, you're all right," she told Charlie, and in the same breath, to June: "You could have really hurt him! Don't ever, ever push someone on a flight of stairs!"

June burst into tears. Then Nicole had to pull them both together and comfort them, awkwardly, because she was their friend and not their mother.

They cleaned up in a café restroom and went home holding hands, all of them shaken. "Charlie had a bit of a fall," she said when they walked in the door. Marion ran upstairs at once for Band-Aids, pulling Charlie with her. June followed slowly.

Nicole stood in the foyer for a while, listening to the running of the tap as Marion cleaned the scrape. "He tripped, Mom," said June. Then quickly: "It wasn't Aunt Nic's fault."

"We'll see," Marion said.

As she was putting her coat back on, Marion came downstairs holding the two Buddha figurines Nicole had bought for the children. "What are these?" Marion asked. Her voice was cold.

"They're figurines from the Met," said Nicole hesitantly, hating the way she so often felt like a disappointing child with Marion.

"No. What are *these*." Marion pointed.

Nicole squinted. "Oh. They're swastikas." They were etched on the arms, unmistakable.

"Can you explain to me why you would want to give them toys with swastikas?"

"I'm sorry. I didn't notice them. They're an ancient Indian symbol." She fell silent, debating how much to say. The swastika was a symbol of peace, found on many Hindu and Buddhist statues and paintings; Nazi Germany had taken the spokes of the wheels and turned them in the opposite direction, to symbolize war. But whenever she had tried to tell Marion trivia, she'd failed to interest her. Her sister-in-law was not in a mood to hear it now, the small features of her face close and furious. "I'm sorry," she repeated. "I didn't see them there."

Marion handed the figurines to her. "I just don't think they're appropriate."

She got on the train for home, but a few stops down the line she got off and walked, needing the time to think, afraid that when she got there her Master would call, more afraid that she would listen. He'd been feeding her koans about monks and lovers, daring her to read between the lines of the story. "Listen to this one," he'd said the night before.

The nun Eshun was very pretty even though her head was shaved and her dress plain. Several monks fell in love with her. One of them wrote her a love letter, asking for a private meeting.

Eshun did not reply. The next day the master gave a lecture to the group, and when it was over, Eshun rose. Addressing the one who had written her, she said, "If you really love me so much, come and embrace me now."

She dropped the statues in the trash.

. . .

On Saturday she was in the lobby of a sleek obsidian skyscraper on the Upper East Side, searching for her new Zendo. The listing said it was on the fourth floor, above a law firm and below a massage parlor.

In the whisper-quiet elevator, she took deep breaths and tried to remember the correct procedure for meeting a new master. She pressed her hands to her face, practicing the deep humble bow. She covered her mouth with her hand and made a soft sound, her last for a while, sucked up by the plush red pile of the carpeted space. The first moves, she knew, would be in silence.

The door opened on a long hall lined with rice-paper walls. A monk greeted her and took her shoes, and led her past open doorways; she saw the bare meditation rooms, along with a more modern reception area with a desk and computer, and a temple room, holding its shrine studded with incense sticks. The monk stopped at a closed door. "This is the private meeting room of our *roshi,*" he said gravely. "Do you know how to proceed?"

She nodded and entered the room, bowing deeply. The *roshi* was seated on an elevated wooden platform, the wide sleeves of his robe making him look like an equilateral triangle. The small room, covered in tatami mats, was bare except for a jade Buddha, a lone stick of incense, and a bronze bell at the *roshi*'s right hand. If a student tried to explain a koan and gave an unsatisfying answer, the *roshi* would ring the bell, sending him away for weeks of more work. At any moment he could lift the bell and send her bowing and scuttling away.

His hand rose; silently, he was gesturing to the space in front of him. She made a quick prostration, then tucked her legs under herself, pressing her thighs tightly together to still their quivering. In the dim honey-colored light, she couldn't help thinking that the *roshi* looked like *her* Buddha statue from the Boston art museum's meditation room, his skin flecked amber like old bronze, his face and body grave and still, his shaved head gleaming in the recessed lights.

"I hear from my assistant that you have studied for several years," he said. His Japanese accent was strong, softening his *r*'s and blurring his *o*'s. "I would like to hear from you your understanding of the dharma. If you please, what are the Four Noble Truths?"

She sat up straighter and readied herself. So it was going to be a test. She had to show him her skill, the library of knowledge she had amassed, if she wanted to pick up where she'd left off with her Master and become one of this *roshi*'s private students. She began to recite, aware that her demeanor was being evaluated as much as her words. He was looking for signs of *kensho* in her, the spark of insight. She would have to tell him what she knew of suffering and its cessation, the complex cosmology of Buddhism, the vast scales of time and space, wheels turning within wheels. The lotus flower and the dragon daughter, the blood bowl and the Pure Land.

What are the steps of the Eightfold Path? the *roshi* asked. She struggled to remember the concepts she had seen when flipping through the paperbacks with rock gardens on their covers that her Master had rarely grilled her on, preferring gauzier sermons on existence, on dependent origination. "Right view, intention, speech, action, livelihood, effort, mindfulness, concentration."

This was another catechism, a second codified world. You could be born into belief, be a member, without knowing a thing. But as a convert, you had to know it all.

And what did Master Dogen teach? the *roshi* asked, unsmiling.

Master Dogen brought the principles of Zen from China to Japan. What is *zazen*?

Zazen is seated meditation, the cornerstone of Zen practice.

What is *sanzen*?

A private meeting with your Zen master. It is essential to advancing in your training.

What is recorded in the heart sutra?

The Heart Sutra tells us what the experience of liberation is like, and how the body is inseparable from the mind.

The Lotus Sutra?

It contains the final teaching of the Buddha, it assures us of the possibility of enlightenment for all, and it explains that faith in the sutra is itself sufficient for salvation.

How many Buddhas are there?

Innumerable.

How many are contained within a drop of water?

Innumerable.

What is the *nembutsu*?

The recitation of the Buddha's name.

Recite, please.

Namu Amida butsu.

How many times must you recite it to achieve enlightenment?

Only once, with perfect clarity.

What is the Pure Land prayer?

The prayer to be reborn in a world free of defilement, where enlightenment is easily obtained.

What is nonbeing?

It is neither being nor not being.

The questioning continued. How will Amida Buddha help you? How will Quan Yin protect you? How will Mara deceive you? What turns the wheel of samsara? Recite, please. In Japanese, please. By what process does its turning cease?

She could feel panic arriving as a lowering of her blood pressure, a gradual blackening of her peripheral vision. Her feet were numb. Her answers petered out without reverberation, sadly, in the densely quiet room.

Finally, the *roshi* reached his last question. "What do you hope to accomplish?" he asked.

"I—" She fell silent. This was a question she couldn't answer. "I don't know."

"Why did you come here?" he asked more gently, trying to help her along.

There were no easy answers she could give: I want to feel centered. I want to live in the moment more. So many nice reasons. "I had to come," she said. "I have always wanted to live clearly. With purpose. I have always wanted to be awake, fully awake, every minute of my life."

The *roshi* nodded and raised his hand. For a moment she thought he would ring the dreaded bell and send her away. "You understand the basics. But there is still much to be learned."

"So you'll take me as your student?" she asked tentatively.

He gave a small shake of his head—whether a refusal or an acknowledgment that things weren't so simple, she wasn't sure. "I would like to put you in my Saturday class. It is starting soon—you can join us now."

She nodded, and bowed again, once to him and once to the Buddha statue. A monk entered after some invisible signal and led her down the hall to a large studio space. She saw the easel set out by the door with its humiliating script: BEGINNING MEDITATION.

Inside, the studio was crowded; people were straightening themselves on the floor, assuming the familiar position, waiting for the *roshi* to take his place at the front of the room. They wore a strange combination of church clothes and workout gear, some there as practitioners, some there as hobbyists, chatting amiably as they laid out their mats and lined their shoes (sparkly ballet flats, heels, pink Converse sneakers) along the wall. She stopped in the doorway and scanned the room to make sure she was right: they were all women.

She laid out a mat for herself and put down her coat to claim it, then went out into the rice-paper hall. She followed it deeper into the building. A few rooms down, she could hear a distant, throbbing sound, like the repeated plucking of the lowest string on a guitar. She followed it, sidestepping a standard saying, RESIDENTS ONLY. She pressed her ear to a closed door: the *roshi* was leading his monks in a prayer session. She could hear them chanting in a deep repetitive bass, singing the words to a sutra and ringing a bell at intervals to maintain the rhythm. Their chanting climbed a long hill of verse, then paused to gather a collective breath and continued to climb. She knew the words they were chanting. She knew the purpose of the bell. Through the thick door, their voices sounded like the humming of many bees.

She returned to the meditation room, listening to the women talk around her, catching up on the week's gossip. "You're new, aren't you," one woman said, large and wavy-haired and smiling. "I'm Jeannie." She made introductions: Lucille, Maxine, Georgia. Each person tossed off a frank declaration of what they were doing there: Lucille had anxiety; Maxine was trying to expel toxins from her body. She'd started with gluten and white sugar, and now she was busy ridding herself of cortisol, the stress hormone known to shorten the life span of your cells. The women smiled, agreeing. "What brings you here?" asked Jeannie.

She shrugged. Now the answer she had given the *roshi* sounded pretentious. "I'm a student," she said.

The *roshi* entered and the women hustled back to their mats, whispering like guilty schoolkids. "Let us begin with one hour of silent meditation," he said.

But it was no kind of quiet at all. Impatience rippled through the sunny mirrored dance studio. The women in the group could manage only half an hour, and then it was like the minutes in a movie theater after the lights have dimmed, when a sudden torrent of whispers and throat clearings fills the darkness. The room buzzed with restless shiftings, coughs, phlegmy snorts. A cell phone rang. Nicole watched the guilty party check her phone—the nerve!—before shutting it off. Gum was unwrapped, audibly, and chewed, resoundingly. It reminded her of Helen's Zen cow joke. *Mu. Mu.* She sat near the back, using most of her energy to control her anger.

She took the subway home in a confused state. There were no seats on the train, and she swayed back and forth among the bodies, feeling her irritation grow every time a warm sweaty hand touched hers or a swinging bag bumped her ribs. On the crowded escalator to the street she felt a sudden explosion of rage, as if an organ had ruptured inside her body. She wanted to kick the person in front of her. *If you would only move one stupid step to the right—just move!* She wanted to scream. She looked behind herself, down the long mechanical slope, at the prayerful heads bent over phones. She wanted to snarl, spit, swear. They would think she was a madwoman, another lunatic lost in this city.

In her little studio, still cluttered with boxes, she fed Kukai and sat on the floor, pressing her back to the cool white wall, and ate noodles from a bowl in her lap and listened to the sounds of her neighbors coming home. The stamp of shoes on tile, the squeak of a chair, friendly voices greeting each other. She heard silverware chime, the sizzle and chop of cooking. The sounds weren't unique; they were utterly generic, the sounds of dinner, talking, laughter, things you could hear anywhere, in a million different rooms in any city. Sounds of normalcy, family, happiness or unhappiness.

She picked up the phone and called Sean.

During the first three rings, she dug the nails of one hand into the other wrist. Then he picked up, and when he said, "Hello?" she half-cried, "Where have you been?"

He laughed, sheepish. "I thought you told me not to call."

"I didn't think you'd actually listen to me."

"Well, I didn't want to. It's been lonely here."

At those words she felt a glad rush, mixed with a curious sadness. She didn't want him to feel lonely. He didn't deserve it.

"How's New York?" he asked.

"It's good. Yeah—good."

"Don't be too enthusiastic. I'll start to think you don't miss me."

"Ha. Well, I do."

"I do, too. Come back and visit soon. Will you?"

"Oh, I don't know. My father, you know."

"Maybe you've forgotten what I look like." He had a funny streak.

"No, I remember," she said. "Have you forgotten what I look like?"

"No, but I'd like to see more of you. Half the time we were in the dark."

She moved to the couch, tilted her head back. "I've been missing you nights especially."

"Me too."

She said, dreading the response, "Are you thinking about what we'd be doing if I were there?"

"Yeah. Yeah, I am. I wish I could touch you right now," he said.

She arched against the back of the couch, letting pressure and warmth seep into her, imagining Sean's weight on top of her. It had been a while, too long, since she'd talked to anyone this way. But it was difficult: there were some words she couldn't bring herself to say. They were words that didn't belong in her, that Catholicism had excised from her mouth, her body. Words like "cock" and "pussy" and "fuck." And how could you get what you really wanted without them, with only a voice on a telephone line. Instead she listened to the huff of static that came each time Sean breathed too harshly into the receiver.

"Sean," she said softly. The road outside began to hiss with rain. Above the grocery, a shadow moved by a lit curtain and stopped there, watching. Somewhere beyond that building and the next, beyond the big dirty rivers, the woods and highways, a ten-year rope was tugging. Her Master had told her, I've taught you so many things about yourself. Even about your own body, about what you want from it. How could you want anything else?

If she stayed on this line, if she held on, perhaps Sean could silence that voice.

"Sean. Sean. Oh, Sean."

. . .

"They're going to drive me crazy," she told Jocelyn.

They were drinking coffee in Nicole's apartment, and she was explaining about the other women in the meditation group. Jocelyn was a ready audience, not just for her conversion story but for her current problems. She brought baby Emmeline and sat her in a bouncy chair and told Nicole about how hard it was to be married to a doctor, how for weeks at a time he was not much more than a harried, smiling face at the door. But Jocelyn never complained. With her sweet face, her languid sprawl across the couch, she absorbed Nicole's frustration beautifully. She explained wearily that having a baby is one of those times when you see your life change in front of your eyes. She said, "You have to figure out where you fit into it. Are you a mother now? Is that all you are?"

Jocelyn was the only person whom she'd told her story from the beginning. There was something exhilarating about that. A friend, a real friend.

"So you're sticking with this new teacher?" Jocelyn asked doubtfully. "This one isn't taking you seriously, and the women are amateurs. Maybe you should talk to your old Master."

"I can't go back," Nicole said. "But I don't know if I'm going forward."

Jocelyn smiled. "You're wasted on them."

"No, no. I understand how hard it is." There was the part where you forgot to count your breaths; the part where your body began to itch uncontrollably, first your scalp, then your back, then your groin; there was the part where your knees began to ache and your head to fill with the loud, tuneless humming of whatever song you hated the most.

If you sat through that, and managed to go deeper into the dense black mess of your brain, you might find something, like the entrance to a tunnel you didn't know was inside you. You'd feel your way along the damp walls in total blackness, the silence beginning to lap through the channels and chambers of your heart, your brain, the way the fever of noise had before.

But you had to get there on your own. She'd done her time.

"What's it like, afterward?" Jocelyn asked. "Are they nice?"

"Well . . ."

When the bell rang and the meditation session was over, the women began to talk at once, filling the room with relieved chatter. The *roshi* had to call for order. "You ladies are like birds, always hopping and twittering," he said. "Your minds are wild monkeys." The women laughed.

Once he was gone, they rolled up their mats. Jeannie always began with an update on her fibromyalgia. And Lucille with her panic attacks, and Maxine with those toxins lodged in her body. Everyone knew. They were sick, full of poison, aching with syndromes they couldn't name. No one really knew why. But they were on a ceaseless search for relief.

Nicole was learning that there were three basic categories of people who came to practice. There were the purifiers. They compared notes on juice cleanses, cell phone radiation, and BPA-free plastics. Cortisol, the stress hormone, was clogging the brain, causing early-onset Alzheimer's, increasing the risk for cancers of all sizes and shapes and kinds. Meditation was one more weapon in the battle to live.

There were the spiritualists. They spoke cheerfully of opening one's chakras, of getting in touch with their Buddha natures. Anything foreign—a Japanese kanji, a Qur'an, an incense stick—was beautiful and strange and pulled them helplessly in like moths.

And there were the sufferers. The women undergoing chemotherapy. The women embarking on divorce, nervous as horses before a storm. The women who had lost spouses or parents or children. The women who had been raped, long ago or not so long ago, and still did not feel whole.

They were tired and overworked, irritable and overpaid. Lonely and restless and panicky. In the most recent session, Jeannie had said, "Sometimes I think I'll never be out of pain. I'll just never get better at this."

"At what?" someone asked, and she said, helplessly, "Being alive."

"The meditation will help," Lucille said.

"But I never get better at that, either. Ten minutes and I tap out."

"If you hold something in your hand, you can concentrate longer," said Nicole.

Everyone looked at her. She went on, beginning to sweat: "It's a technique—in the oldest sutras. Hold something simple, like a rock or a lump of clay, and concentrate on its feel. Focus on the experience of holding it."

"You know, I think I will try that," said Jeannie, and heads began to nod around the circle. "Where did you learn such a thing?"

"From my old Master," she said.

Jeannie considered this, tapping one spectacular red-polished nail on her chin. "You're a sleeper, aren't you."

"What do you mean?"

"A quiet type. But still waters run deep, right? You've been holding out on us. Listen to you, talking about sutras. You tell me," Jeannie said, and there was a challenge in her voice. "Tell me what I should do about chronic pain. Tell me something Zen."

Nicole took a deep breath. It was Helen's test again. *Give us a blessing.* She recited, "Mara the deceiver god asked, What is being? Where does it come from?

"The nun replied: Why do you harp on the word 'being'?
You have strayed, Mara, into confused views.
A mere bundle of compound aggregates:
There is no being to be found here . . .
Nothing but suffering comes to be,
Nothing but suffering ceases."

"What does it mean?" Jeannie asked.

"When we are in pain, we tend to think it is part of our identity, our being. If we remember there is no permanent being—that we're constantly changing—it's easier to think of pain also changing. It can fade and cease to be, just as we change."

The room was quiet. No breathing or sighing or shifting. The women were listening. For the first time in Nicole's life, a small voice spoke hesitantly inside her: *I could teach. I could even become a master.*

"What brings you to New York?" asked Maxine.

"My brother wanted me near him. He's very protective." Then, in a blurt of honesty: "I'm a bit of a screwup in the family. I went AWOL for a while."

Jeannie smiled. She stood up and walked across the circle to Nicole, and touched her shoulders. "Honey, everyone needs to get away from their families once in a while," she said. "That's not screwing up. That's *life.*"

"You like them," said Jocelyn now, splashing more coffee into Nicole's mug. "I can tell."

She did like them. They reminded her of the old gang back in Boston. They were laughable and foolish, snobby and judgmental, safely ensconced in their privilege. But they tried hard. They wanted things so strongly.

And they kept coming up to her after sessions and telling her things.

In line for coffee in the lobby, Lisa said her husband was becoming impotent just as she was discovering she actually enjoyed and wanted sex for the first time in her life. "We're out of sync," she said. "All my life, I've discovered things too late."

In the hallway, waiting for the advanced meditation class to end, Lacey whispered to her, "I get these night terrors. I see my husband, the kids in their car seats. I see myself buckling them in and driving off. Then we're going the wrong way on the freeway. I read an article about this woman who drove the wrong way on the freeway and killed a carload of children."

Georgia told her, as they waited in the subway, "I think of myself as made of sand. And every day you give away a handful of yourself to someone else. You give yourself to your parents and your children and your lovers, one by one. By the time I'm fifty, there'll be nothing left."

The stories came out involuntarily, whispered to her when they were walking down the street, pressed into her ear before she had fully turned around to see who it was.

"My friend's cancer has returned. I'm not supposed to say anything. She hasn't even told her husband."

"Do you think meditation would help with ulcerative colitis?"

"When we sleep together, it's good. It's good because it's not all weird in the morning. But then he doesn't call for a week."

She nodded and knit her brows and gave them proverbs: *This life is realized here and now, not later. The ten thousand things and I are of one substance.* Mostly she listened and did not say anything. They wanted to tell her, they were hungry to tell.

. . .

On the phone that week, her Master listened to her recite her answers to the koans, her explanation of nonbeing. In his silence, she could feel his impatience. "Very good. It's time for you to come back now. You've had your time wandering in the desert. Now we must resume our important work."

"I don't know if I should come back," she said, surprising herself.

His voice grew thin and taut. "Soon you will have to return. Without me, what teaching will you receive?"

"You aren't only my teacher. You can't pretend that's all we are." And now you're not even that, she thought.

"You are mine. No other teacher will want you, once you have been shaped by my instruction."

She was having trouble swallowing. Her mouth was too dry.

His voice was gentle and imploring again: "Did you know I was married, before I became a sensei?"

"No." He had shared almost nothing of his life. Early in her training, he'd said it was better for her to think of him as a disembodied voice: that would make the transmission of the dharma more absolute.

"Well, I was. We were not very happy together. In fact, we were miserable. We both wanted different things. She wanted a cozy sit-down life. I was restless. I was discovering the Way."

"What happened?"

"We parted. It was no one's fault. But now I know. It's only with you that I can be free. We have such important work to do together. We are like two stars circling, attracted by our mutual gravity. You can't turn that gravity off. Even if the space between us is greater, we continue to orbit each other. And we only have so much time. We must act. We must hurry."

That voice! When she had been afraid, grief-stricken, disgraced, his voice had surrounded her, protected her. She couldn't turn from it. She'd be ruined by it.

"I will give you a poem," he said. "A young nun is meditating by the side of the road. A man walks by and calls out to her. He says:

"You're young and innocent.
What will leaving home do for you?
Throw away your saffron robe.
Come! Enjoy the flowering woods.
Sweetness falls from the tall trees.
Flower pollen whirls all around.
The beginning of spring is a time of joy.
Come! Enjoy the flowering woods.

The treetops are in blossom.
They call out when the wind shakes them."

. . .

Five years into her training, her Master begins to let slip threads from his earlier life. He says offhandedly, "I hurt my shoulder playing baseball. I was recruited for college, but I dropped out." Or: "We can't let ourselves be constrained by the expectations of others. My family will never understand me, but still I go on, teaching the Way."

She gives him details in return. He knows she ran away, but he doesn't know about Jules or Eddie. He knows her father is dead, but he doesn't know about sitting by his bedside, listening to days of his rattling breath. He knows about her difficulties with her brother, but he doesn't know Paul had periodically rescued her when no one else would.

These threads of story they offer each other are deliberate lures, leading them deeper into danger. She's trying to win his sympathy but doesn't realize that she is the one ensnared. When she tries to avoid an unpleasant memory, he is there, telling her not to run away. When she is crushed by guilt and can't help crying, he is there, stroking her wet face, promising that their relationship is not contingent on her goodness.

He gives her a small bracelet of Japanese prayer beads, a beautiful chain of dark polished wood with a tassel of red silk. He shows her how to roll the beads in her hand to help her count her *nembutsu* prayers, and she laughs and says she knows how a rosary works. There are 108 beads, for the 108 afflictions people are said to have that prevent enlightenment. The 108th is made of cloudy glass. If she holds it to the light, she can see a tiny painting of a monk inside.

She's fingering the beads, flushed with gratitude at the specialness of the gift, when he says, "I gave beads like these to my previous student. But that student did not have the discipline, the patience required for the Way. I know you will not fail."

It's the first time he has ever mentioned other students. Of course she isn't the first; she feels stupid for even assuming.

She studies the other practitioners entering the Zendo with a new watchfulness. Are they being trained, too? Who is the student who existed only in the past? Did she lift the cup to his lips with the same solemn devotion?

She is certain the student is another *she*.

Over the years she has watched other students attend *dokusan,* or private meetings. There is diligent Buffy wanting to get her A in Zen, skeptical George looking to hash out some point of doctrine he takes issue with, other former Catholics seeking a confessional, the anxious hoping for reassurance, the treasure hunters wanting Eastern mysteries. And occasionally there were girls like herself who knocked on the door and vanished into the back room. They never stayed long, though. In a month or six months, they were gone, moving on to the next thing in their lives: a yoga class, a juice cleanse, a return to the Orthodox Judaism of their childhoods. Like curious tourists, they stopped for a while and took pictures and moved on.

She tells herself, I will be the patient one.

Other students come and go and then stop coming, and she is still there, doggedly persisting. He hasn't invited other women into his private chambers for some time. Five years in, he kisses her on the neck and rests his head on her shoulder and sighs with contentment. On Buddha's birthday, called the Flower Festival in Japan, he brings her red flowers from his garden and tucks them into her hair, smiling and serious. "There," he says. "Beautiful." Soon, she tells herself, he'll need her the way she needs him.

Who knew that all she had to do all those years was disappear?

. . .

In the morning, the buzzer rang: she ran to the door in her bathrobe and accepted a bouquet of white chrysanthemums from a delivery-man. The card said simply, *Come by when the flowers bloom in Boston. You are running out of time.* She didn't know how he had gotten her address, but she did know what they meant. In Japan, white flowers were given only at funerals. They were a symbol of death.

She stood in the doorway and wondered how her life could have possibly arrived at this day, this moment, these flowers in her hands.

. . .

"Have you forgotten about me yet?" Sean asked on the phone that afternoon.

"No, of course not." She pulled the phone into bed with her. It was her day off, and after the arrival of the flowers she hadn't been able to get herself moving. She'd watched the light from the window travel across her floor as though she were a prisoner in a cell.

"Why don't you tell me your story, and I'll tell you mine."

"What would you want to tell me?"

"I'll start with the old neighborhood. And the kids I played street hockey with. And my family's church. The priest who went to each family's house and each of the moms served him tea and brought out the good cookies. It was something, having a holy man over for tea." He paused. "Where would you begin?"

"Let me ask you a question. Do you remember this protest that happened in Boston, over ten years ago now, when all the churches were closing—the Communion on the Common? Did you go?"

"Yes! I remember. I did go. Seemed like every Catholic I knew was there, and that's a lot of Micks."

He laughed, and Nicole clutched the bedspread. "What do you remember?"

"Let's see. I remember it had rained the previous night, and with all those people on the grass, it was muddy as hell. I came with my wife, and with Frankie. She would have been about four. We had the stroller."

"What side of the Common were you on?"

"It was the east side—near Park Street station. I remember because we got pretzels from one of the vendors that's always there. They were making cross-shaped ones that day."

She remembered the funny pretzels. She tried to summon him from her memory, assigning meaning to this turned head or that one. She'd been only a teenager; he was a man, with a wife and child. But still: they'd both been there, bowing on the muddy green of the Common.

"That day is important. You're giving me a clue," Sean said.

"Maybe—I don't know."

She could hear him thinking. "That was the day you fell in love," he guessed.

"Not quite."

"You met a nice Catholic boy on the green, and your girlish heart fluttered."

"No."

"Tell me," he said. He was getting frustrated. "Or write it down. Write me a letter, and tell me what you can't say."

"I—I don't know if I can." *I don't know if I'll still be lovable to you.*

"Try," Sean said. "Just try. Write me a letter. Write me your story and tell me where we stand."

"We stand about two hundred miles away from each other."

"That's not an answer."

She looked at the flowers on the mantel. "Don't you know what a mistake I am?"

"You're not. You're not."

"Oh, but I am, sweetheart. I am."

"I don't care. I don't care. Don't you know I'm a mistake, too?"

. . .

The women were getting unruly. Now the sharp looks, the hisses and whispers that filled the meditation sessions, seemed deliberate. Nicole half-closed her eyes, tried to settle. On Fridays she was working late at Nordstrom, sorting inventory and flagging new items for the weekend sales; then on Saturday morning she had to hurry uptown to make the session, still blurry with sleep. She wanted to pay Paul back for the deposit money as soon as she could. It made her uneasy, these favors hanging over her head.

At the end of the meditation session, Jeannie bowed low to the *roshi,* blocking his exit from the door. "Excuse me, Morimoto-sensei. May I ask a question?"

"Of course."

Others busied themselves with their mats, but quietly. Listening in.

"Why is Nicole in our class?"

Tying the laces of her sneakers, Nicole started.

"Why do you ask?" the *roshi* said politely.

"She's studied for many years. She's much more advanced than us. Why is she studying with us?"

The *roshi* said calmly, "I do not teach women in the private setting that more advanced study requires. Shakyamuni Buddha said, 'In whatever religion women are ordained, that religion will not last long. As families that have more women than men are easily destroyed by robbers, as a plentiful rice field once infested by rice worms will not long remain, even so the true dharma will not last long.'"

"But—women can be ordained. They can study at an advanced level."

"That is true, yes. But there have been cases of misconduct in mixed-gender teaching, and it is better to avoid these situations. A woman who wants to be ordained must find her own teaching lineage, through a convent perhaps. And," he added regretfully, "It is more difficult for women to make the sacrifices of family and home that are required."

He bowed; she bowed; he left. The rest of them resumed rolling their mats. Nicole bent over her shoes, her face burning. As soon as the laces were tied, she hurried out of the room. But downstairs in the lobby, when she paused just to take a long breath, Jeannie tapped her on the shoulder. Maxine and Lucille were there, too.

"I thought I might get an answer like that," Jeannie said. "And I knew you weren't going to ask. But I just wanted to know."

Nicole shrugged and tried to smile. It was embarrassing. Like having your mother call the basketball coach to ask why you weren't picked for the team. "It's not that simple."

"No, it's not. But we wanted to ask you something. Would you be our teacher? We think you'd be perfect."

"But I'm not ordained. Or registered as a sensei. I'm not anything."

"That doesn't bother me."

She stared into their trusting faces. Something was growing in her chest, making it hard to speak. She wanted to grab their hands. *Let's get out of here.*

But that wouldn't be very teacherly. She squared her shoulders, took a deep breath. "All right. You'd better come with me."

THE THREE JEWELS

I want to know the reason you broke your family's heart, Jocelyn said at their next meeting. They were in Jocelyn's apartment, folding laundry. Nicole liked being helpful while she talked, and she had lots of sweater-folding experience.

Where were we. I was seventeen, she said, and you know better than to take a seventeen-year-old's word for how something happened. One day I was a Catholic, and then one day I knelt and took refuge in the Three Jewels. I thought it would be like a spell, like transubstantiation. You know, when the wafer and the wine become the body and the blood.

Did you transform? Jocelyn asked.

I don't know. No one saw me except some statues. Does what you whisper in a dark room with no witness have any weight? If a Catholic girl converts in an empty museum, does it make a sound?

Come on, Jocelyn said. I want to know what makes a person do such a thing.

Well . . . there were the churches that closed. My mother. And the cats, all those cats that died. I guess it started with the cats.

. . .

A virus was going through the town's strays, herpes or feline AIDS, something like that. You'd be walking down a quiet lane and see a limp, furry shape stretched out in the road. Sometimes there'd be kittens there, still huddled in the cooling warmth of the body. They'd gaze up at you with their glinting, witchy eyes.

Her mother took in a pregnant queen, who gave birth to sick little premature babies. The kittens lost weight and died one by one, like clockwork, the littlest first, then on down the line, a new still body among the squirming ones each morning. They knew how to purr and knead their tiny claws while sucking on a bottle, and they were just starting to open their eyes, which were the deepest blue Nicole had ever seen, like milky jewels. Lapis. The one thing they didn't know how to do was keep living.

The last kitten was too weak to hold up its head. But it kept trying to suckle on her mother's hand. That was what got her: the trying. It was only a dumb animal, the alleys and dumpsters were full of them, but this one wanted to live, it wanted it desperately.

. . .

She was seventeen; it was early spring. The ground was thawing beneath her and groaned at night, changing shape. When the scandal broke wide and the church closings began, she and her mother watched the news in the mornings before school.

The Catholic Diocese of Boston, nearly bankrupted by private settlements in sexual abuse suits, was due to close more than sixty of its 357 parishes. The parishes that had named towns and schools and roads would now be split into new allotments, shuffled among other churches. The Assumption of the Blessed Virgin, the Holy Family, the Blessed Sacrament, the Holy Rosary, Our Lady of Pity—all closing. Polish churches, Hispanic churches, powerful Irish churches. In a panicky meeting demanded by the congregation, their priest explained that there was a calculated "sacramental index" of a parish's vitality, amounting to the year's baptisms and funerals plus twice the number of weddings. When a pastor was alerted of his church's closing, he raised a black flag on the church flagpole. The cameras of the local news stations lingered on these flags, whipping in the spring winds.

She and her mother watched the story unfold: the exterior of a rainy Gothic building, a few gravestones out of focus through the fence, angry protesters circling, a beleaguered priest at a microphone. And the people she knew from photographs on St. Augustine's bulletin boards: bishops and the powerful Catholics of Boston, angry, woeful, resigned. There was archbishop Bernard Law, red-faced and jowled, rheumy eyes squinting. He would be accused of covering up child abuse, one of the highest-ranking church leaders found to be skillfully shuffling predators from parish to parish. There would be letters and documents. There would be suicides. Years later he'd be made a cardinal, receive a special appointment under the Vatican. She'd be clicking through the news and be shocked to see that bulldog face framed in red, arm in arm with the pope.

Then the camera shifted to the protesters, signs jabbing at the air.

The reporters always seemed to interview the craziest speaker they could find: a frizzy-haired woman in a Pats jersey with a rich Boston accent, shouting that the archdiocese was burning good Catholics. How no one even cared any more about the Irish people that made the city. Why weren't they closing more of those Mexican churches? Where was the respect for the sacred? The church her grandmother, her mother had gotten married in, now closing. It was blasphemy, pure and simple. It's like losing a part of your body, Boston's Catholics said.

Nicole's mother was busy marking the black-flagged churches on a map of Boston, looking for a pattern. "Look, some of the oldest parishes are closing," she said, tapping the scattered X's on the map. "It doesn't make sense. They're screwing us over. They're screwing over good Catholics, Nic. Where's the justice in that?"

It took so long for everyone, Nicole included, to believe. It took story after story in the news, the victims growing in number, filling town hall meetings, gymnasiums. Church leaders were caught in cover-ups and taking hush money. It was the first time in my life, she told Jocelyn, that I saw how holy men could lie.

Once, years later, she'd tried to bring up that time, remind her mother: you were more upset about those churches closing than about what was really going on.

So was everyone, her mother replied. The one thing was a private matter. The other was that they were razing the city. Making it into something else. A new Boston.

Nicole didn't say a word. She nodded and retreated, spent more time lying on the couch reading. She was taking a class called World Religions that was moving slowly across the globe. She'd read with interest about the familiar faiths, examining the questions Judaism, Christianity, and Islam sought to answer. She'd dressed up as a nun (shades of childhood) and given a report about life in a medieval convent. But it was the paperback book *Understanding Buddhism,* with its cover of a line of saffron-robed monks walking beneath a stone Buddha, their faces composed with a kind of quiet joy, that intrigued her. All those shepherds in the desert with their sheep metaphors. They spoke so confidently of that old external figure, God; the way she pictured him as a child, he was the intangible hand on the basement stairs, grabbing her shoulder. The hand on her head. Sometimes he was God the judge, doling out laws for your own good, God the parent, loving you in a disappointed, Catholic way.

Buddhism seemed to respond to all declarations with intriguing questions. Her teacher sometimes called Buddhism a philosophy. They watched a fuzzy VHS of monks filing into a monastery, Zen gardens raked into exacting concentric circles, the sound track the chiming of bells. A smiling monk told an audience of long-haired American followers, "All you must do is chant the single phrase 'Awake, I breathe in,' and you will be liberated from your sorrow." The teacher invited parents who were practitioners of different religions to come in to discuss their faiths, but no one could be found at the school who was a Buddhist (Kumiko had moved away, taking her model horses, her shrine and incense with her). This silence seemed fitting.

Nicole loved reading about the gods in the Buddhist universe, who were jealous of human beings. It was better to have a body, to experience hunger and pleasure and suffering. Only with the lesson of suffering could you attain enlightenment.

While her mother watched the church closings at high volume, listening to priests denying that they knew anything, Nicole lounged in headphones, reading about the cycle of suffering. Anger, greed, and delusion kept the giant wheel turning, rolling relentlessly through time. The cock chasing the swine chasing the snake.

The mother cat, still making nests, kept dragging wool sweaters into closets. Nicole had held the kittens in her hands and felt their heartbeats like moth wings. She'd felt the last, lightest flutter. The last beat. Her mother held the little body to her ear to be sure. "That's it. Gone to heaven," she said.

"Even though it's a cat?" Animals didn't have souls. Everyone knew that.

Her mother looked at her. "Go add this one to the box."

Nicole added the last kitten to the plain shoebox in the garage. They'd been told it could spread the disease if they buried the bodies, and so they went into the trash. When she returned, the kitchen chairs were all upended on the table, as though they were in a restaurant closed for the night. Her mother was scrubbing herself furiously in the sink, working long red tracks down the pale skin of her arms. Then she went into her bedroom and closed the door.

Nicole sat on the floor of her own bedroom, listening to the hushed negotiations, muffled sighs. Her father was standing in the hall. She could see him through a crack. The flat of his palm was pressed to the bedroom door. "Liza, just let me in and let's talk."

"I can't talk to you, Bill. You don't listen or understand. I'm sick of it. They're coming for us. They're coming for *us*."

"Who?"

"You know who."

"Is this about—"

"They're coming for good Catholics. My *home*, Bill. I grew up here, on the next hill. I used to wake up and see those steeples across town and know everything was all right. Or even if it wasn't—if I wasn't—there was a place I could go. I thought I'd see our children married in the church where we were married. But everything's been ruined."

"I'm coming in so we can talk about this like reasonable—" His rattling the knob was interrupted by her mother's cry: "What the *fuck* are you doing? What the *fuck* are you doing?" Nicole opened her door and saw her father rubbing his temples. He saw her and smiled. "Let's get out of here for a while. Give your mother a little air."

They went walking through the park where she used to play softball and where he would coach her, throwing endless underhand fastballs, trying to get her to follow through instead of flinching. Neither of them were natural athletes; the balls flew wildly, sometimes at her head, sometimes in the dirt. But she remembered the time she finally trusted him, sent the ball soaring up and away over the green meadow, and the look on his face—this unabashed surprise and delight.

"Your mother—" he began without looking at her. She expected him to say that she was going through a rough time, that we all had to pitch in, the usual familial clichés. But he didn't.

"Your mother was so exciting when I met her," he said instead. "She had all these crazy ideas. Plans for great adventures we'd have. And then she'd get these moods. No one could bring her out of them. Except sometimes when she went to church and prayed, it calmed her."

If the Buddha was right, her mother had lived many lives. Even inside this one, she was many people, many different mothers. Nicole had always known this to be true. There was the mother who loved you and the mother who didn't want anything to do with you. The mother who cooked resplendent French meals. The mother who told you not to take as much of them as your brother, potatoes were fattening. The mother who pressed a hand absentmindedly in your hair while reading to you from a favorite book, *Kidnapped* or *Treasure Island*. The mother who wondered who would ever want to marry you, with your hair in that state.

The mother who was afraid of shadows in the stairwell and lakes where you couldn't see the bottom.

The mother who was afraid of what she called her "blue period."

The mother who was afraid of the contents of her own mind.

The mother who might never forgive you.

The mind is everything, Nicole read in *Sayings of the Buddha. What you think you become.*

" 'The mind is its own place,' " her father began softly, amused and sorrowful. Occasionally they shared this surprising moment of thinking the same thing. "How does it go? '. . . and in itself can make a Heaven of Hell, a Hell of Heaven.' "

He scrubbed her hair with his hand, as though she were much younger, still his silly goose, his nickname for her because of her honking bronchial cough. She waited for him to say that everything would be all right, that this too would pass. But he said nothing.

Here they were in church, all dressed and scrubbed and jostling in the narrow pew. Her mother, bright-eyed, her hand steady on Nicole's shoulder. Here they all were, singing the old favorites. The haunting "Ave Maria," the imploring "Faith of Our Fathers." Paul home from college for the weekend, leading the family with his strong baritone. Her father, warbling off-key, shifting up and down octaves. And high and straight, running like a taut thread through their family's voices, her mother's fragile soprano.

Here was the priest, gliding by in his silk stole; here was the lantern of incense, filling the air with the smell of holidays. Here was the fervent prayer of St. Augustine: "Breathe in me, O Holy Spirit, that my thoughts may all be holy. Act in me, O Holy Spirit, that my work, too, may be holy. Draw my heart, O Holy Spirit, that I love but what is holy. Strengthen me, O Holy Spirit, to defend all that is holy. Guard me, then, O Holy Spirit, that I always may be holy. Amen."

Filing up to receive the sacrament, Nicole watched her mother close her eyes and open her mouth. Was that what ecstasy looked like? Rapture?

Many of the closing churches had been taken over by their members, in round-the-clock vigils. As long as someone was in the church worshipping, went the thinking, they couldn't tear the place down. There was something sweetly naïve about this. She pictured construction crews removing their helmets as they entered the space. Respectfully skirting the faithful.

Walking home from the T one day, Nicole saw the black flag flapping high from St. Augustine's steeple. Already there were signs on Augustine's stone wall: KEEP THE CANDLES BURNING. DON'T CLOSE OUR CHURCH. KEEP FAITH ALIVE.

She found her mother in the kitchen, tying packs of bottled water and saltines together. "We'll take it in shifts," she told Nicole. "We all have to do our part. I'll go during the day, and you can go after school. And Paul can come on the weekend."

"Mom, we're not actually doing this vigil?"

"Of course we are." Her mother handed her a crate of clementines to put in the car. She was impeccably dressed, sleek and stern in a blue blazer and skirt, wearing the good Chanel shoes. "This is our church. We have to protect it."

"You go if you want. I don't care whether it closes or not."

Her mother slapped her, hard against one cheek, and then clasped Nicole's face in her hands, gently. For a moment she looked puzzled, then concerned, the way she'd looked when Nicole was sick with bronchitis as a girl. "Remember Hildegard? Remember how you loved her? You were going to be a nun. What happened?"

What happened was that what she did at night, a hand in her underwear under the covers, stroking herself into a nervous exaltation, meant she could not be a nun. She knew she was not built for it, but she did not know what she was built for.

Her mother straightened. "You're not your own. You are my daughter. You're a part of this family, and you're a part of this church."

Nicole agreed to go; there was no way she couldn't.

She watched the light changing on the old plaster statues, the deep bronzy gold of the altar. The priest told them that when good Christians were truly in need, their Savior would help them. It was the higher law that all the universe obeyed.

There is no savior in the world except the truth, said the Buddha. She had read it in the books she was taking out of the library.

The priest told them that the church was more than a physical place; it was a sanctuary for their souls. It had protected generations. It would protect them again.

Men, driven by fear, go to many a refuge, to mountains and forests, to groves and sacred trees, she had read. *But that is not a safe refuge, that is not the best refuge; a man is not delivered from all pains after having gone to that refuge.*

She stayed with her mother for many hours on the hard pews, long after the color in the stained-glass windows left them and only the watery candles lit the pews. Each time she fell asleep, her mother shook her awake.

In her daydream the priest said, There in that corner, a boy stayed after choir practice and a youth pastor asked him to hold something in his mouth. On that pew a priest sat next to a girl whose brother had died and he consoled her and fondled her. In that corner, there, with the plaster statue of the Pietà, the one where Mary is holding her dead child in her arms, boys were held and caressed. They were told they were different, that no one would love them. They were told they liked it.

Of course the priest didn't say that. Nicole shook and straightened, tried to stay awake. But surely he would say he was sorry. How could he be such a hypocrite? Here was the time to acknowledge what had brought them to this brink—abuse and corruption and lies. You looked away and looked away, for years you did this, she thought, staring at the priest. To children, your brothers said, Put your head down and take it. To children, your brothers said, There are no words for what is happening to you, so remain silent.

Your brothers said, Here is your first taste of suffering, and it's good for you. Drink it up.

The priest's voice grew high and frantic in the great space. He read from Matthew. *I also say to you that you are Peter, and upon this rock I will build my church; and the gates of Hades will not overpower it.*

Nicole clutched her mother's arm. "Can we go? Please, can we go now? I feel sick."

"We'll go in a little while," her mother whispered.

When they left the church, she staggered into the yard and retched among the gravestones. There were still people inside, starting the late shift now. She heard them singing as she leaned on a headstone, panting, her mother stroking her hair. They were singing "Softly and Tenderly Jesus Is Calling."

"It's beautiful, isn't it?" her mother asked, gently.

. . .

She was supposed to go straight to church after school each day. And for the first week or so, she did. Each day, the vigil was thinning out; there were fewer people with signs outside, fewer faithful in the chilly pews in the middle of a cold spring afternoon. One day, she was the only one there. She drifted through the shadowed apses and behind the altar, where normally only altar boys were allowed. She had never been alone in a church before; it was eerie. She poked through cramped little back rooms: the offices, the custodial closet. Here was the music room, where she and Paul had practiced their Christmas carols, and a tiny girl with a lisp had been chosen to read: *In the countryside close by there were shepherds out in the fields keeping guard over their sheep during the watches of the night. An angel of the Lord stood over them and the glory of the Lord shone round them. They were terrified, but the angel said, "Do not be afraid. Look, I bring you news of great joy, a joy to be shared by the whole people."*

She kept looking up to the sad eyes of Jesus above the altar, which watched her from every angle. She wanted to ask him what would happen next, who would keep her safe. But she was not a child; she knew he would not speak.

Finally, she went to the stone basin of holy water and dipped her fingers in and brought them to her lips. She had always wanted to know what it tasted like. But as she'd expected, it tasted of nothing. She put on her coat and slipped out.

. . .

That week she looked up the address of the Tibetan arts and crafts store in Cambridge and took the T there, then stood shyly in the back by the colorful Nepali wraps and scarves, stroking the fine silk, the scratchy linen. She drank in the vermilion dyes and the scarves of lapis blue, the color of the kittens' dreamy unseeing eyes. She pored over the posters of mandalas, blushing at the gods copulating with goddesses. The gods, horned and fierce as bulls. Erect and enormous. Here, the *dakini* of wisdom, a lovely cat-eyed goddess, impaled herself on the god of compassion, her legs ensnaring him. Nicole looked and looked.

The shopkeeper, a small, round man, kept his eyes on the security TV, watching her. She was only a teenager in a sweatshirt, and she knew he was waiting for her to stuff something into her pocket. What was she doing here, anyway? What could she possibly want? She listened to him chat on the phone, in Nepalese or Tibetan or Hindi, she couldn't possibly guess. When she reached for the Buddha statues under the glass counter, he waved her hand away. "Too expensive for you," he said.

On Friday, Paul returned from college. They ate ice cream in his car before they were due at church. She felt like a child, being rewarded for good behavior. "This won't last," he said abruptly. "Just hang in there a little longer. Either the vigil will break—"

"Or Mom will," she finished for him.

"She's in one of her blue periods."

Paul had no idea what it was like. He was away at college; he hadn't seen the way their mother prayed now, in a frantic breathless rush, appealing to Mary, to all the saints and angels alike. He hadn't heard the shuddering cries that came from her room at night, the way she pleaded with their father, then raged at him. "I'm not going back," she said.

"Back where?"

"To church."

"You have to go. It will kill Mom if you don't." Paul turned off the low buzz of the radio, and they stared at each other. "Look, once you get to college, you won't have to go anymore. I tell Mom I do, but I don't. Just pretend for a little while longer."

She knew there were plenty of people who went to church because their families did, or because they had always gone. People who didn't demand anything more than habit and ritual and the same old songs. "So lie and fake it?"

"That's what growing up is all about, sister. We'll go to church tonight with Mom, and then you can come with me to my friend's party tonight." He smiled. You have your fun, and you do your penance, and the scales stay even.

Paul had a way of sweeping through the front door and making things right. In the past, when black silences had spread through the house, he had returned from college, cheering up their mother, cooking, inspiring Nicole to scrub the bathroom tiles or bag leaves on the lawn. She could see the way their mother's tight, brittle mouth loosened into a smile, and the way she held on to him as he left, reminding him how much he would be missed. With his blond prep school hair, the cheerful way he called, "Hello, family" and stamped his boots on the mat, he exuded sanity. Even when Nicole hated him, which was especially right this moment, she knew that he was good for them, that he wanted what was best.

A crowd was gathered in the graveyard when they pulled up to St. Augustine's. The parishioners were milling uneasily, but there were no picket signs. Their mother broke loose from the group, running to the car, her hair flying. "They've locked the church," she said. "Those bastards have locked us out."

Nicole followed her mother to the great oak door. A giant padlock and chain secured the handles. There was no sign, no explanation. The message was clear.

"How about a back entrance?" Paul asked.

They circled the building, looking for a way in, poking through overgrown shrubs. But lines of gray caulk filled the back door and the basement bulkhead. Every window was barred, every spare opening sealed. This was careful work; the church officials must have had people working through the night. These protesting churches were an embarrassment to the archdiocese, and they were being dealt with this way across the city. Wait until the last member leaves; then hurry in with concrete and chains.

"I guess that's it, Mom," Paul said quietly.

Their mother turned. She didn't seem to recognize them at first; her eyes were too strange and wild, too uncomprehending. Then they found Nicole. "You were here yesterday, weren't you? Until dinner? Who else was here?"

"I—" She couldn't say, *I haven't been all week*. She couldn't say, *I've betrayed you*. "No one I knew."

Her mother ran to the front steps. She banged her delicate fists on the church doors. She rattled the padlock on its chain. "Let us in. Let us in." The crowd took up her chant for a few rounds, banging on the doors. But no one was inside to hear them.

She was making a spectacle of herself. Here was the mother who hid in the upstairs bedroom, the frantic and fearful one. But now she was out in public, beating on the locked doors. "It's over," Nicole called, embarrassed. "Stop."

Her mother whirled toward her. "If you'd stayed, they couldn't have done this," she cried. Then Paul's hands were on her shoulders, ferrying her back to the car.

. . .

That night she stood in the backyard of a shambling old Victorian up in the woods somewhere close to the train tracks. Paul's old high school friends were passing red cups of warm beer around a low campfire. Someone offered her one, and then she was alone again, holding the beer, staring into the fire.

That was where she met Jules. He was the only one who talked to her that night. She saw him emerge from the house, black against the deepening sky, and move down to the fire next to her, downing his beer. "You look familiar. You came with Paul?" he said.

"Not *with*. He's my brother."

"I can see it." He looked her up and down as if searching for things in common: the mouth, eyes, wide straight shoulders. It allowed her to look at him as well—pale skin, thin nose, knowing dark eyes—and she realized she did know him: he went to the all-boys school they shared plays with. When she'd had a bit part in a play last semester, she had seen him hanging out at rehearsals; he was dating the star.

He wore a leather jacket and was painfully thin under it, the way she always looked naked in the bathroom mirror—spindly and flat-chested.

The play gave them something to talk about. He knew girls in her class; she knew that he had been suspended from school for drinking on campus. "I heard you got in trouble" was how she put it, and he laughed.

"Yeah, I got in trouble." He shook his head and crumpled his cup. "Those pissy little headmasters and headmistresses like getting all tangled up over me. I'm just one more in a long line of disappointments."

"Okay, I get it," she said. "You're a bad boy." Inside the house, she saw Paul laughing with his arm around a girl she knew—Jennifer, his friend, the girl he seemed to find again whenever he was home from college. Through the lit windows, she watched him take the girl upstairs, where no lights were on.

"That's me," Jules said. "The one you've always been waiting for, right?"

Not always. But now, she thought. *Maybe.*

She let Jules come closer and touch her hand as they moved away from the fire. She led him into the sheltering dark, and they found their way out of the yard and into the woods.

It was a warm spring; the woods were marshy and damp, full of mud. They climbed until they reached a dry patch of pine needles. Jules was immediately upon her, kissing her and gripping her waist.

She kept quiet, terrified but thrilled, unsure of even how to kiss back until something softened in her and let her move her lips gently, relax her tongue until it was liquid and compliant.

"You're sweet," he said. "Where are you going after this?"

She didn't understand; she was going home. Home had an impossible gravitational pull. Home was everywhere.

He shook his head, grinning. "You're not going home yet, are you?"

In answer, she wriggled out of her jeans. Part of her wanted to say, Stop, stop, let me keep everything the way it always has been. But part of her didn't.

At first it was difficult, and painful, and mortifying. A lot of wrestling and fumbling, the wrong angle, the wrong fit. But at the very end there was another feeling, not quite pleasure but getting there, something deep and awakened now.

He lay back. "First time?"

She nodded, and she saw his teeth flash in the dark. Then he squeezed her shoulder. The earth was still under her; somewhere around them, an owl called, and then the train went by. She was still here, coated in pine needles, disheveled, trembling, but alive. *Awake, I breathe in.*

"Yeah," she said. Then, awkwardly: "Thanks." She was glad it had not been someone who was tender and who cared that he was her first. She had wanted to get it over with and feel nothing.

"Anytime." He rose, straightening his jacket, brushing the dirt off his pants. She wanted to roll over and grab his leg, pull him back down to her, but she knew this would be a terrible breach. She lay very still instead, watching him stretch and adjust himself, the very maleness of him.

"Maybe I'll see you around," he said.

She nodded. That was all she had been expecting. She stood, yanking up her jeans, and brushed away his offered arm. "I'm not a baby. You don't have to hold my hand." She walked away down the hill, feeling his eyes on her as she moved steady and straight.

She rode home with Paul in a tired silence, then waited until the house was dark before creeping to the bathroom and burying her blood-streaked underwear at the bottom of the trash. In bed, she opened her copy of *Understanding Buddhism* under the covers. When explaining dependent origination to a great Indian king, she read, the monk Nagasena asked what part of him made him Nagasena. Was it his ears, his eyes, his body, his hands? What part of him was him? No one thing was him, the monk explained. But neither were they not-him.

The monk gave a parable:

> It is precisely as if some man or other were to choose a young girl to be his wife and were to pay the purchase-money, and after a time that young girl were to become a grown woman, and then a second man were to pay the money and marry her and say, "I am not carrying off your wife; that young girl of tender years whom you chose to be your wife is one person; this grown woman is another person." Whose side, great king, would you take?

I am the young girl, she thought. But now she was the grown woman, too. She was neither and both. The split between them was exact.

. . .

The next morning, the family went to the Communion on the Common, the giant Catholic sit-in where priests would be giving Communion in protest of the closing churches. The crush began blocks away, and the four of them held hands like schoolchildren, struggling to stay together. They passed the First Church in Boston, now Unitarian; the First Baptist Church of Boston; Emmanuel Church (cross-denominational), the Arlington Street Church (Unitarian Universalist), and the Church of the Covenant (Presbyterian). All of their doors were flung wide, and people were streaming out, watching the Catholics go by.

They crossed Charles Street, which was awash with crowds and closed to cars, and began to climb the damp brown hill. There was a curious dual air among the people: half day out, with balloons, funnel cakes, Bible stories, and skits for children, and half protest, with grim-faced picketers, angry shouts, tight-spun groups marching with military ferocity. The paths were lined with cardboard tombstones, labeled with the names of the closing churches.

Nicole clung to Paul's arm, letting him carry her forward. She was sore from last night with Jules, or not sore exactly but strangely open, like there was a new place of feeling in her that hadn't existed before. A new star. A bright center. She walked slowly among the busy clumps of people, wondering if she looked as though she'd changed.

At the top of the hill, she could see the speakers shouting into megaphones, but it was difficult to hear. "What did he say?" her mother kept asking her father tensely, and he would repeat phrases for her. She was struck by this now, she told Jocelyn: the tenderness and patience with which her father had treated her mother, always.

Others were pushing forward, trampling through the rare breeds of roses. Balloon animals were twisted into crosses. Children cried and were hushed. A phalanx of protestors bristled with signs. Young priests, with straight, serious thatches of hair and quick, angry voices, passed by. Women and children parted before them in the crowd. A mother lifted a baby out of a stroller, holding it out, and a priest blessed it without looking.

"We cannot unconsecrate our holy ground," chanted the crowd.

It seemed like all of Boston was on that hill, clamoring to be heard. The four of them held on to each other, sensing danger, as if they might become separated. "We're all here, Liza," her father said to her mother. "I think he meant not just us, but everyone around us," she told Jocelyn. He meant all these sons of Irishmen, all these dock-workers and mailmen and police officers, all those guys leaning over porches in the South End and drinking in dark pubs in Somerville, all the mothers telling their kids to mix shame with a fearful kind of love.

She knew that the noise would miraculously fade when the prayer began, because they all knew what to do. It would be magical, even sacred. But it was not a silence for her anymore. She'd gotten herself tainted somehow. It had not begun with Jules, after all. This was what she had to tell Jocelyn, she saw now. It wasn't just about sin and exile. She'd begun to feel her separation when she and her mother held the dying kittens in their hands and she *wished* with all her power to save them and could not. She wondered why suffering was permitted, and what kind of god would permit it, and all the things that she knew people had wondered before but were nonetheless important, and were her right to wonder about.

There was a wall between her and that Communion. She gripped Paul's hand and tried hard not to cry. She was still very young. She wanted it all better, Paul back from college, her father opening a door to speak to her mother instead of walking away, her mother hushing their boisterous dinner table to say grace, and all of them falling silent to listen, gathered up into her quiet reverence.

. . .

The next day, she took the train into Boston. She walked to the Museum of Fine Arts, which was near her school, the grand white-columned museum she had often visited on school trips. She remembered that in the MFA's Art of Asia collection, along with the flattened kimonos and painted screens, there was a Japanese Buddhist Temple Room. The room was always kept dark, and it was well insulated from the sounds of the tourists outside. On one side were benches, and on the other was a Buddha.

She was alone in Art of Asia. The corridors were half-lit, each doorway a small vanishing point in the dimness. She paused to look at the screens and drawings on the walls—crowds of monks and nuns, bowing and praying; dragons and saints perched high on cloud tops; cherry blossoms and lotus flowers on yellowing paper. At the door to the Temple Room, she bowed. It was cool and dark. Behind a wooden barrier sat three statues of stone and bronze going cloudy green. To one side, the deities: behind their heads, licks of bronze flames cast eerie shadows that seemed to move. And she could just make out, seated on a dais of lotus flowers, the Buddha in the center, shadowy gold.

In her dog-eared copy of *Understanding Buddhism,* the first chapter described Siddhartha the outcast, climbing the hill to the bodhi tree, weak from his years of prayer and fasting. The other ascetics had turned their backs on him because he had chosen to eat a bowl of rice. But I'm hungry, I need to eat, he told them. I must live. Why are you afraid of such pleasure?

The Buddha was smiling at her, welcoming her. *Come in, come in.*

She knelt. Then before she could help it, she was crossing herself. "Sorry." Then she touched the floor—the earth is my witness—and breathed the words:

I take refuge in the Buddha.

I take refuge in the dharma.

I take refuge in the *sangha*.

"That was the part you wanted to see, wasn't it?" she asked Jocelyn.

And still in her mind, it was a moment in time she couldn't look beyond or behind.

Here is her heart tolling like a bell. Here is that frightened girl, looking for a refuge, a house that will have her. Here is her body, beginning its disgrace.

Dear Sean,

Siddhartha, certain that he is close to the truth of why peo-
ple suffer, sits under the bodhi tree through the night. Depend-
ing on which folktale or epic poem you read, he defeats Mara
the deceiver, or he sits by himself; he fights armies and conquers
death, or he sees the dawn through the leaves and finds himself
alone and aware.

So he's enlightened. What happens now? Does he look any
different? Does he feel triumphant or sorrowful, or is he now
above all human emotion? Is there a serene smile on his lips?

But maybe he feels thin and tired, as any forty-year-old who
has sat on the hard ground all night would. Maybe he staggers
a little as he walks down the hill, and goes unnoticed by the first
few wanderers and mendicants on the road. He feels the terrible
loneliness of the truths he's discovered. He's thinking of his fam-
ily at home, the family that is afraid of what he might become.
Maybe when a girl gives him a bowl of rice, and asks him if he is
a god or a man, he eats in silence, pregnant with what he is and
what he knows.

Can you unknow something you now know? Can you put
the genie back in the bottle? It never felt like a choice. All my life,
I drank the wine and it was blood. One day, I drank and it wasn't
anything anymore. I think I would have given anything for it to
be blood again. Still would, sometimes.

THE TEACHER

New York was full of gurus. Unlike Boston, provincial and suspicious, sunk deeply in its own traditions, New York was ripe for self-improvement, for transformation, for charismatic leaders. All you needed was the confidence to tell other people what to do. A couple of brass balls and the right story.

On the first day of her new class, Lucille and Jeannie and Maxine unrolled their mats on the floor of her studio apartment. She'd leaned her mattress and bed frame against the wall and hung a silk curtain over it, then set up the little shrine with her brass Buddha; otherwise the floor was bare.

She began the session with a recitation of the Fire Sermon, but Maxine quickly interrupted. "Sorry—can I ask a question?"

"Of course."

"What first brought you to Buddhism?"

"At first I joined just to rebel against my family, I think. To be something they weren't. But when tragedies visited me—it was Buddhism that kept me alive. It helped me go on living."

Now they were quiet, ready to listen.

"To become one with whatever one does is a true realization of the Way," she said. And they began.

. . .

"They're so hungry. They're looking for something I can't give," she remarked to Jocelyn.

They were walking back from Emmeline's baby yoga class, jostling through crowds at the Fort Greene farmers' market. Jocelyn put Swiss chard in her basket, her brows knitted thoughtfully, while Nicole wrestled with the stroller.

During meditation, she gave corrections, offered advice. Don't try to hold yourself up from your shoulders; let structure roll up from the base of your spine. Count your breaths until you lose count. When you feel fear, annoyance, anger, don't try to block it out; just acknowledge it, then let it move past you like weather.

As her students were rolling up their mats, they had other questions. When you're home and your husband is asleep in the den in front of the lit box of the television and you're suddenly crushed by loneliness, what do you do? If you wake up with the old chronic pain sneaking down your spine and into your hips, if you know it will be there all day, that now your day is ruined, how do you get out of bed? If your sister has cancer, do you get tested to see if you have the same awful gene, or do you lie awake listening to the thumping of your pulse at night?

Was this how her family priests had felt when widows came to them for comfort, when fighting siblings asked for advice, when husbands and wives sought marriage counseling? The clergy had trained in chapter and verse, in the esoteric nature of the divine—not in family and marriage and steady love. But apparently these things went hand in hand. She did her best to answer, sometimes making it up as she went along. You are never lonely as long as you have yourself. Let each day contain its own possibility. Each moment, you are a new self and have a new chance at happiness, she said. Whatever you choose to discover, do it prudently. Fear comes from dread, our anticipation of the worst. To be wise, let go of your desire to see the future.

After practice, they seemed to leave soothed. That was all she could offer them. She could see how being a teacher meant giving everything you had, offering up the example of your life. She could almost see how a teacher or a student could confuse that with love.

"What do they want?" Jocelyn asked.

"Everything. They want all of me." They called her up at odd hours, weeping into the phone. They wanted to be comforted, to be told that life would soon be better than what it was, that this was the absolute best use of their valuable time, that their children would get into the right schools, that their parents were proud of them, that if they just did this and this, all would be well.

Jocelyn sighed. "Isn't that always the way?"

When the Master called her now at night, he was gentle. "I've missed you," he said into the line. She listened to his voice with the lights off and rain streaking the windowpanes. It was almost like they were lying in bed together. This was the kind of intimacy she had imagined as a teenager, the thing she'd hoped she might share one day with Jules. Even when they were very young, she had looked forward to being old with him, the touch of their bodies all she needed.

When her Master had guided her through a meditation session

back in Boston, steering her away from the hurts and pain of memory, she had felt a powerful relief; but he, too, had been moved by their progress together. Sometimes when she cried, his eyes also shone with tears.

Now he whispered on the phone that she was the only one of his students who understood what a spiritual life required; that it was not just comfort and reassurance, it was hard work, it was questioning and wandering, it was anguish and doubt. He would show her how to be; she was his responsibility, he would not let her fail. She worked the prayer beads he had given her in her hands, listening.

· · ·

Sean had not called her back since she'd told him she was a mistake. She wrote letters to him and then crossed them out. ~~Dear Sean. Dear Sean. Dear Sean.~~

At work downtown, she managed the women's department's layout and folded sweaters under brilliant lights. The fashion for retail these days was stunning museum minimalism and brightness; in places like Nordstrom, wrinkles had to disappear in mirrors, diamonds had to sparkle. She sometimes felt like a lab mouse, folding the sweaters under the black globular cameras mounted in every corner. The women in jewelry had their bags weighed before and after their shifts to make sure they weren't smuggling out gold.

Her coworkers in corporate told her how to dress more New York: crisp blazers and soft, silky blouses. "Everything has to be a mixture of hard and soft," they explained. If her jewelry was geometric, then her hair had to be teased into soft waves. If she wore boots, she had to wear a dress. Strong eye makeup had to go with girlish pink lipstick.

The next week, Alison and Kathy from the *roshi's* class came to her apartment, too. "What are your qualifications?" Kathy asked. She was a psychiatrist; she needed credentials.

"I've studied Buddhism for ten years. Buddhism teaches that we're all in a burning house together. If we can help one another out, then we must," she said. She was just realizing that she could help.

She told her students about emptiness, samsara, and nirvana. She told them that when Buddhism spoke about life as suffering, the word was a mistranslation, a poor choice in English. It was not that everything was pain; there was so much pleasure and joy to be had, too much. The better translation was "unsatisfactory." Pleasure makes us hungry for more. We are never sated. We demand more and more. We think we are entitled to pleasure and happiness, when the universe has made no such promises.

"Think about a time in your life when you were happy," she said. "It's fleeting, isn't it? 'This is happiness,' and then it's over."

Now a few times a week there were women buzzing at her door, filling the hallway with their stories, their anxiety, their laughter. There wasn't enough room in her studio anymore. Jocelyn connected her with a sculptor wanting to teach ceramics classes, and they arranged to share a studio space in a converted warehouse in Alphabet City. She looked forward to arriving early, laying out the mats and lighting the candles, donning the silk robe that made the ritual feel real. The students seemed to like her, too. After a *zazen* session, she sometimes took them out into the city, teaching *kinhin,* walking meditation, which the Master had taught her. They practiced monitoring their breathing, taking slow, graceful steps. They snarled traffic and got honked at; Nicole told them it was a good test of their concentration. When they reached the river, they leaned over the fence and whooped into the wind like children, letting their hair fly. Enjoying the moment. She told her students, You are best at achieving no-mind when you are listening to the body. So run, dance, shout.

"And sex?" asked Alison, a younger painter living in Bushwick.

Nicole hesitated. "Like any other pleasure—it's over too soon." The women laughed.

At first, she didn't charge. But the students had kept leaving checks for her on her kitchen counter in embarrassing, Upper East Side amounts. Finally she left a basket by the door with a note saying, "Suggested donation $30," and they obeyed. You had to let people pay you or they'd feel guilty, and she needed the money.

And at night she performed her prostrations for her Master, as she had promised on the phone. Ten, twenty, thirty, forty, fifty. Slapping the wooden floor with her open palms. Knees creaking. Submit and submit and submit. She had to be perfect for him, she had to prove she was his best. She told herself she could do this and stay independent as long as her rebellion, her secret teaching, continued. It gave her a strange feeling. Like she had taken a book out of the library and left it on a bus. Like she had left a light on somewhere in the dark house of herself.

Teaching without the permission of your master was a grave sin. The oldest tales warned of a Judas: Devadatta, an ambitious monk who believed he had become greater than the Buddha. He could create illusions that impressed the weak-minded: snakes would fall from the sky and into the laps of astonished princes. He wanted to lead his own order, but the Buddha told him he wasn't ready. He broke away from the Buddha's *sangha,* taking five hundred monks with him, and tried to kill the Buddha by poisoning an elephant to make it go mad. The Buddha quieted the elephant by raising one hand, and Devadatta was condemned to hell.

Every time she spoke to her Master on the phone, she considered her betrayal. But now she had already poisoned the elephant. Word was spreading, one student telling a friend, and then that person telling another, and strangers were showing up at her studio space, bowing low, asking, Please, help.

. . .

Family dinner night: at her brother's door, June and Charlie pulled her in by both arms. They wanted her to pick a name for the new pet turtle scrabbling grumpily at the glass walls of its tank. It had to be something Buddhist, June insisted. Nicole chose Hotei, for the Laughing Buddha: god of contentment and protector of children.

Downstairs, the door slammed. "Halloo," said Paul, in the funny voice their father had always used when coming home from work.

"We've named our turtle, Dad," June yelled.

"Don't yell between rooms," Paul yelled back. He appeared in the doorway, his coat over his arm. "Hi, Nic. Hi, scoundrels."

"His name is Hotei," said June, staring wide-eyed at her dad. "The Laughing Buddha."

Paul looked slightly pained. "Why not something a little more—I don't know, petlike? Fido or Sparky or something?"

"No. I want Hotei. He's Hotei," June insisted. And then, trying on a much older girl's voice: "Jesus, what's your problem?"

"Language," said Paul. "Everyone wash up for dinner."

Under Nicole's parents' heavy brass chandelier, Paul circled the table, filling wine glasses. "This bottle's from Mom's stock. She wants you to call, by the way. She's so glad you moved here."

"She can call me, if she's so eager."

"We both know she doesn't make a lot of overtures." Paul sat down, overfilled his own glass. "Anyway. You remember your friend Eddie? He's living in New York now. We crossed paths a while back—his company managed some investments of ours."

Nicole's mouthful of food became cold mush. "Eddie?"

"I thought you could reconnect with him. Who knows, maybe talk to him about getting a better job."

"Oh." Nicole put her fork down, careful not to drip on the white tablecloth, her mother's tablecloth with the fragile Irish lace. "Did you."

Eddie, the third member of her runaway party; the car had been his. Eddie, whom she hadn't seen since that final night. She wondered what he looked like now.

She knew he had returned to his family; she had hoped never to see him again. If she saw Eddie's face, she wasn't sure what she would do. It would make everything too real.

"I've decided I'm never getting married," June announced.

Paul and Marion smiled indulgently. "What makes you say that?" Paul asked.

"I'm going to be alone, like Aunt Nic." She delivered this small, sad pronouncement, her thin little girl's voice loud in the room.

Nicole began to offer some benign advice. But Marion didn't wait. "I'm sure Aunt Nic wouldn't want to be considered a role model," she said.

A silence settled on the table. Nicole felt a curious relief. Now it had been laid bare, Marion's feelings about her. According to Marion, she was not just a lovable screwup. Her story, her whole life, was dangerous.

"Aunt Nic will find somebody," Paul said, forcing a smile. "And you will too, when you're older."

"No! I'll never!" June fled the table. After a nod from Marion, Charlie left as well. The three adults fiddled with their napkins in the quiet. Somewhere outside, a dog barked; on this side street, they could almost be in the suburbs again, the remains of their dinner congealing on their plates.

"It's a difficult age," said Marion.

Paul put down his fork. "Do we have to speak about our children in platitudes?"

Nicole stared at her lap. She had never seen Paul and Marion fight, but it was remarkable how similar they sounded to her own parents, right down to the shame she felt at witnessing it. Marion's eyes narrowed; Paul hunched his shoulders and turned to Nicole. "Want to help me take out the trash?"

They hauled a few bags to the dumpster shared by the neighboring apartments. The night air was heavy with rain; no stars could be seen in the clouds. "Why Hotei?" Paul asked suddenly.

Nicole laughed. "Because she knew you wouldn't like it. She wants to piss you off."

"Why?" Paul asked again. Under the dim light from the streetlamp, his face looked young and innocent. "I don't get it. She used to be happy. She used to love me."

"She still does!" Nicole reached for her brother's shoulder. He was so good, so clearly good. Kind and loving, constant, stable. "You know, I still loved all of you, even when I left? I never stopped."

Paul shrugged her hand away. "She's not you, Nicole. She's not going to do what you did."

"I know." Nicole stepped away, sensing that Paul's mood had changed. "You've just done something to piss her off, that's all. Perfect Paul, own up. Admit what you did."

"I don't know what you're talking about." He hoisted a bag into the dumpster. "I wish I smoked. It's nice out here. Quiet."

She considered that Paul might have his own share of loneliness, the kind you could get even in a crowded room. "Mom would kill you," she said.

"We don't have to do what Mom wants."

"You always do what she wants. You're the one who makes her happy."

Paul's gaze had a veteran emptiness. "It's because I lie so as not to offend her delicate sensibilities."

"You do?"

"I did what she wanted when it mattered. I told her I went to church, and I told her Marion and I hadn't slept together before we got married. Yeah, she asked. I take care of her the way she wants. I call every few days, do what needs doing."

"Why don't you stop, then?"

"Because she's my mother and I'm part of a family, and that means doing things you don't like. That's what people do," he said, enunciating the words as though she were a child. "They lie. But you knew that already, didn't you?" He hurled the last bag into the recycling bin. "Come back in for dessert," he said, and went inside.

She lingered for a moment, watching him through the windows of the warmly lit house. He and Marion floated from kitchen to dining room, putting things away. Then Marion moved toward Paul and held him by the shoulders. They spoke, but Nicole could not make out the words. It seemed right to her, that she couldn't know what was said. Someone else's marriage was like a house. You could only watch from the windows.

She turned and looked at the apartment building behind Paul's townhouse; it was an old brick tenement with fire escapes zigzagging across its surface. In the checkerboard of light and dark windows she could see other silhouettes moving—husbands, wives, cats on sills. One caught her eye: a woman moving in a kitchen, swaying to music while she stood at the sink. In the other room, a light on, but no one there. "That's me," Nicole whispered.

. . .

We are all in the great god Indra's magnificent net, her Master tells her, seven years into her training. You move and I feel it. You grow, you change, and you tug on the strings of the net. Try to tear free, and you snarl things even tighter. The people all around you are affected.

She nods; she can understand that. But the confines of the net are becoming more constraining every day. She meditates with her Master's shadow stretching over her shoulders and imagines herself growing, her neck straining, her limbs restless, struggling to open, to move. Tell me the answer to the koan, he says. Show me your original face, before your parents were born.

She says, I have always had this face. A true master never asks to see something that isn't already there.

But even when she gives the right answer, her Master seems angry. Being self-satisfied with your own progress, he says, leaning over her, is a barrier to enlightenment.

But I'm not, she says. Satisfied is not what she is.

I know. I know. His hands cup her shoulders, slide downward, claim each part of her piece by piece. In truth, she loves the way he touches her into being, as though each piece of her body, her life, has no meaning until he has gotten his hands on it, shaped it a little. He is going to make her excellent. And there is so much work to do.

You are on a journey to discover the origins of joy, anger, sorrow, and pleasure, her Master tells her. Let's figure these out one at a time. Go to the source, as they say. Let's start with pleasure. Let's see how it begins.

· · ·

"So go on," Jocelyn said on the phone when Nicole got home from Paul and Marion's that night. "Tell me about when you ran. What made you leave? Where did you go?"

THE GONE YEAR

My mother wasn't doing well, and she decided she should take a vacation to visit her cousins in North Carolina, Nicole began. There was a beach house there that the family often shared in the summer. It would be a little rest cure. This was right after St. Augustine closed.

"Take care of your father while I'm gone," she told Nicole, packing her suitcase. "It'll just be the two of you." She sighed. "You'll have to break in the new church for me. They won't have as nice a benediction. I thought you and Paul would want to be married in the old one." Her mother knelt suddenly on the carpet in her stockings, clasping her hands on the bed like a child. "Nic, say a Hail Mary with me. It's good luck. Before a journey."

Nicole froze. "Do we have to?"

Her mother looked at her. "What's gotten into you?" Then her eyes roved over her daughter's face. "Have you cut your hair?"

She had cut a few ragged inches around her face with kitchen shears. It was part of her new allegiance to Buddhism: monks and nuns shaved their heads or sliced off a topknot as a symbolic cutting of ties with their families. But that wasn't all that her mother was noticing. *It's me. I'm different.*

"Come on now, for me." Her mother's eyes were closed in prayer. Nicole knelt next to her.

Hail Mary, full of grace. Our Lord is with thee. Blessed art thou among women, and blessed is the fruit of thy womb, Jesus, her mother said in her fragile voice.

Once her mother was away, she read stacks of introductory books on Buddhism. The library's copies had long lists of red and blue checkout stamps, going back to the sixties; the more advanced the book she took out (*Esoteric Buddhism* or *Special Topics in Japanese Zen Sects*), the fewer the stamps, as though she were winnowing the list of Buddhists in Boston down to a committed few. She read the lancets and koans of Dogen, the hysterical prayers of Nichiren, the metaphysical wanderings of Ch'ang-sha. Ch'ang-sha wrote, "The entire universe is your eye; the entire universe is your complete body; the entire universe is your own luminance. The entire universe is within your own luminance. In the entire universe there is no one who is not your own self."

In her morning meditations beside her bed, she began to see that every move she made threatened the world around her. Karma, the law of cause and effect, meant that every action had its reverberation out in the world. The universe, her books told her, was not a stony firmament, a Catholic certainty, but a fragile web. She was ready and willing to believe it.

Jules called her a few days after the party. He'd gotten her number from a school directory. "Do you want to hang out or what?"

He parked down the street, as she'd asked, and then she walked out to meet him and they drove to a park with a few jogging trails. It was misty out and they could just see a big old house up on the hill, sea-gray. "You know, I have a girlfriend," he said, walking ahead of her quickly.

She thought he had broken up with the theater girl, but she didn't say it. She ducked her head and murmured, "I know," wanting to seem serious and respectful. She wondered if this was why they were at this park instead of the movies or the mall, hidden from public view.

In his tight jeans his legs were slightly bowed, and it gave his walk a little hitch, a jaunty swing. It was the way a cowboy would walk, a boy acting like a cowboy. "Then why did you take me here?" she said.

He laughed. "Man, we can go back if you want."

"I'd just like to know what I am to you." It was a desperate ploy, this frankness, but she was pretty sure the only attraction she had for him was her directness. If he was looking for the usual things a girl could offer, he already had plenty. She knew those Boston girls from the big-lawned suburbs, the girls who went to her school, who clattered into ice cream shops in their field hockey cleats, with their dark blond hair and their freckled rosy-glowing skin, smelling of baby powder and body glitter—those demure entitled girls stalking down Newbury Street in packs, those brisk beaming ponytailed girls, too busy, too accomplished even to be mean, assembling their résumés for the Ivy League schools where they would meet drunk blond boys, those girls, who were trained to attack on the soccer field, on the debate teams and model U.N.'s of the world but were still called "sweet"—those girls, diligently turning the keys of their palate expanders—those Boston prep school girls.

Jules shrugged, a thin-lipped smile on his face. "You're like all the other good girls, looking for somebody who'll give you flowers."

"No, I'm not." Hadn't screwing in the muddy backyard of a friend's house during a party been bad enough for him? "What'll it take to prove I'm not?"

Jules dug into his pocket, came up with an orange prescription bottle. "From my dad's knee surgery. They're sick." He palmed two pills, swallowed, and offered the bottle.

"I don't know—"

He smirked. "Go home. Go home to Daddy."

"Asshole," she said, and swallowed.

She began to feel as if she were wearing special glasses that let her see the fog hanging on every new leaf of every tree. She laughed and glided on a cushion of nauseous elation. The worry that had been like a second shadow—her mother, her conversion—began to retreat. Jules pushed her gently into a pile of moss and unbuttoned her jeans. "Want to? Want to?" he kept asking, and she kept saying, "Yes."

But he didn't actually. Just caressed her a little and held her and lay very still. She thought, Ah! This is what everybody was really talking about. Not all the lust and the wrestling around. That could be good. But this was far more dangerous, this closeness. This was what could pull you in.

"You gonna go gossiping around school about us?" Jules asked after a long time.

"What's to tell?" That was an easy test to pass: she had no one she cared to gossip to. But he seemed pleased by her nonchalance.

"You act cool, man. I thought you were some good girl."

"You were wrong." All right, she would be his secret for now.

"Man!" He slapped his thigh. "Where'd you come from?"

"You're making fun of me," she said warily.

"Yeah. But it's because I like you."

This moment, she could see now as she told Jocelyn, was the beginning. It showed how easily she was governed by that simple, wordless, adolescent need: the need to be liked. She'd spend the next year chasing it, needing Jules to see her as adventurous and dangerous. By the time they ran away, it was bigger than that; it was her own pure, beautiful dream. Together they'd drive away from everything they knew to be safe.

Jules hugged her from behind, ground against her. "You like me too, bad girl. I can tell."

She shrugged. It was a hard gesture to make when your heart was pounding with joy.

. . .

She believed everything she read in books. It was books that would signify her allegiance to the truth. So now she carried a copy of *The Blue Cliff Record,* a collection of Zen koans, in her bag at all times, and dipped into every book she could find about Buddhism, reading urgently, wanting to know, to believe, in everything.

> *Boundless wind and moon—the eye within eyes,*
> *Inexhaustible heaven and earth—the light beyond light,*
> *The willow dark, the flower bright—ten thousand houses;*
> *Knock at any door—there's one who will respond.*
> —*The Blue Cliff Record*

Her nights began with her tapping on the bulkhead door behind someone's house in the twilight. Then a friend would open the hatch. She'd descend the crumbling cement steps, pass the rumbling washing machine, duck under hissing New England pipes. There, Jules and the others welcomed her in.

That spring, when she had converted to Buddhism but still barely knew what that meant, was the beginning of her basement year. In math, in English class, ignoring her teachers' puzzled glances, she kept *The Blue Cliff Record* open in her lap and read koans. She was deciphering a code, the runes and diagrams of a non-Catholic world.

The couches in the basements where Jules hung out were always furry and matted with lint and potato-chip crumbs. They were surrounded by the detritus of suburban childhoods: Nerf guns, video game consoles, Ping Pong mallets, Halloween masks, Christmas lights in snarls. They played Ping Pong and smoked and talked. You could fill a night that way.

At these hangouts, Jules introduced her as a friend. They talked as if she weren't there for a while, but they were watching her, she knew, and saw how Jules had his arm around her, passed her the joint and showed her how to inhale slowly.

"You're a nice Catholic girl," said Holly. "Not Jules's usual type." She had sleek ink-black hair and wore lots of bracelets.

"Not anymore," said Nicole. "I'm a Buddhist."

That made them interested.

"There's a monastery in Tibet where you go off and live in a cave for seven years."

"What, all together?"

"No, everybody gets their own cave, and you don't talk to anyone. You just meditate."

"That's insane."

"What's so insane about it?" Jules asked. "They're on a quest.

Everyone should try just being alone with themselves for a while." He squeezed her hand.

"I bet they jerk off in there, like, three times a day. Nuns, too." Eddie grinned.

"Jesus!" Nicole said.

"What?"

"It's just not a pretty image."

"You just can't stand the idea of them being less than perfect, Nicole. It says a lot about you."

Holly rose to her defense: "I think it says a lot about *you,* Eddie, that you assume everyone jerks off three times a day if left to their own devices."

"If they're not, they're going crazy. It's a surefire way to go crazy. The human is *the* social animal." That was Eddie, fervent and political, dabbling in communism. "Why do they do it?"

"They value the mind so much that they want to free it from the prison of the body."

Much of what Nicole said was about things she didn't understand then but wanted to. She talked to Jules in a constant stream, reciting haiku and telling him about the emptiness at the heart of all things, loving the easy way he kept his arm around her, the way he listened. They talked about South America and the Gulf War. Eddie, freckled and red-haired, whose basement they hung out in more often than anyone else's, wore soccer jerseys with the names of Chilean teams on them and sat cross-legged on the coffee table. The others—Jon, Colin, his girlfriend, Holly—sat around listening to him talk about Chile and Venezuela and the prisoners there. He told them about his favorite revolutionaries, listing their manifestos and arrests as if describing his favorite baseball players and their stats.

Eventually they drifted away in ones and twos. Eddie went

upstairs, and she and Jules humped quietly on the couch until she heard a cough and saw Eddie's red Converse tennis shoes in the line under the door. They hastily rearranged themselves, and then Eddie came in and sat on the recliner facing them, grinning, rolling an empty beer bottle between his hands. "This guy, Nicole," he said. "You found yourself quite a guy."

"Yeah?" She was still flushed and sweating, trying hard to look composed.

"Yeah. Knows how to treat a lady, if you know what I mean. Or should I say 'ladies.'"

"Shut up, Eddie." Jules struggled into his jacket.

"Ask him," said Eddie, still grinning, rolling the bottle, his eyes on Nicole. "Go ahead, ask him. He's got quite the reputation."

"Enough." Jules stood up and got in Eddie's face.

Eddie shrank back. "I'm a pacifist, dude."

"Then be a little more passive."

Jules borrowed Eddie's car to drive her home. Throughout that year she'd find he was good at borrowing things—someone's car, someone's basement to spend the night in. Once they arrived, they sat at the curb, beyond the streetlights, and Nicole took a comb from her bag and fixed her hair, sniffing her clothes for smoke. "I'm gonna be in trouble if my dad's still up."

"That's what you get, for being with me," Jules said. "See you tomorrow?"

"Yeah." She felt her heart lurching. She knew her father would be angry and worried; she didn't care. Nothing really mattered except for Jules's languid hand on her thigh.

She told her father she'd been to the candlepin bowling alley with friends. And later, that she was studying at the library. Just lie, she told herself. If it means nothing to you, then the lie, too, is nothing.

. . .

While she and her father were seeding the lawn for new grass, she felt that companionable silence between them, the easy way they worked together. "There's this monastery I've been reading about in Japan," she said. "They meditate for hours under a waterfall. The point is to maintain this incredible focus while the water is pounding on their heads."

"Jeez. What are they? Franciscan?"

"Actually, Zen. They're Buddhists."

"Hmm," her father said.

Nicole pressed on: "There's this other monastery out west, in Colorado. It's run by this guy called the Karmapa. He's second-in-command under the Dalai Lama. They send the really advanced monks up into the mountains with nothing but a wet blanket. They have to dry it with their own body heat. They can control their body temperature."

Her father straightened over the seed spreader, wiping his brow. "I knew people who got taken in by this craze when it first started," he said. "All these swamis and gurus were popping up all over the place. People poured their life savings into these communes or the swamis themselves. And it never came to anything. They lost their money, or they got hooked on drugs, or they died. I wouldn't want you to get taken in by the same things, Nic. There are a lot of snake oil salesmen out there."

Nicole sighed.

Her father ruffled her hair, that gesture for which she was too old. "Let's have a nice green lawn for when your mother gets back."

. . .

The Path has no byroads; one who stands upon it is solitary and dangerous. The truth is not seeing or hearing; words and thoughts are far removed from it. If you can penetrate through the forest of thorns and untie the bonds of Buddhahood, you attain the land of inner peace, where all the gods have no way to offer flowers, where outsiders have no gate to spy through.

—*The Blue Cliff Record*

When she hung out with Jules and his friends, they talked about "the system" and "the establishment" and how they were all getting processed like cornmeal through the gears of the capitalist machine. Eddie pounded a point home with his fist on his shoe. ("It's dank, man, fucking dank, the way the world is now.") Jules argued with Colin over whose father was worse (Colin: "At least your dad isn't breathing down your neck about getting into Duke and perfectly replicating this messed-up line of multigenerational Colins." Jules: "At least when your dad's drunk, he complains about Clinton instead of locking you out all night because you didn't empty the dishwasher.")

They watched pop stars laugh and grunge acts growl on TV, and they wondered what lies they were being told about what was in the milk they drank and who really had a shot at the American dream, and why no one was marching or singing or writing about it anymore.

And sometimes in the later hours of the night, the talk would start about going. Just what if. What if one day you weren't here. No note, no *sayonara*. Just gone. When Jules was fighting with his father, Nicole would ask:

What if we get out of here?

What would it be like just to be gone?

She read *The Dharma Bums* and reread Japhy Ryder's grand vision for what would soon be happening in America. He said he pictured a great "rucksack revolution." Millions of Americans on the move, traveling to mountains to pray, making old people and young people happy. Just a great big bunch of Zen lunatics in motion, spreading wildness with their steps. That was 1958. Had his prophecy come to pass? Nicole felt keenly that they'd missed something important by being born when they had. Battles had already been fought and lost. Kids had been dressing as hippies for Halloween for years.

She read about the girls in these books, simpering, foolish, half-naked. The girls were there for spice, Kerouac wrote.

Where were the girl wanderers? Where were the girl lunatics?

And if it was late enough, the thought of running away would lie out before them on the table like some rare artifact discovered buried under the house. They'd paw around it, look at every angle. Where. When. And they'd all get quiet, imagining.

· · ·

It got to be just her and Jules and Eddie more and more—Colin overwhelmed by SAT test prep, Jon joining the swim team and actually becoming popular, Holly impatient with all of them. They were going nowhere, she said. They weren't revolutionaries; they were wastoids. She delivered this pronouncement one night and then vanished from their lives.

Once Jules took her to his dad's because he had forgotten his wallet. He asked her to wait in the car and left her parked in front of a small brick colonial with a fallen-in chimney. The lawn was covered with dead leaves and fallen brush, untouched since the fall.

Jules was strict in showing her only careful, regimented portions of his life. Well, enough of that, she thought. She got out of the car and pushed open the kitchen door.

Pots were in a jumble across the counter, with mail, papers, old receipts scattered in loose piles. One cabinet hung by a hinge. A drawer gaped ajar, the silverware inside scattered randomly.

"You're new," said a voice behind her. She turned quickly; a tall, bearded man with Jules's cheekbones and his shell-shaped ears was leaning on the counter.

"Hello," she said. "I'm with Jules. You must be his dad."

She offered her hand, but he didn't take it. "Yeah, I'm Jules's dad."

Jules came downstairs with his wallet. "Dad, this is Nicole," he said. Standing wary.

"We've met." His father picked up the beer bottle on the counter and swallowed. "So where are you going tonight? When will I see you? In a week or two?"

"I'll be back tomorrow. I always am."

"Whatever." He drained the bottle and tossed it into a bin with a crash. "Watch out for this one, Nicole. You seem like one of these nice girls. His mother warned me not to take him, but—" He threw up his hands. "Here we are."

In the car, Jules opened and closed his hands on the steering wheel. "See? See why I didn't want you to meet him?"

She didn't know what to say: the dim kitchen, its disarray, his father's cold disregard felt ominous. She knew what her mother would say: this was no kind of home; they were not the right sort of people.

But she could feel only compassion for Jules. "You wanted me to see him. Otherwise you wouldn't have taken me tonight."

"I don't know. I guess. I guess I wanted you to see—"

"What you're up against?"

"No. Where I'm coming from." He smiled. "You can't change where you come from. It'll always be a part of you. And I come from nothing good."

When she got home that night, she hugged her father, who was sitting in the den. She wanted to crawl into his lap as if she were still a little girl. "Are you all right?" he asked.

She couldn't raise his suspicions any further. "I'm fine."

Later that week she saw Jules with the drama girl, the one he had said was still his girlfriend. They were standing in the parking lot of her school by his car, kissing. She stopped with her armful of books, feeling suddenly small and foolish. She'd been warned, but somehow it hadn't been real until this moment. Was she one of many?

When he called two days later to meet, she walked to the corner in the twilight but wouldn't get in the car. "Give me a good reason to go with you."

"What do you mean?"

"You know. I saw you. With your other girl."

He smiled and stretched back in his seat. "Julie, you mean. You saw us."

She had expected angry denials or pleading apologies, not this smirking self-assurance. "So you want to tell me what the hell you were doing?"

"I told you I had a girlfriend."

"So—what am I?"

"You know. You're my girl. Friend. My girl friend."

"Oh. I see." Her mind worked furiously. It seemed like the only thing to do was walk away. She did, fast, heading home.

She heard the car door slam. "Nicole, wait." She didn't pause. "Nicole." His hand on her shoulder.

She turned, furious. "What do you want? You think I can just put up with that? Be one of your many girls?"

"I thought you were cool." He sounded hurt. But he was teaching her a lesson as well. Don't you understand what being cool really means? What detachment really is? Don't you see that you've got to take whatever comes with a mixture of equanimity and disdain? Was this a Buddhist thought or just a teenage boy's?

She looked up at him. "I guess it's harder than I thought."

He shrugged. "Yeah, well, you can date other people, too. I get that. That's how it works."

"Yeah." She knew she wouldn't.

"Come on." He shepherded her to the car. She put the seat back and he climbed on top of her, but they couldn't manage to make things work. The back seat was full of Eddie's dirty laundry and a case of beer. They squirmed and cursed for a few minutes more; then Jules slid into the driver's seat. "Let's go somewhere."

They cruised through town for a while, scanning the buildings for opportunities. Break into the library? A park bench? Each suggestion seemed more depraved than the last. Finally they returned to the woods and crawled up the pine-needled hill to where the lights were farthest. This time, though, the ground was cold and hard; dirt slipped into her clothes. The things she'd been willing to overlook before were too real now. The next day she'd find herself covered in scratches from tree bark and pine needles, and have to invent a story for her father involving a trip to the park, hide-and-seek, a fall down a hill.

Still, it was exciting. Driving back home sore and silent, Jules's hand on hers. The game they were playing: *I won't care if you won't.*

. . .

Julie, the drama girl, was always starring in the school's latest production of *West Side Story* or *Guys and Dolls*. Her bright, heart-shaped face shone in the lights, her voice making up in robust volume for what it lacked in tone. She wore argyle sweater vests and little short skirts.

High white socks and pink scrunchies. There was a different polish on her nails every day. Nicole noted the changing colors: orange, saffron, turquoise, maroon.

One Saturday when she was walking through Waban, she saw Julie ahead of her on the sidewalk. Julie stepped into the ice cream parlor, and without hesitation Nicole followed.

The parlor was crowded, and from several groups away Nicole sat and watched her order one scoop of mint chocolate-chip ice cream. Normally drama girl was never alone, always the type to travel in packs. She coasted confident and queenly through the school, magnanimous to the little others. But here she was, quietly staving off her melting ice cream cone in a sweatshirt. Did she eat ice cream only when she was alone? Maybe her crowd tolerated only fat-free frozen yogurt. Why else would she be eating alone here with no one to adore her? Maybe her life wasn't as airy and wonderful as it appeared.

She thought, *I slept with your boyfriend. Your boyfriend, he's the one who took my virginity. Just a few days ago, his hands were here and here and here.*

She thought, and wished the words could seep out of her and into the air, *Your boyfriend prefers the strange girls, the ones like me.*

The drama girl got up, licking her fingers, and left the parlor. Nicole followed her out the door and down the sidewalk. The words she wanted to say circulated through her blood, a hot, toxic sludge. She knew that this girl, a stranger, had done nothing wrong. But still she followed. She was a malevolent ghost, a bad spirit, whether Catholic or Buddhist, and she would stalk this girl, would hunt her to the ends of the earth like the dogs of sin, the swine of greed, the cock of wrath. She walked fast, dodging people on the busy shopping street. She watched the girl pause and look in windows, her movements easy and unhurried, the long, strong ponytail swishing and flicking like it was alive.

The words moved through Nicole's body the way the words of a mantra were supposed to become flesh: *I slept with your boyfriend. He wanted me. He would choose me. He will.*

The girl ducked into a pharmacy. Nicole stayed an aisle away, fumbling with the mints. She saw her contemplating a wall of greeting cards. She examined those cheap, maudlin cards as though they carried the secret of love. Nicole picked up a candy bar and gripped it until the chocolate softened in her fist. How laughable this girl was, how un-special. *I'll show you, Jules. I'm screwed up. I'm wild. I'm dangerous. That's what you want, isn't it?*

Nicole walked down the aisle. She was beside the drama girl now, pretending to flip through the Father's Day cards. "Hey, don't I know you from school?" she said, her voice coming out low and husky.

Drama girl stiffened, looked her quickly up and down, figuring out if she was somebody important. "Oh, yeah. You were in *Guys and Dolls,* weren't you? In the chorus?"

"Yeah." Nicole kept her eyes on the cards, carefully turning them one by one.

"What's your name?"

"Nicole."

"Nicole, right. How's it going?" How blandly friendly this girl was willing to be.

"Do you know a guy named Jules?"

"Jules, of course—you know he's my boyfriend?"

"Yeah, I know him." The words were close, very close. "You could say I know him."

Now drama girl was suspicious. She couldn't miss the edge in Nicole's tone. "What, did you guys used to go out or something?"

"Something like that. We are now."

The girl put down the card she was holding. Looked her up and down, closer this time. "What the hell is that supposed to mean?"

"Just what it sounds like. Jules and I are dating. And I wanted to tell you—" She gulped at the words. "I wanted to tell you you're wasting your time with him. You're not the kind of girl he wants."

Drama girl didn't speak at first, just kept staring at her. "Yeah, I know you. Everyone thinks you're a fucking weirdo. What the fuck do you think you're doing, messing around with my boyfriend? Why don't you get a life?"

"You should talk to him about that. He asked me out. I didn't know he was seeing you, but now that I do, well—you're wasting your time. You should give him up." They were standing next to the giant plastic tree filled with greeting cards. Around them, through the throbbing of her heart, she could still hear the monotonous whirr of the automatic door opening and closing, the clerk ringing up someone's items, the bell chiming each time a prescription was ready. Both of them facing each other, surprised, not sure what would happen next.

Drama girl found her footing first, seemed to remember the next thing to say in the script. "And what'll you do if I don't?"

"You don't know what I'll do. I'm a fucking weirdo, remember?" And without a pause she grabbed the card tree, toppling it in one magnificent crash. Greeting cards rained down all around them: cartoon bears hugging cartoon hippos, floppy-eared puppies and kittens in oversized shoes, all of them falling in chaos.

· · ·

Look at the body, diseased, impure, rotten. / Focus the mind on all this foulness. / Your body is like this, / And this is like your body. / It stinks of decay, / Only a fool would love it.

When Jules drove her home from their late-night dates, spent smoking and chatting on Eddie's couch, they crawled along the dark streets, watching for overzealous suburban cops. She remembered staring at the little houses shut up for the night in a hazy awe. They were so safe, so impregnable, such tidy, sweet Colonial houses. High many-paned windows. Lace curtains. Swing sets in the backyards. Half-frozen snow piles that wouldn't melt until April. Clapboard, brick, and slate, all weatherproofed for storms and snow, their gutters choked with leaves. People sleeping inside, enclosed in their private worlds.

And she, stinking of skunky weed, of beer, sweat, of saltier body fluids, her hair clammed to her skin—she was welcome in none of these houses.

"So you're some kind of freak, I hear," he said to her without looking over. "Causing chaos in CVS and whatnot."

"Maybe." So word had gotten back about the incident with the drama girl. She watched his hand drift easily on the steering wheel. "Is that what you think?"

"I think you're not the good little Catholic girl I thought you were." He pulled up at the corner as always. "See you tomorrow?" He leaned in for his kiss, and he put his arm around her, drawing her close in a new way, something that felt more tender. They did not mention the drama girl again, but word went around school that she was now dating the lacrosse star.

. . .

Every few weekends Paul visited from college in New York and they went to Dairy Joy, the joint out in Weston famous for its homemade soft-serve. By fall it was really too cold for ice cream, but they were New Englanders and ate sitting in his car in their parkas.

"What's going on at school?" he asked.

"Jeez, you're consulting with Mom and Dad now? Do they send you my grades? I've been busy."

Paul had come home from college wearing a suit and tie and had tucked a paper napkin into his collar to protect it as he ate. His new girlfriend, Marion, had picked out the tie, he'd said. It was the most expensive article of clothing he'd ever owned. "Busy doing what? This Buddhist stuff you told me about on the phone? What exactly do you *do*? Chant mantras and wave incense around?"

"No, Paul. That's what you do when you're a Catholic, remember?"

He laughed and said, "Got me there," but it was the first time she had implied that she was not a Catholic.

"A lot is at stake," he said. "Wait until you get to college; then you can be whoever. But don't fuck up your life now, before you have a chance."

"You're so dramatic."

"I mean it."

She thought he was her best chance for understanding. She wanted to tell him about the Karmapa in Colorado, the books she'd been taking out of the library about him. He had fled terrible slaughter in Tibet and set up a temple in the Rockies, attracting new followers. She'd read, *You keep going. That is the bodhisattva's way. As long as it benefits even one being you have to, without any sense of discouragement, go on.*

"There's this trip I want to take, maybe next summer. There's this monk, called the Karmapa, in Colorado. He's the next ranking lama under the Dalai Lama, and he's the head of this—well, like a monastery, but for the laity."

"So it's a commune."

"No! More like a spiritual retreat. I want to meet him."

"I don't know. You, going alone, to some camp for unwashed hippies—"

"Thanks, Paul. Is that what you think? Making fun of a religion practiced by only about a billion people."

"Do you speak Tibetan? What are you and this Karmapa guy going to talk about?"

"It's a quest, okay?"

"What do you mean?"

"It's just something I have to do."

She was lucky, she knew, to have Paul, even when he made fun of her. They'd knock on each other's walls at night in the code they had established as children. They knew where their mother's antique dolls were buried in the yard.

. . .

The lowest of places, on examination, has a surplus; the highest of places, when leveled, has a deficit. Holding still and letting go are both right here, but is there a way out?

—*Commentary on the Blue Cliff Record*

Her mother returned, freckled and a little more relaxed, and the basement year trickled by. She was seventeen and she began hiding her report cards and faking her parents' signatures on letters sent home. The spring air held its annual promise. On a blustery Sunday after church, Nicole's family went walking at World's End, a harbor and nature preserve on Massachusetts Bay. Nicole's parents walked arm in arm, both of them shapeless in their old blue barn jackets. Paul and Nicole walked behind in a companionable silence. The wind tore at her hair. It ruffled the golden-green cattails down by the water.

Their mother climbed out onto an overhang of rock as the wind pulled at her playfully, and she planted her hands on her hips and shouted, "I can see around the world from here!" She looked beautiful, and Nicole felt a hopeful pride.

Clouds gathered in the narrow neck of the bay. They all ran for cover and sat in the car without starting it while the rain pounded around them, falling across the windows in thick silver curtains. Thunder went off like a bomb, and they saw lightning, a strange alien green through the clouds.

After a while, Nicole's father turned the engine and pulled away. She looked around the car, at Paul watching the trees flash by, at the back of her mother's head. In church the priest had read from Corinthians: *Do you not know that your body is a temple of the Holy Spirit within you, which you have from God? You are not your own; you were bought with a price. So glorify God in your body.* But she *was* her own; she was unique, something her family could not understand.

. . .

Later that spring, Eddie brought his new girlfriend into their basement world. Willa came thumping down the stairs of Eddie's basement in giant black lace-up boots and surveyed them for a moment before declaring, "Some party, Ed." She was a proto-Goth, wearing a black skirt and an oversized black shirt, and she had thin black lips. It was the first time Nicole had seen the look. In small towns in the Midwest, teenagers had been accused of Satanism for years, but it had yet to reach preppy, mainstream New England. "I'm Nicole," she said.

"Willa practices Tantra," Eddie announced. "You know, she's a Buddhist, too."

"Tantra?"

Willa shook her necklace, a chain of skulls the size of marbles. "It's the only way to access the authentic truth, you know?"

Nicole's hands tingled; this was the first other Buddhist she had known since Kumiko. She felt suddenly ashamed and nervous. Now all the talk she had been putting out about Buddhism could be challenged. She would be revealed as a tourist, a gawking fan.

Willa sat with her large white legs in Eddie's lap, swigging her beer and laughing at Jules for being too cool and Eddie for being too geeky. She threw the Diamond Sutra into the conversation ("No one is liberated until we're all liberated. That's what it says. Sounds a lot like communism, doesn't it, Eds?"), her big knees dwarfing Eddie's, talking about how cute Eddie had seemed when he'd asked her out. "We were in the 7-Eleven. He looked like some poor puppy somebody'd left in a box. Right, Mr. Ed?"

Eddie laughed nervously.

"You meditate?" Willa asked Nicole.

"A little. I'm not very good."

"I hear that. But it's not about tamping all that mental energy down. It's about letting it out. Finding doors to open." She grinned, ran her tongue over her teeth so they could see its silver stud.

"How else do you pray?" asked Jules. "I hear Tantra is all about the body." Of course he would ask that. They'd already been there for hours, grinning at each other in the light of the muted TV.

Willa smiled, playing with her chain of skulls. "You don't know the first thing about it, buddy boy. Tantra is pure joy." She took Jules's cigarette right out of his mouth and pulled on it. "You've got to loosen up, crack your head open, let all the good stuff in."

They smoked a joint and Jules produced a handful of pills that made the walls of the room creep in and pulse with warmth.

Willa wanted to investigate the rest of the house. "Come on, Edster, let us out of the dungeon."

"All right, all right. But don't make a mess—my parents will kill me." Eddie had kept them corralled in the basement all this time, insisting that they enter through the bulkhead.

They trooped upstairs. Eddie's parents were away on vacation; they never missed the ski season in the Alps, apparently, but Eddie had school to go to, and so he was left to his own devices. The house was still, the gleaming countertops, the stainless steel appliances all undisturbed. Nicole wandered from room to room, seeing esoteric artworks and African sculptures, fine mid-century modern furniture, the chairs and tables all sleek and minimal and arranged at perpendicular angles. Here and there, a small corner of Eddie's existence: sneakers fenced in a tray; a soccer ball up on a shelf; a single report card on the fridge.

Jules saw it, too. "Man, do they ever let you out of the basement?"

Eddie shrugged. "I chose it."

"Your bedroom?"

"They turned it into an exercise room. I liked the basement better." Of course, it suited him, Nicole thought; it suited his romantic fervor. He wanted to be the misunderstood Communist ranting from his garret, his *Notes from the Underground* at his side. How many suburban kids wished they could lead their own rebellion or thought they were leading one already? It was kind of sweet.

"They don't bother me, and I don't bother them," said Eddie fiercely. "As long as I bring the grades in, they don't know I exist. And one day I can go."

"You shouldn't wait around for them to notice you," Willa said. "*Make* them notice."

She slid open the back door. Out beyond the lawn there was only darkness; Eddie's house flanked a protected bird habitat. In the lights from the house they could just see a stand of trees at the edge of the darkness. "Come on," she said.

She started off across the lawn, and Nicole and Jules followed. "It's off-limits at night, you can't go," Eddie yelled from the door. But Willa didn't stop, and Nicole, heart thumping, followed. "Nicole," Eddie said, as though he knew she was the only one who might see reason. "Nicole, I just wanted—"

"All ashore that's going ashore, Eddie," Willa called over her shoulder. Nicole went on.

"Come back," Eddie cried again, forlorn. But Willa, with her necklace of skulls, was the only one leading the real rebellion. Nicole wanted to impress her, show her they were worth her time.

"I am the night Buddha," she whooped into the darkness. "I am the Buddha with no name!" She grabbed Jules's shoulders from behind and he piggybacked her across the wet lawn.

They climbed the low fence at the edge of Eddie's lawn and took a few cautious steps on the pine needles. It was already so dark here, the lights of the house far away. The three of them ran, calling to one another, making ghost sounds and jumping out from behind trees. Nicole ran until her hands touched a scratchy tree trunk, the blackness around her so thick it felt like a second skin. There was something happening, a dizzy wildness in her. Then Jules was there, a tiny cell phone light reflecting on his face. "Where's Willa?"

"Here." Willa's breathy voice was a surprise on the back of Nicole's neck. She moved lightly around them, just skirting the flashlight, laughing. "Hey, we could have some real fun," she said.

Nicole and Jules stared at each other in the cell phone's blue glow, and then Jules made a face, startled but excited, and she knew Willa had her hands on him. She waited, heart thumping, wondering what would happen next. Then a hand was on her waist. "You can open yourself to the universe of the dharma if you practice Tantra," Willa said. "In the Tibetan temples, the *dakinis* are the goddesses of wisdom, and they dispense pleasure freely." Her voice, her hands kept traveling around them. Jules's eyes didn't leave Nicole's. "They make the holy union of the Tantra possible," Willa said.

Jules reached for Nicole, kissed her hard and hungrily. She was hungry, too. Willa laughed in the darkness. Nicole imagined walking back to the lit house, rejoining Eddie. They could listen to their Kurt Cobain albums and play at being revolutionaries and everything would still be all right. But it was too late for that, wasn't it? She'd made her choice, walked out willingly. Willa's trespassing hands, her generous body, drew the three of them together.

. . .

If you have a home, leave your home. If you have beloved ones, leave them.

—Dogen

She came home late, her body raw, her lips and legs hurting. And maybe it was this that made her enter through the kitchen door instead of slinking through the garage, slamming it without any attempt at deception. Her parents glided downstairs, belting their matching robes, Paul, visiting from business school, behind them in his boxers, his hair wild. She stayed behind the kitchen counter, afraid to let them get too close, afraid of her own smell.

"You want to tell us where you've been?" her father began. She knew the script; they all did.

"Out. Out with friends."

It was her mother she was afraid of, pale and silent, bleeding disappointment.

"Who?" Her father demanded. "With the same friends you've been sneaking out with every goddamned night?"

Nicole waited for her mother to say, "Bill, please," or to put a hand on his arm. But she remained quiet, waiting for the answer.

"I can see whoever I want."

"We're worried about you," said Paul, from the doorway.

"Who the hell asked you? Why is he in this discussion, anyway?"

"Because he cares about you, like the rest of us," said her mother. "And it's not just the late nights. It's the books you've been reading— the things you've been talking about—"

Nicole could feel their eyes, diagnosing her. She turned around again. "I'm sick of going to church. I can't do it anymore. I don't want to be Catholic." She was warming up now. "All the sin and shame! Am I supposed to be afraid of, of *life*? It's corrupt."

Silence fell; they all sat at the table and listened to the buzz of the refrigerator, the gentle nautical swish of the dishwasher. Her mother stood up. "You will always be Catholic. You were baptized." Her voice was grimly triumphant. "I don't understand you."

She had to explain. "There's this Buddhist monk in Colorado. I have to meet him. If you would let me go and see him—"

"You're not going anywhere," her father said. "I've seen this happen to people—they think they want to join a New Age cult or chant 'Hare Krishna.' You don't understand. You'll end up ruining your life. You're too young to understand."

Her mother began to cry. "Look what you're doing to me. Just look." Paul put his hand on his mother's shoulder. Nicole hated him then.

Her father said there would be curfews and check-ins from now on. In a glimpse she saw what the next weeks and months of her life would look like: her mother's black silence in the house, forced marches to church. She couldn't do it anymore. She was tired. Her father's argument didn't matter. None of them mattered.

She went to her bedroom and crouched on the floor beside her bed, and heard them all come upstairs after her, shutting off lights. She waited for her mother to open the door and press a hand into her hair, to tell her all was forgiven; there was still that chance. But she didn't come.

"I was already a runaway, long before I left," she told Jocelyn.

She waited until she was sure they were asleep. They were so trusting, still; every door was unlocked. They thought the power of their disappointment could hold her here. She called Jules.

"No note," she said. "Just go."

. . .

"So you just left?" Jocelyn asked.

"Jules called Eddie. We needed a car, and I knew he wouldn't want to be left behind. His parents were gone for a month—he thought he'd be back before he was even missed."

"And you didn't tell anyone?"

This was the most difficult part of the story, the part she feared no one would understand. All the cruelty and joy of it mixed. "You have to understand what it was like," she began.

PART TWO

The week after she and the Master have sex for the first time, she comes to the Zendo as always and chants and meditates along with the others. She keeps her eyes down, and she tries to hide the trembling in her body when he passes along the aisle. He sees, though; he knows she is on a razor's edge, struggling to keep herself under control, to pretend she doesn't care, that she's all right. After the other members have dispersed, she's still there, kneeling on her mat, and he waves her into his private room, careful not to touch her, to startle or hover.

"You came back," he says. "I'm happy."

Last week she'd bolted up and out of the room, fleeing her own embarrassment and confusion. "Of course, I wanted to apologize," she says. "I was—confused. I don't think we should—" She stops, begins again, tries to explain.

He listens to her patiently. "And you think what happened was wrong?" he asks finally.

"Well . . ."

"That's the old Catholic in you. It's going to take some work to drive that thinking out of your head, I can tell."

You have to destroy all the old gods, he knows, if there's any hope of changing your perception. Even the idols like guilt and shame and decency are distractions, old tribal ways of keeping people in line. For his students, especially all these American girls and women who grew up with a sense of themselves, he has to start with the concept of *muga:* no-self. It's painful, learning that you are not an immortal being, and that no one is judging you, weighing every thought and feeling that passes through. All your adolescent fears and desires don't have the special weight of sin.

She's still talking: "I think I made a mistake. I think we should—"

"You think, you think," he says irritably. "Who are you?"

"I—"

"Have you learned nothing?"

She flushes; even her scalp under her fine hair is pink. Now she will listen to anything he says. In Zen koans, struggling monks are often slapped or hit by their teachers, spurring them on to revelation. He rises and walks to the corner of the room, where the teaching stick is waiting. He picks it up, tests the light, springy weight of it. "Do you need a lesson?" he asks.

There are so many warring emotions on her face; he loves how poorly she hides them, pride and shame and confusion and desperate need. He loves the storm of her. "Yes, I do," she says.

He is gentle; just one strike across the shoulders, not enough to raise a bruise. It's the thought that counts, the lesson. She'll remember the dread, the delight of his walk across the room, the sound of the stick swishing through the air. And the tenderness that can follow.

It takes time to discover what no-self really means.

INDRA'S NET

She was just barely eighteen and at a pancake chain sometime early in the morning, sitting across the table from Jules and Eddie. She pulled out her book and read, sipping lukewarm coffee.

Far away in the heavenly abode of the great god Indra, there is a wonderful net which has been hung by some cunning artificer in such a manner that it stretches out indefinitely in all directions. In accordance with the extravagant tastes of deities, the artificer has hung a single glittering jewel in each eye of the net, and since the net itself is infinite in dimension, the jewels are infinite in number. . . . If we now select one of these jewels for inspection and look closely at it, we will discover that in its polished surface there are reflected all the other jewels in the net, infinite in number.

— Francis Cook, *The Jewel Net of Indra*

She closed the book and spread out the road map stolen from her mother's car, gapping in the folds, nubby at the corners, with her family's summer trip to the Catskills marked in ballpoint pen. The roads were a tangle of colored threads. They were on Route 9 now, still the road they always took to the outlet mall, still barely away from home. In an hour, they'd be out of Massachusetts, farther on the road than she'd ever been. Eddie wanted to go to South America. Colorado was on the way, sort of.

"Will your parents come after you?" Jules asked.

"I don't know." She put her hand on the sticky table and pulled it back in disgust. It was a few days after the blowup. She'd left a note saying that she was going to visit Paul for the weekend. Then she sent him a letter. *Tell them not to worry,* she wrote. *I have to go and do something. Remember the quest I told you about? It'll be all right.*

She wasn't sure what he would do. Whether he would hold them off or not. A police car whisked by, its siren going. She slouched in her booth.

They took the back roads when they could, afraid of cops stopping them, sure her parents had called the police and given them the school portrait of her in her navy sweater. Jules wrote in his notebook, chronicling the trip. It's going to be like *On the Road,* he promised. But better than a novel, because it's our lives. It's going to be *monumental.* They found the quiet roads, where dense green trees walled them in and deer flickered through the branches. As Jules drove she leaned her back against the door and rested her bare feet in his lap.

Eddie propped his chin on his hand, staring out the window. They passed still, small lakes that looked like mirrored lockets, and familiar houses—clapboard and square, Colonial prim.

They picked up a hitchhiker who claimed he'd been to every state and Cuba too, who carried a burlap sack on his shoulder and told Nicole that travel, seeing the country like this, would change her life. He'd heard of the Karmapa; he knew some people who'd joined the monastery in Colorado. He had all the badges of a home-leaver: his gray-brown hair, in dreadlocks under a bandanna; his T-shirt, rumpled; his fingernails, black. He could tell they were rookies, but he was willing to give some pointers. He showed them how to forage in dumpsters, sliding in the slick black sea of garbage bags, how to steal old bagels off the carts they were loading up for the homeless shelter. They weren't at that point yet, but they would be, before this was all over. The hitchhiker smelled like pot and motor oil. The smell was wildly exciting.

When she went out into a grove of trees in the dark to pee the hitchhiker tried to grab her and hurl her to the ground. He grabbed her underwear when it was down around her knees and yanked it the rest of the way. She kicked and hissed like a cat, and cried out her mother's prayer, *Saints preserve us.* He backed off. Catholic magic is strong, she told Jocelyn.

She convinced Jules and Eddie to leave him there by the side of the road, and they peeled away with the tires screaming. Jules didn't say anything but he knew why, she was sure of it. His arm was tight around her. Already she was grateful for these simple gestures of comfort.

"I wonder what my dad's going to think," Jules said, driving one-handed. "One day, I'm gone. No note, no nothing. I told him for months I'd do it. He said, 'Good riddance.'" He chewed his lip thoughtfully. "He doesn't give a fuck."

Days after leaving, at an all-night diner, she called Paul and listened to him say, "Hello, hello." Hearing his voice made her feel like crying, but she didn't; she gently lowered the phone to its cradle, listening to his voice grow fainter and then disappear.

They traveled through the big northern cut of New York, carefully pooling their loose change for a budgeted meal at rest stops once in a while. Eddie fighting with Jules one-handed while driving, Jules punching back good-naturedly. Past Delhi, Sidney, then taking Route 88, wandering up and down through the state. Through Horseheads and Big Flats. On through the Cinnamon Lake State Forest.

. . .

The recollected go forth to lives of renunciation. They take no pleasure in a fixed abode. Like wild swans abandoning a pool, they leave one resting place after another.

— The Dhammapada

They got sidetracked for most of the summer, smoking weed in Toledo in abandoned buildings with gangs of not-quite-homeless teenagers. Jules wanted to stay. These were his people. There was time enough for the monastery, for the robe and bowl, plenty of time. She could panhandle pretty well, sitting on sidewalks with cheerful cardboard signs. She knew not to look too dirty or needy, not to look like she was going to use the money for pot, to smile but not make eye contact. The people don't want to have to look at you. Don't make them feel sad when they're tossing money, make them feel they're doing good. Say thank you. Say God bless.

At night she walked along the riverbank and threw stones in the water, whistling to the dark bands of people on the other side. The kids who settled on the bank had codes for cops, for social workers, for scary homeless people, for parents. Parents were always coming to the campouts by the river, looking for their kids because the cops had given up. They came armed with handfuls of wallet-sized photographs, distributing them to the blank-eyed kids sitting around campfires with their school backpacks on one shoulder, their good shoes full of holes. The parents were thin and tired. They spoke in monotones, asking if anybody had seen their child. Sometimes she looked at one of the photos and wondered how this bright-cheeked boy or girl in the school picture, with the little vest, the flower barrettes, could possibly be one of the wary gremlins she sat with each night. They were slippery and wise as stray cats. They knew the right dumpsters, they knew where to get weed and coke and whatever handful of candy-colored pills you wanted. They had friends in camping shops who gave them iodine tablets so they could fill their bottles from the river. They knew to sleep with their belongings under their heads, like indigents or inmates, or else their things would be gone by morning. They knew to burn the edges of a cut with a needle passed through a flame. In a few months, she learned these things, too. Her hair grew long and wild and she hacked some of it off and it grew back in ragged bunches. She got used to the smell of not washing: oniony and too sweet.

She stared hard at the photos of missing kids and wondered: Girl, where are you?

For the two months she lived on the river she talked to the other kids about impermanence and what she was learning about the Middle Way and the Eightfold Path. She told them about the realm of hungry ghosts, where the greedy and selfish go after death. The ghosts have caved-in bellies and skull-like faces with giant open jaws. They are always starving and never satisfied; they shove dirt into their mouths in their desperate hunger; they wander the world, restless and rapacious. The Buddha says we should pity them, because we are no different, she told the kids who would listen, who still liked hearing stories. If you're here on this river, it's because you're never satisfied, you never have enough, whether it's food or money or love.

She saw Jules on the edge of the circle, listening without any trace of irony in his eyes. Afterward, when they were walking by the river looking for a place to sleep for the night, he said, "That's true, what you said. About the ghosts."

"What part of it?"

"That we're no better than them."

While they sat under an overpass he told her that when he was a kid, his mother used to punish him for being bad by locking him in his room without dinner. He would howl and whine, but nothing would get her to open the door. In the morning she'd be sober and sorry and make him a giant breakfast—pancakes and bacon and mounds of eggs. "But only a few bites in, I'd start to feel awful, because I knew that pretty soon, the food would be gone, and she'd be angry again. I couldn't eat, I was so miserable." He laughed bitterly. "My mother never understood it. She always thought she could bribe me into forgiving her."

Nicole put her arms around Jules and hugged him as tightly as she could, wanting to press the sadness out of him, convince him of her constancy. She thought she might have made him a convert. He wouldn't meditate with her; he scoffed at any prayers she tried to recite from her book. But every night he was there with the others, listening.

It wasn't that he had converted to Buddhism, she was beginning to realize. He was in the process of converting to something else. One night they were lying together on the damp concrete slab under an overpass, a nest of scuzzy sleeping bags underneath them, the kids in the distance quiet, the cicadas blasting out their hopeful song. He said,

"Everyone back home is so obsessed with looking good, they don't even think about what they look like on the inside, or whether they're even interesting people, for chrisssakes. . . . But you're not like that. You live with such a clear motherfucking beautiful sense of purpose. I love that. I love it."

She was afraid, because they had never used the word "love." She couldn't speak for the fearful pounding of her heart. Jules rolled closer, kissed her on each cheek, on her forehead. "You're like an arrow. Like the sound of a bell. You're clear and straight and pure. You're beautiful."

. . .

She'd been hanging out with a girl called Skunk, whose ears were studded up and down, her head shaved except for a dark center stripe of hair. Skunk wasn't good at panhandling. She kept staring at passersby with her "yeah, keep walking" glare. Mostly she bummed burger scraps and the occasional handful of pills off her friends. Nicole would find her sitting on the concrete pilings by the river most days, glowering at nobody and sharpening toothpicks for her growing ashy tattoos.

"Why are you so angry, Skunk?" Eddie asked her one night when they were around somebody's fire. Eddie was in his element, impressing kids with his political screeds. Many nights he wandered away from the fire with a scruffy Mohawked girl under his arm. "Why'd you run away?"

Skunk spat into the fire. "I don't know. Same reason you did."

From the dark they heard someone whistle. They had laid out their shoes and socks to dry after wading, and they were still getting dressed when a woman entered their circle. "I'm looking for my daughter," she started to say, then stopped. One raised arm fell slackly to her side, and a flutter of school photos fell to the ground. Nicole picked one up. It showed a mousy little kid with long brown hair, heavy bangs. Smiling.

The mother pointed at Skunk. "Molly. Molly. Oh my God." She stood without moving.

Skunk tried to run, but Jules stuck out his leg and tripped her. She leapt up, but by then her mother was on her, hugging, sobbing. Skunk was stiff in the embrace, but she didn't fight.

Nicole and the others retreated to a safe distance. Sometimes the parents started asking about kids that weren't theirs. *Go home already. Go home.* She watched Skunk put out her shaky arm and touch her mother. They walked away together, and for a moment Nicole wished she, too, had been found.

"Why did you trip her?" she asked Jules.

"I don't know. Just thought she wanted to go home."

They went down an alley and leaned on a wall together and he held her close. "Hey, flower girl," he said. "Hey, lotus blossom. What about the Karmapa?"

She realized with surprise that he cared about the quest, too. That at the end of it was the promise of peace and freedom from pain that he'd maybe never known. That night they found Eddie and went back to the car and drove on. They weren't like those other kids; they had someplace to be. Somewhere they had to go. Enlightenment was waiting.

. . .

Will you turn toward me?
I am lonely too,
This autumn evening.

—Basho

They snuck into a YMCA in Michigan to shower, and when she was in the girls' locker room, slowly pulling on her threadbare jeans, a crowd of elderly women in floral swim caps surrounded her. "You look like you're lost, hon," one said.

"I—" The women looked at her, the faces all alike in their bathing caps, the council of the wise and motherly. She was surprised to find tears crowding at the backs of her eyes. "There's just somewhere I have to go." She pushed the tears away.

"Your mother is shedding a tear for every moment you're gone," said one woman, clasping her shoulder. Nicole wondered how they knew she had run away. She remembered the times her mother had taken her bra shopping and had looked over her body appraisingly, tugging a strap here or there, ownership in her eyes. *You're mine,* she might as well have said.

She found Jules and Eddie on the basketball court, playing with a bunch of local Vietnamese and Somali kids. The Vietnamese kids, two brothers, were short a player, so she joined in, glad to forget herself in the game. The boys called to each other in Somali, in Vietnamese.

After they told him about their quest, one of the Vietnamese boys brought them all to his local Buddhist temple. She mumbled her way through the prayers she'd read in books. Women came with paper bags of wet fish, the bottoms of the bags transparent with oil, and offered them to the golden Buddha at the front of the deep red room. The boy who brought them there said, You can only visit this front room; the back rooms are for the members only. She was kind of a member, wasn't she? But she had no witnesses, no one who would believe her. She didn't have anything to offer. She dug through her dirty pockets and found a single green penny. She dropped it in the offering box; a monk bowed his thanks. She looked at him wordlessly, begging with her eyes, not sure what she was begging for.

Afterward Anh and his brother, Van, brought them home for dinner and their mother served bone-marrow *pho* in little palm-sized bowls. She, Jules, and Eddie ate like animals, ravenously, without speaking. The boy's mother peered at Nicole over her bowl. "Homeless? Homeless?"

She shrugged, and the mother shook her head. "So young. Too young for homeless. Parents?"

"Yes, parents." The woman's stilted English was contagious; it hid greater profundities within.

"Why leave?" she asked. "Argument? Do drugs?"

"We're only taking a trip. Then we'll come back."

"That's what I said to my parents in Vietnam," remarked the father gently. "By the time I returned, my father was dead. Don't wait too long."

After dinner, Anh and Van's mother touched the top of Nicole's head; she was praying for them. "Careful, okay?"

Nicole clung to her flowery apron. The last stop for warm kitchens with magnets on fridges. Last chance to grab hold. But Jules pulled her arm. "We can make Nebraska by morning."

"Okay," she said. She let go.

. . .

They passed JESUS SAVES signs and old men walking alone on the side of the road. Fast food chains lit up late at night, eerie glowing islands in the darkness. Employees leaned on counters, laughing without sound. The dark country knew her. She was ready to be known; soon it would take her up, claim her once and for all.

Somewhere in Nebraska they got a room in a Red Barn Inn; they needed showers. There were two double beds in the room, and after a quick spliff she crawled in with Jules in her sweatshirt and underpants. In the dimness she saw Eddie's shape in the floral bedspread beside them, still as a log. She tried to push Jules off but he made a whining sound and wrapped a leg around hers, and before she knew it they were rocking gently together.

In the morning, gray light awakened her, striping her body through the vertical blinds. Jules was splayed across most of the bed like the overindulged family dog; Eddie was gone.

She found her underwear, her sweatshirt, her tattered jeans. Standing at the window, she saw that the car was not in the lot. The motel was right on the highway, and she watched a car whine past into the gray horizon with a clutch of panic.

She waited in the parking lot, wondering what to do, but after twenty minutes Eddie pulled into the spot next to her, leaning out the window. "What? Thought I'd left you here?"

"Yeah," she said, relief making her honest.

He held up a paper bag, his face expressionless. "Doughnuts."

When you were cold and hungover and your stomach was pinched with emptiness, doughnuts could seem like a religious experience. She ate three, getting powdered sugar all over her face. Eddie laughed. "You're an incompetent geisha."

"Pinko."

"Hare Krishna."

They drove back to the doughnut shop for more and sat outside on the curb, eating them. With only the highway near her, the sky seemed enormous, a cloudy white bowl cupping her near its rim. Eddie sat with his bony back to her, the knobs of his spine showing through his plaid shirt. "Can we keep the screwing in front of me to a minimum?" he asked.

"Oh. Sorry."

"You know, I was fine with it in my parents' basement. Really. But

I always wondered if you were. I wondered if Jules wasn't just being a jerk." He looked at her sidelong; her mouth was full, and she couldn't respond. "You know, I always hoped—"

"God, Eddie," she snapped, spitting crumbs. "You need to get a girlfriend."

"You left me," he said. "That night with Willa."

Many times in their basement year, he had appealed to her in the middle of an argument with Jules; he'd always appreciated her intelligence and tried to draw it out of her. He had this lonely sensitivity that she often forgot about. When they'd stumbled back out of the trees that night, she'd heard music drifting out of the house: it was Eddie, playing Chopin on the piano.

Thinking about the night with Willa always made her ashamed; she covered it with anger. "You wouldn't come with us. You missed out."

He pressed his lips together; for a moment she thought he might cry. "You can be a real bitch," he said.

She realized she had really hurt him. "I'm sorry," she said.

"Yeah, well." Eddie picked at something on his shoe. She remembered his bright museum of a house back in Boston, and the basement cave he had carved out for himself, and the way he opened the bulkhead door each night, inviting them inside hopefully.

She pulled *Understanding Buddhism* out from her bag and flipped to a remembered page:

Although they may play with my body
And make it a source of jest and blame,
Because I have given it up to them
What is the use of holding it dear?
Therefore I shall let them do anything to it. . . .
And when anyone encounters me

May it never be meaningless for him. . . .
May I be an island for those who seek one
And a lamp for those desiring light,
May I be a bed for all who wish to rest
And a slave for all who want a slave.
May I be a wishing jewel, a magic vase,
Powerful mantras and great medicine,
May I become a wish-fulfilling tree
And a cow of plenty for the world.

—from the Bodhicaryavatara,
the Library of Tibetan Works and Archives

. . .

A Buddhist seeking enlightenment must follow the Noble Eightfold Path. Dharma, the teaching, is the wheel that must turn, and the eight parts of the path are the eight spokes of the wheel. That summer and fall, these were the things she learned:

RIGHT VIEW: when it is night somewhere in Iowa and you are driving down a farming road in a car with rapidly fading headlights, watch the road, even when someone has his hand up your skirt. Otherwise you might get confused, and crash the car into a fence, and find yourself suddenly surrounded by a herd of curious donkeys, all of them ghost white, drifting about the black field like the spirits of jackasses past, present, and future that you are doomed to meet.

RIGHT INTENTION: When you are in a bar in Columbus, flirting so that you and your weary friends lurking in a booth can get drinks, don't take it too seriously. Don't smile too deeply or feel a pleased flutter in your chest when a young man in a silly denim vest tells you you're beautiful, like some honest-to-goodness flower child. Don't imagine what his story might be or why he might like someone like you. Otherwise your boyfriend might come over from the corner of the bar and ask the poor sweet boy to step outside, and someone's mouth will get bloodied.

RIGHT SPEECH: When you are in the car afterward, refusing to help clean his face, don't say, "Why can't you just grow up?" or "You fight like a girl. I saw you go for his eyes." It will be a mistake. You can yell at Eddie. Make fun of his politics. It's always okay to make fun; he can handle it; he absorbs insults like bread. But watch what you say to Jules. He takes in everything you say; he believes everything fervently, good or bad. He, too, is waiting to see what redemption the Karmapa can provide. So the next day, when you are all sitting outside a barbecue-and-pork-belly restaurant with miraculous one-dollar ribs and Eddie is impressing the local kids you're hanging out with, talking politics, and the air is thick with lightning bugs, the ones that had faded and grown fewer with each year in New England, tell Jules about what you'll do when you get There. Tell him you'll get jobs at the monastery, and listen to the Karmapa's lectures, and lead pure lives, but not too pure—pride, after all, is a sin whether you're a Catholic or a Buddhist. And it might not be cool to say it, but you will be loved. The Karmapa tells us we must learn how to love so that the beloved feels free, and that's exactly what we'll do. When Jules presses, asking how long can we honestly keep that up, tell him, Forever. When you get old you'll just be a couple of monks sweeping together in the temple.

RIGHT ACTION: When you are passing through Kansas on a bright, cool day that hints at autumn, do follow signs for the Renaissance Faire. Spend the last of your money on fruit pies, tickets for the stained-glass workshop, and old tomatoes to throw at the smiling man in the stockade. All these odd, cheerful people seem to enjoy transforming themselves, treating the day with the same concerted seriousness of children playing dress-up. Drink sour home-brewed beer from wooden mugs and watch the jousting, the archery, the strangely anachronistic Ferris wheel. Ride to the top, look out on the green country reddening with the approach of fall, and know how far you still have to go.

In the dusk, when the bonfire has been lit, ooh and aah with the others, and when it has died, accept the Buddhist certainty of this death. Jump over the ashes hand in hand with your lover, feeling old, ageless. You are eighteen but you have already lived more than one life.

RIGHT EFFORT: Try to call home. Listen to your brother's voice, or your mother's, or your father's. Try to gauge from their hellos whether they are all right, how many trick-or-treaters came to the house, whether the first snow has fallen. Try to speak; try as hard and as often as you can.

RIGHT LIVELIHOOD: Remember that your job, your purpose, is to leave home. You are beginning to realize that this—leaving home—is what you will be doing for the rest of your life.

RIGHT MINDFULNESS: Be aware of everything. When you are high or drunk or coldly sober, be aware of all the smells and sounds. Read the maps and mark where you have been, the strange detours you have taken. Record things, the way you see Jules scribbling in his notebook.

RIGHT CONCENTRATION: At some point you'll find yourself lost in a city whose name you've forgotten, but it's close, very close to There. You're in the middle of a raging party in a warehouse somewhere and the place is packed with grinding bodies. You and Jules have palmed a few pills crushed into the drinks someone bought you. Somewhere in the third song, the bass vibrates its way into your chest, and your body expands, becomes a galaxy, large beyond all knowing. Your people are below you, your mother and father, Paul. You can wrap them all up in the folds of yourself. You're Indra's net, the web of the universe, and all the connections are you.

Stumble out of breath into the back room, where people are sitting on pillows on the floor and passing around the nozzle of a hookah. "It's so nineties out there," someone says. Even though you were exhilarated a moment before, agree. This is better, much better. In here the weather is 1968 or so. The girls lay their long-haired heads in the boys' laps. The dancing is limp-armed, vague, and white beyond belief. A couple is relentlessly making out in the corner.

Tell them where you're going. Righteous, one girl says, and smiles dreamily.

You never really had a strong enough stomach for drugs. Sometime later, puke in the alley out back. Now it's time to find the car, but it's not where you left it. Someone has stolen the car. You're too sick, too stoned to go to the police. All you can think is to wander, dragging through the empty streets, the three of you getting colder, hugging each other. You stay instinctively in the rough chewed-out part of town, knowing that the car is likely to be there, and that you don't belong anywhere else. Here the street murals are spattered with bullet holes; human feces drift by in the rain gutters. You're too sick to stand. You want to lie down, but you must concentrate on finding the car, you must keep walking. Jules helps you up. You're scared that you're not cut out for this, but you can't think about that now. Keep going. Concentrate.

And you do; somehow, in the early morning, you find it. Kids or junkies stole the car for a joyride but left it half on the sidewalk, out of gas, the radio taken.

Climb into the back seat, which now smells of piss and liquor. Press your head to Jules's shoulder while Eddie turns the engine. Jules is gamely duct-taping the window. A gray false dawn is creeping past the unfamiliar buildings. On the sidewalk next to the car, a thin old woman has settled onto a bus stop bench for what looks like a long wait. "Read your Bible! Read your Bible!" she brays at you without warning. You must look sorely in need of salvation. "It's not too late," she pleads. "No one can read it for you. You've got to read your Bible. It's the only way."

Dig and scrape through the car seats for coins. Call Paul's number, and hear his voice, and finally say, "It's me." But don't let him talk. Just say, "I'm okay. But I need money."

Tell him about the quest. Remember? The Karmapa? It was this thing you had to do, but now you are on your way home, your trip is over, you just need the money to make it back. Promise you'll be on the doorstep in days if he'll only stay quiet a little longer. Your parents will never understand, but you and Paul have always had your secrets.

Let him absorb the lie. Wait, hunched miserably in the graffitied phone booth. Wait for him to demand your whereabouts. Wait in the beating silence. And give the address of the nearest Western Union when he quietly agrees. Wonder if he's as trusting as you hoped, or if he knows the lie and is going along anyway. Poor dupe.

Lie in the back seat of the car and cry because you have failed, you are not truly independent, not liberated at all. Silly girl with your stupid dreams: the minute things get tough you go begging for help, lying and deceiving for cash. Then Jules will be there, sliding into the seat beside you. He'll hold you quietly, he'll make no demands upon you, he'll not tell you you have failed. He'll tell you instead how brave you are, how far you've come together. He promises you that you're the girl he's always wanted. You are just as wild and free and dangerous as you hoped to be. Be glad of the principle of impermanence. Feel a small comfort that your shame will not last. Your eyelids grow heavy; he'll soothe you into sleep, watch over you, love you.

. . .

Three business days after the phone call, Paul's money arrived. It was enough for five cheeseburgers and three Cokes in the booth of a Burger Shack at nine in the morning; enough for a motel room for the night with a hot shower and cable TV showing *Gunga Din* and *The Dirty Dozen;* enough, even, to let her put aside some, to get her where she needed to go. In the cold morning, she huddled under blankets while Jules and Eddie slept and read her book on Tibet. Time to bone up now that they were so close. She drank in the photos, familiar as friends, telling the faces of the smiling monks how close she was. The Karmapa beckoned, his face creased and glowing, like cracked amber.

For the first time, she paused on the page to read the photographer's commentary.

At this time, the Karmapa had a serious case of kidney stones, but to the amazement of all around him, he seemed to feel no pain from this frequently agonizing condition. His doctors, in particular, expressed astonishment that His Holiness remained his smiling, affable self. "I may be witnessing a minor medical miracle," said one. By the spring of 1980, he was back to leading sermons. This would be his final world tour.

The spring of 1980.

Of 1980.

She looked at the other photo taken of him. Fall 1975. Then she flipped to the copyright page: © 1982. For some colossally stupid reason, she hadn't thought to check the date of the book until this moment. It was Scripture; it was timeless. The monk would always be there for her, waiting on the mountaintop; he could be nowhere else.

She pulled on her jacket. *Have to go to the library,* she wrote on a hamburger wrapper.

She'd seen a city branch when they were wandering the streets two nights ago. At the card catalog, she searched for Karmapa. Her book came up, along with one other: *The Life of the 16th Karmapa.*

She found the book near the bottom of a tiny, pathetic shelf labeled EASTERN RELIGION. It was crisp in its plastic dust jacket; no stamps on the card. She flipped through its pages and found the beloved photo, the one showing the wise, crinkled smile, the ridiculous golden miter. "His Holiness, fall 1980," she read, "shortly before his death in 1981."

She slid to the floor, clutching the book, and didn't move for a long time.

Even now, she struggled to tell this idiocy to Jocelyn, this laughable oversight. She wasn't using the Internet much then, she said. It wasn't the first thing you reached for when you were digging into ancient texts and secret dharmas. Someone must have written a page on the Karmapa, all the information was there waiting for her, but she hadn't thought to check. You could only believe everything you read in books. The Karmapa was as alive, as dear, as real as Ishmael, Huck Finn, Holden Caulfield.

Leaving the library, she was stopped by an onset of rain, cold enough to remind her that winter was closing in. She stood under an awning with the book clutched to her chest, under her coat. Across the street, a woman took shelter in the open doorway of a fabric store, watching people hurry by with their sweatshirt hoods pulled up. The rain clouds were fast-moving and dark. In the apartment above the fabric store, a light came on, and a woman loosened her head scarf, kissed a golden painting of a saint on the wall. In this moment, every ordinary act, and every common melancholic face, seemed charged with tragedy. She wondered if this was what it felt like to lose belief. It was not rejecting things as absurd. It was not loving what was sacred any less. It was merely saying good-bye to them, to the last of her Catholicism, the part that told her that she was special, she was loved, the world existed as a rune for her to decipher, and it would wait for her to solve its riddles.

She remembered that girl. So adolescent. Such a child. She couldn't forget the way the cold rain whisked through that unknown city. She could have called Paul right that minute and told him the jig was up, she wanted to go home. At that time, pay phones were still scattered across any city; there was one across the street. If she'd called, her parents would have been on the next plane. Everything would still be all right, in its own way.

Winter was coming; she could feel it, bitter and dangerous, seeping into her boots.

But she didn't call. She didn't go home.

Jules found her still huddling under the awning an hour later. "Man, what a dork," he said. "Rushing off to the library."

When she didn't move, he sidled up next to her. "What's wrong?"

"I'm an idiot," she said. "He's dead."

She showed him the book. He looked through it several times, flipping through the pages. "Fuck."

"What do we do?"

"How the hell am I supposed to know?" He got up, jerking free of her arm. It wasn't until this moment that she realized how much he had come to care, that the story she'd spun for him was one they both believed in. She remembered that Jules, unlike her, had no one to call, no one who would shepherd him back into an embrace.

"Is that it?" she asked. "The quest?" But he was already walking away, jamming his hands into his pockets.

She walked back to the motel, but he wasn't there; only Eddie came to the door, in his graying underpants.

She told him, too. They sat on the edge of the double beds, facing each other. "What are you going to do?" he asked. It had been the three of them all this way, but suddenly this was her problem.

She waited all day. She and Eddie lay side by side while he slowly read the paper from front to back, licking his thumb each time he turned a page. She wished he were not there. She wished he would disappear so she could lie there alone with her sadness.

Jules returned by nightfall. He blasted into the room and paced around it, stuffing hotel towels into bags. "Who cares if one guy is dead," he said. "Let's see the monastery. Was all this just about him, anyway?"

"No—"

"Exactly. None of this trip was. None of it—it was about something else, wasn't it? Yeah?" He grabbed her off the bed, clutching at her waist, her hair. "We're going."

"Going on?"

"Of course we are. We're going to see whatever lousy plaque has been put up in this guy's honor. And we'll go right on to the ocean. To San Francisco! Where everybody like us ends up!"

She knew then that he'd taken the money and spent it on whatever shit was making him grind his teeth like crazy as he threw Eddie's socks at his head, yelling, "Pack, motherfuckers, pack."

There was enough money to fill the tank of the car. She could hear it idling out front, its healthy gurgle and roar. As she crunched the yellow pills he'd brought, she could feel his mood spreading like a candy-coated infection, making her heart beat harder. His words were magic. They would take her and hurl her back out onto the road, where she belonged.

. . .

Jules drove them on a wave of Adderall and high spirits. They did not eat or sleep. She curled up on the passenger side, alternately nauseous and euphoric, staring down the white lines of the highway, trying to count them all, to stay clear and focused.

The Rockies looked like big brothers in the windshield, giant shattered shapes powdered with white. They were close. Most of the time the radio was full of static, but when it spoke, it warned of snow. First blizzards of the season, it told them. Whiteout conditions. "Damn, it's going to be hot to drive through that," said Jules. One of their car's windows was only duct tape; the cold drove her under blankets, whatever flimsy fall coats she could pile on. It drove hard little flakes of snow onto her arms. "I'm going south, I'm going south," Eddie kept repeating, as though it were a mantra that could protect him from the cold.

It wasn't fully dawn when they reached the foothills. Morning gave the sky a sad, faded light. They began the hairpin turns up the mountain, the car filling with wind and snow. These weren't the soft, heavy blankets of New England that she loved; this snow was hard and driving, like little needles on her skin. The car squeaked on, shimmying and jittering around each turn. The white mountaintops were all around them now, like the tips of a lotus blossom, ready to close. "Is the monastery at the top?" she asked.

Jules shook his head. "We're going through the pass. The monastery is on the other side."

The snow accumulated in giant drifts by the road. "We have to make it through or we'll be stuck here," said Jules. He pounded the gas. The engine whined; they bucked and skidded through a snowdrift on the road. "Jesus," she said, but she felt no fear, only wonder. At her right was the drop into space, the tiny pipe-cleaner trees below, the little lit gingerbread houses of the town they'd left behind.

Home was far behind.

Jules hit the brakes and they slewed to a halt. To the right, the road moved gradually downward again, back toward the town; to the left, it led steeply down through the pass to the other valley. It was blocked by wooden sawhorses with signs. ROAD CLOSED.

She opened the door and stepped out. Snow was seeping into all the last warm recesses of her body, but she couldn't feel it. She crunched to the edge of the road and looked down: lights, a town of some kind, a network of low covered buildings like barns or dormitories. Then her view was obscured by a sweep of snow. "It's there," she said. "It's real."

"Yeah, it's real. And we're going." Jules was out, too, and he had one end of one of the sawhorses blocking the road. "Come on, come on, we're wasting time."

"Are you crazy?" Eddie called from the car.

"Yes," said Jules, and then there was nothing else to say. She helped Jules drag the sawhorse through the piling snow. *I am the snow Buddha,* she chanted to herself as she pulled and panted. *The goal is within reach. The goal is me.*

Then they were back in the car. Jules gripped the hand brake. What was waiting for them in the valley below? The sleepily alarmed part of herself woke up a little and looked around at the steep slope, the landscape rapidly filling with white. "Jules, wait," she said.

But he shook his head. "What?" The hand brake was already up. They were already beginning to slide.

Time was no longer theirs. Time belonged to the car and the road and the whiteness that was sucking her in, burning down her throat. The car spun on one set of wheels and then the other as Jules careered around a turn, his brow sweetly furrowed with concentration, the rocks and trees around them a blur. Eddie was yelling in the back seat. Jules was telling her, so earnestly, "Almost there—almost there—"

For a while the car disconnected from the road and flew disembodied, and they were creatures of only snow and air. She screamed but nothing came out, only silence. Jules's hand grabbed her knee. Later she'd find his fingernail embedded there.

The car struck a pine tree on the far side of the road and plowed into it entirely on its left side. Eddie, in the back seat on the right, was unharmed. Her left ankle, braced on the dash, was shattered.

Her eyes opened, and her second consciousness began. The car, torn open on one side like the belly of a whale, steaming blood. Her body burning, every hair, every pore, awake and shivering. Snow falling, cold now, real.

Buddhism teaches that moments of powerful feeling can be used to fuel awareness. Even awfulness. Even despair turns the dharma wheel. She told Jocelyn, "That was my true conversion." Here is her body, lying in sweat and melted snow. Here is the smell of wet coppery blood, the earthy rankness of someone's bowels. Jules, dead. Here in the crushed body beside her is the end of something, maybe the end of her.

Eddie would walk the snowy road to get help, and she'd fly home, her ankle in a cast, her parents flanking her in the narrow seats. The wreckage left somewhere behind in the mountainous dark. Looking out the small plane window, she'd see the great gridded webs that were the cities she'd crossed. Now the places where she'd lived homeless and ragged were drawn in lines of light. She could make out all the places she'd been and the place she couldn't reach, zooming away into the dark. Then the plane dipped over the great black nothing of the Great Lakes. She saw the drop-off into a deep ocean of lightlessness: perfect, austere. Zen.

Dear Sean,

In Japan, the monks are called home-leavers, and are granted a privileged place in society. They are doing the most difficult thing, breaking the scarlet cord, and this is the first and hardest step.

It is how the Buddha's story begins, too. In the tales, when he realizes he must go, he stands in the doorway of his wife's bedroom and watches her sleep with their newborn son in her arms. He does not approach. He knows that if he touches her, his resolve will break, and he will never leave. So he turns; lets the curtain fall; leaves.

So the story is about the world's greatest deadbeat dad.

Did he come close to their sleeping bodies? Was he near enough to smell his baby's milk breath? Did he think about his wife's arms around him? Did he see all the items of their safe, precious world: the ornaments and jewels, the baby blankets, the neat lines of shoes? Didn't he think, once, My self is here—I cannot leave?

And when he returns—fifteen years later—his head shaved, his face now serene, his son grown—can he say, "I'm home?"

Of course not. There is no home for him. Every religion has its sacrifice. Jesus gives up his life; Abraham gives up his name; Muhammad gives up his pride; and for Buddhists, Siddhartha gives up his home. It's the only way we can prove we are good: we can give something up, the thing we love the most.

EDDIE

"Your brother's right, you know," Jocelyn said. "You have to see Eddie."

"You think?"

"You have to. Then you'll be able to put this behind you. You'll be able to forget him."

By "him," she did not mean Eddie.

Eddie lived in a high-rise condo called the Brooklyner. On the phone he was effusive. "It's time we sat down and finally had a long talk," he said. It sounded almost nice: just the two of them in a cluttered room like his old basement, with his Che posters and his Ping-Pong mallets hanging on the wall.

But when she arrived at his door, she heard the clinking of glasses and voices of a party. A woman in a black dress and pearls answered the door. She threw her head back without looking at Nicole. "Eddie?"

"Who is it?" Eddie came to the door. He was still himself, still with that wiry red hair, the pale wash of freckles, the same sleepy eyes. But he had filled out; he bore his own weight with a more dignified air. "You forgot the guest of honor, Mel. This is Nicole."

He stepped over the threshold and hugged her, hard, and whispered in her ear, "You're just the same."

"So are you," she said, though maybe it wasn't true. Eddie seemed to hear her uncertainty, because he backed away, and smiled with a little shake of his head. How extraordinary it was to see him there, having arrived safely into the prime of adulthood.

"Well, come in," said Mel. "I'm Eddie's fiancée. We're having cocktails."

They stepped into a brilliantly lit, spacious apartment in stark black and white. Black granite countertops, white velvety carpet, black leather sofa studded with silver grommets, black-and-white cowhide by the window. The only color came from the guests, five of them, arrayed around the coffee table in jewel tones. They sat in a low slouch and looked like they'd been sitting and drinking for a while. I've walked into the wrong room, the wrong story, Nicole thought.

"Everyone, this is Nicole," said Eddie, ushering her over. "They've all heard of you," he told her. He went hastily through the introductions: Emma and her husband, Bob; Mark and his fiancée, Jenna.

"I wish I'd done something like that when I was young and reckless," said the woman introduced as Emma.

Her husband patted her shoulder indulgently. "We went on that safari, hon."

Emma turned back to Nicole. "Anyway, it must have been an adventure. Did you have a wild time?"

"I suppose so." Nicole sat down at the end of the stiff, glossy couch; Mel poured her a glass of wine, then said, "Or don't you drink?"

"I drink." She took the glass. *Tonight I drink.* She took a large sip and held it in her mouth before letting the wine burn its way down.

"What was Eddie like then?" asked Jenna, a thin woman in a fuchsia sheath dress with matching clawlike fingernails and blank, bird-bright eyes.

"I was a raging little Communist. Ask Nicole," said Eddie from the kitchen.

"Really?"

She nodded.

"And you were going to some sort of—commune?"

"No," she said, but did not want to explain further. She was exhausted already, a little sick. Eddie came out from behind the counter. He was anxious, too, she could tell, trying to set the story straight. This was his chance to tell it right, the way she had told Jocelyn. Perhaps these friends of his would understand.

"I was going to South America to fight for the proletariat," he said. "Nicole was going to join a monastery and get enlightened. We had very different goals, and one car."

Everyone laughed at this. She felt their eyes move along her body, from the rain boots to the dragon skirt to the moon barrette in her ruffled hair. She'd worn the dragon skirt for Eddie, to remind him of their time together; now she could see how perfectly she fit into his plan of show-and-tell. How entertaining it all was.

"Nicole, they're finding it hard to believe that a person such as yourself and I would be friends," said Eddie. He was explaining the joke to her, thoughtful him. "With my job—"

She raised her hand. "Let me guess. It's the kind of job they didn't have a name for fifty years ago."

"It's the kind of job they still don't have a name for," said Bob.

"You know, it's simpler than most people think," said Eddie. "You see, Nicole, if you have a lemonade stand, and you want to buy insurance for when you don't have enough lemons to meet demand—"

Oh, Christ, thought Nicole. He's going to very patiently explain the dogma to me, with kid-friendly metaphors, so that a layperson like me can understand. And then he's going to explain to me why he changed, grew up, put aside childish things. He's going to laugh at himself, at the fool that he was, at how natural it was to put that person aside. Well, we *were* fools. But weren't we brave as well? She pressed her palms together, looked for any place in the austere apartment where her gaze was safe, where she could avoid their scrutiny.

"Of course, you know what I'm talking about," Eddie finished. "We were wild then. It's so strange to see you here."

"Was Eddie a good survivor?" asked Mel. "Did he scrounge for your food? Did he panhandle? God, how did you bathe?"

Nicole tried to think of what to say. "We survived. We did a little of everything. We were cold and dirty. But it didn't matter. None of that mattered. We were young."

"Did you sleep under bridges?"

"Mostly we slept in the car."

"That wreck," Eddie inserted. "You wouldn't believe what it looked like by the end. I had to junk it."

"Did you have sex anywhere crazy? Like in a telephone booth? I always wanted to have sex in a phone booth, and now I fear I've missed my chance."

"Jesus, Mark." Mel jerked his empty glass from the table. "A little decorum."

She was beautiful in the way only New York women seemed to be: possessing a kind of savage elegance. Moving swiftly from kitchen to living room and back again with cutting boards of cheese, bottles of vodka and gin. Her black dress severe and fashionable, the plunging V exposing a marble, jutting breastbone. The lines of her jaw and chin, aristocratic in their force.

"Eddie and Nic's excellent adventure," laughed Emma.

"And Jules," Nicole started to say, but Eddie interrupted: "Guys, enough with the third degree."

"It's always so interesting to get a glimpse of a friend's past," Emma said. "Nicole, you have the secret of Eddie. And Eddie, you have the secret of Nicole. Has she changed much?"

He hesitated, looking at her. Everyone was studying her now. In a flash she was back in Buffy's living room at the party that had first driven her to flee Boston. So many people looking at her then as now, thinking they knew who she was. And they were always wrong.

"It's a fricking twenty-first-century miracle," said Eddie. "We could have pulled her right out of the time capsule." He leaned on the back of the couch, gazing out at his view of Manhattan.

Nicole realized that whereas the story of the trip had been her guarded secret, for Eddie it had been his currency, the adventure he had aired for all his friends.

"Why did you give up at the end?" Mel asked. And then, her voice too loud in the small room: "Why did you abandon him?"

"I didn't—our parents came and got us. We had an accident. Our other friend . . ."

"Your other friend?" asked Mark, and the room was silent.

She understood now. She asked to use the bathroom; Mel pointed down the hall. She stood a long while before the sink, looking at the array of creamy purple and pink soaps cut in the shape of lotus flowers, the bottles of lotion in deep blue bottles. The towels were so soft she had trouble drying her hands. She could hear the voices rising and falling outside. They wouldn't miss her for another moment.

She went quietly across the hall into a bedroom and sat on the edge of the bed. This looked like the master bedroom, judging by the hand cream and contact lens solution on one night table. She looked at her own hands; cracked and peeling, as always.

Eddie found her there. He closed the door and stood facing her in the dark. "I'm sorry," he said. "I never thought I'd see you again. It was just a story to tell."

"And you erased Jules from it." She felt almost envious of him.

"Come on," said Eddie, angry now. "He was no saint. I hope you don't think of him that way. He was a bully. An asshole. He never quit pushing me around, and he treated you like crap." He stopped and looked her in the eyes. "It killed me, seeing the way he treated you."

I know. But I liked it.

"We'd better get back," she said. "Mel will think you're still in love with me." She knew it to be true only as she said it. Of course: Eddie had loved her. Why else had he gone, had he put up with Jules, had he been so angry when she'd refused to see Jules's flaws.

He laughed. "She thinks so already. You wouldn't believe the flak I've gotten this week since I said I was going to see you." He sat down beside her. "I've changed. But you haven't."

"That's the problem."

He touched her cheek, and she didn't flinch. "You know that I miss him, too," Eddie said. They had this built-in intimacy already, this closeness that comes from living through something together. Eddie knew her past, and with one confident stroke he had exorcised it for himself. But now he moved away. "I don't think Mel has anything to worry about," he added.

"Oh?" For a moment, she was pleading. Why not? Couldn't we? Couldn't you make Jules disappear, for me, too?

He got up, straightened his tie. "I don't think you'd fit in. To my life now, I mean."

"Right." She stood up. She could give him this gift, and let him be a shit. She owed him one, after all. She'd played the part often enough. "Shall we?"

They rejoined the party.

. . .

She walked home, crossing the Brooklyn Bridge. It was late, and the footpath was empty, the great soaring arches barely visible in the darkness above her. The burly suspension cables were strung with lights, joining the two shores in luminescent constellations.

When she was across, she felt her cell phone vibrate on her hip. It was the Master. She heard his voice roaring before she had even brought the phone to her ear.

"You have betrayed me," he bellowed. "You have lied to me."

"What are you—"

"I know what you've done. You've found another teacher. And teaching by yourself, without my consent? You have betrayed me. Snake. Traitor. Deserter."

She sank onto a bench. Hearing his voice berating her, so close in her ear—it was like he was beside her, leaning in close, full of wounded fury. "How—how do you know? How did you find out?"

"It doesn't matter. I know. I know." And he went on; there was no escape from the assault. "Traitor. Turncoat. Judas."

She gulped down a sob, but she could not turn away from his voice. "I'm sorry," she gasped. "I'm sorry. I had to—"

"You had to do *nothing* except listen to me, *your Master*. You filthy snake." There was an imploring note in his voice, the thing she could not bear. "After all we have shared. All we have done together. And for you to secretly find another to trust—and then to pretend *you* were some kind of teacher—you have damaged those fools who think they are your students."

"I'm sorry, Master. Please, forgive me. Please. I'm yours to instruct." She was desperate. Seeing Eddie had shown her that she couldn't be like everyone else; she needed him, she needed his steady guidance.

His voice was quiet now, as he regained control of it, returned behind his wall of unflappable calm. "I think, sometimes, about the things we have shared. We're both refugees, you know. From another life. Our bodies touch, our minds fit. You are devoted. You want things so badly."

She bowed her head. "What do you want me to do, Master?"

A police car went by with its siren wailing. He asked, "Where are you?"

"On First Ave. I'm walking home."

"I will give you a lesson. Walk to the river."

Beyond Thirty-fourth and First, the road opened into a snarl of on-ramps for the overpass. Navigating it in the dark left her nearly breathless; but beyond it was a thin strip of park with shrubs and trees, and a waist-high iron railing looking out over the water. Beyond that, the shapes and lights of Brooklyn glimmered.

"All right," she said, leaning on the rail to catch her breath. "I'm at the river."

"What do you see?"

"Brooklyn. The bridge. The river."

"Is anyone around?"

She cast a look backward; aside from the rapid whine of traffic, she was alone. It was really so easy to be alone in this city. Take one step out of the busy stream of living, and you were suddenly in a deserted world of rotting piers, narrow alleys, buildings with FOR LEASE signs. "I'm alone."

"Good. Now climb over the railing."

"What?"

"Don't make me repeat myself."

On the other side was a slim concrete ledge littered with cigarette butts, then a short drop to the black moving water. Nicole slipped the phone into her jacket pocket, hiked up her skirt, and straddled the railing. She sucked in a breath when an icy bar brushed her bare leg, but she managed to swing the other leg over and drop to the concrete. "I'm over." Somewhere far away a boat chugged by; the water swelled and lapped the narrow ledge.

"Now dip your legs in the water."

"I won't—"

"I told you not to make me repeat myself. I am your Master. If you want a taste of nirvana, you'll get it from my lips."

She pushed off her boots and socks, beginning to shiver. It was still spring, and a cold breeze whipped off the surface of the water. The lights of Brooklyn winked at her, hopelessly far away. She could feel the creep of terror now, metallic and chemical on her tongue. But she could not stop. She was far from anything that might pull her back. If someone were to see her here, some night runner or lonely smoker, he would think she was a jumper. He would not understand; no one would. She slipped one leg into the water and gasped.

"How does it feel?" The voice, close and harsh in her ear, rough with short breath.

"Cold! Very, very cold."

"What would it feel like to slip and fall into the water?"

"So cold—like death!"

"Get in."

"Please—"

"Get in, and hold on to the side."

She put the phone on the ledge and squatted, lowering herself into the water. Each new high mark felt like ice creeping up her skin. Her feet swayed in the black groundless void. She clung to the ledge, just her head above water, her clothes heavy on her body, pulling her down, and put the phone to her ear again. "I'm in," she gasped.

"What would happen if you let go?" The voice, soft now, purring in her ear.

"It's so cold. I—I would drown."

"Remember the Buddha's instruction to look upon a corpse and imagine it as yourself, so that you might truly understand impermanence. You must experience *dukkha:* the anguish we feel when we glimpse our nonbeing. Now make yourself the corpse. Describe it to me. Tell me of your death."

Her teeth were chattering so much she could barely talk, but something inside her numbly obeyed. "First—first the cold would make it hard to swim. My muscles would seize up. I'd go under. Everything would be black. I wouldn't know which way was up. I'd thrash, but it would be too late; I'd breathe water. I would choke. My brain would begin to shut down."

"Yes, yes, yes. Don't stop."

"I'd lose consciousness. My body would go cold, and sink. I'd go far down. Nothing would stop me."

"Don't stop now!"

"If I wasn't found, fish and flies would eat me on the top and the bottom. I'd rot. It would take a long time. Eventually there would only be bones left."

The cold stabbed at her legs. Inside her head was a dull primordial chant: *I would die. I would die. I would die.*

"Good," said the Master. "Very good. That was good. For now I release you. You understand another koan."

She hung up the phone. The lights of the city jiggled and waved around her head, as distant as stars. She tried to climb out of the water but she was so stiff, she couldn't make it. She fumbled, grasped a concrete edge that cut her hands; it took several tries. All this death-feeling was not for her, not tonight; all the longing to become nothing, to become spirit rather than matter, was so childish—her body was hers to keep for such a short while. Finally she was back on the narrow concrete ledge, drenched and exhausted, shivering uselessly.

There was just one thought in her mind; it was a memory, the only thing that could make her feel again, the memory she'd been saving for a moment like this, when terror and loneliness seemed inescapable.

It was from the last night she'd spent at Sean's place, the weekend before she was due to leave. One cold day they sat upstairs by the window and saw rain move in silver bolts across the marsh. It was very quiet, and for a long time they sat on the couch watching. Sean's lips were in her hair.

At night they crept down to the old furniture in the basement and made love on little old canopied beds too short for their twined feet. His body was very soft, pudgy and dark with downy hair. "You'll write me letters, won't you," he asked. "I want something to hold when I think of you. I want to open a letter and see you tell me your story." She promised she would.

Very early, Nicole awoke. He was beside her, his limbs loose with sleep, but she couldn't see this; she knew only because of the heavy warmth of him on her.

She knew it was almost morning. She knew she had to leave. Soon Paul would be at her apartment, waiting to move her away, to succor her into her new life.

But for now, the darkness surrounded them sweetly. The only light came from the false dawn in a high basement window. This gray square floated without context in the blackness like a funny little moon. For a moment, she felt herself float loose like that lonely window. She was not herself, dense with ruin, but an effect of many causes, a body of intimate demands, a brief wonderful moment in time. Made moving by its approaching end. In another minute she would rise, pushing his leg gently off hers; another minute and she would be gone.

Here in New York, the memory quivered like the reverberation of a bell. Not happy or sad, not unhappy or unsad. Just real, and hers. In the next slip of time, she'd eased out of bed with Sean. It was still dark, and he hadn't stirred. It was just as she'd promised: she was getting away without a good-bye. She pressed her hand to the warm space in the bed that she was leaving. Then raised her hand and it felt cool, the warmth already fading.

Then she slipped away.

. . .

Someone was leaning on her buzzer. The noise was loud and insistent, but she'd managed to ignore it the previous times it had rung in the last few days. The time for her meditation class had come and gone; her students had called many times before giving up. She pulled the blankets back over her head, waiting out the grating sound.

Now someone was pounding on her door. This was a closer and more intimate sound. It could be a fire marshal because someone had called Social Services. It could be her brother, who she had staved off for a while with phone calls. She'd told him she was sick, which wasn't untrue. Now she struggled out of the tangle of sheets, tripping over them on her way. She barely remembered to check that she was decent—T-shirt, yoga pants—before turning the knob.

Jocelyn backed her way into the apartment the moment Nicole cracked the door, wrestling Emmeline's stroller in with her. "You missed two coffees with me. And you just don't seem like the hooky type." She paused to take in Nicole, sweeping her gaze up and down the sweat-stained T-shirt, the rumpled pants, the bowls and glasses accumulating on the counter. "Girl, I was right to come," she said. "Wasn't I?"

"I'd rather you didn't—"

Jocelyn was already putting plates in the sink. "What's up? Are you okay?"

It was such a difficult question to answer. And Jocelyn was so kind; it was above and beyond their fragile acquaintanceship, coming here to check on her. She had a baby, she had the problems of a real family, and yet here she was. Nicole wanted to tell her, *I'm fine. I just need time to recover. And I can never enter a meditation hall, a Zendo, or a temple or a roadside shrine, ever again. I can't teach. I don't know how, but he would know. And he would refuse to save me, I would be unredeemed forever.*

"Thank you for coming, but really, I'm fine," she said. "Just a little—under the weather."

Jocelyn looked around the apartment, at her, at Kukai sitting by his empty bowl. When had Nicole last fed him? She poured him some kibble, then sank back to the couch.

"I don't believe you," Jocelyn said quietly. "I want you to understand. I'm like you. I had this person I worshipped, someone I couldn't escape from. I'm still not fully free of him, I think." She delivered this calmly, staring straight ahead. Nicole wondered how many years had passed, how hard-won this composure was in the telling. "I see you, getting quiet and dropping away," Jocelyn continued. "I can't leave you alone. I just can't."

Suddenly Nicole was angry. "You can't put that on me. You've got your life, and I've got mine."

Jocelyn didn't say anything. She just waited, her gaze direct and patient. She already held so much of the story in her hands. But wasn't it all playing out again, the running away, the finding out that she'd taken all her old sins with her? Nicole said helplessly, "My Master found out I was teaching. I don't know how. But he's like that. He has ways."

Jocelyn nodded. Other people would ask why she could not leave her Master; but Jocelyn seemed to know. "The master-student relationship—in Zen, it's a sacred bond," Nicole went on. "It's for life. You can't ever break it." And suddenly her mother's words from so many years ago were in her mind: *You have to understand. You don't always feel happy. Sometimes you have to say to yourself, "I'm needed here." When it stops being fun, still, you stay.*

"How did you meet him?" Jocelyn asked finally. "Why is he your Master?"

THE PEACEFUL HEALING ZEN CENTER

Her ankle was held together by seven steel pins, and she needed crutches to walk. Her rucksack, covered in mud, held Jules's notebooks, some condoms, some filthy underwear, a piss-soaked newspaper, the book she'd stolen from a library somewhere in Nebraska. (Or was it Illinois?) All that was left of the quest.

In the morning she was in her old bed; her clothes, her stuffed animals were still there, the school reports pinned to the walls. Her father was at work, Paul at the job selling medical supplies in Boston he'd gotten out of business school. The light slanted across her face in the old manner.

She sat up and lifted one slat of the blinds with two fingers, looking out into the backyard. Snow was on the ground, but the day was sunny. She watched her mother step outside and shake a white sheet, whipping it hard in the light, her movements precise. Then her mother stopped; she folded the sheet, draped it over her shoulder, and crossed herself.

Nicole crept downstairs and prowled the house, looking at paintings, at china dolls, at sea-captain lamps and vases of pressed paper flowers. They hadn't moved an inch; there was still the air of a museum, places where the dust had settled and would not stir. Only the family photos on the mantel had been shuffled: a photo of Paul with Marion had taken prominence, flanked by images of her parents. The only picture of her, an awkward school portrait, had slid off into a corner.

After a week at home, she found her rucksack in the trash. She tried to salvage the notebooks. All throughout her trip she had seen Jules writing in them at odd hours, frowning in concentration, crossing things out. She was certain they would contain something important, some final message for her. She'd take anything: a blessing, a curse, an explanation. She hugged them to herself and limped up to her room, closed the door, lowered the shades. The house was quiet enough that she could hear the occasional rasp of a turned page downstairs. The silence of a changed house—changed by her, made empty.

She opened the first book, then began to turn the pages with increasing dismay. All of them were a snarl of shapes, spirals, interlocking triangles, one word or two ("my hand my hand my hand") filling pages. Many had been entirely blacked out by ballpoint pen and were crispy with ink. That was it—just the scribbles of someone on drugs. Meaningless. No story for her to tell, no absolution. She cried for a long time that afternoon, and her mother did not come. She understood then that her mother was not going to come, not now, not ever.

It was her father who stood in the doorway, looking away until she sat up, wiping her eyes. He waited until she straightened her hair, made herself presentable. "Come on now," he said, in a pained way.

"What do you want?" Her nose was running; she spoke sullenly.

"We're going," he said, and gathered up her crutches. "We've got things to do."

They bundled up and drove in silence to the churchyard where they bought their Christmas tree every year. This was normally an all-family task, full of cheer, of passionate arguments over the merits of balsam versus Douglas fir, but she did not ask why it was just the two of them. They shuffled down the aisles of bushy green. "Good batch this year," he said. "Though in Colorado you probably saw bigger ones."

This was the first that he had mentioned the trip; he was trying to broach something. He was so often silent, but she could feel his gentle, worried attention at all times. She struggled to meet him out on his tenuous limb. "Yeah. The mountains looked like they were covered in green fur."

They walked through a channel of trees, feeling the snow dusting their shoulders, the night quiet of the churchyard. There was so little time. They were not supposed to be together. She sensed that by taking her here, her father was violating a code set by her mother. Soon they would choose a tree, and drive home with it tied to the roof, and retreat to their separate quarters.

"This one looks nice," she said, pointing to a tall, stately Douglas fir.

"Handsome. The king of trees," he agreed.

They stood back while a muscular man in three layers of coats hefted the tree onto the roof of the car. Struggling to tie a knot of twine, she heard her father greet someone on the other side of the car. She knew the voice—bright and operatic, projecting even in small rooms. Betsy Malley, another churchgoer. "I heard about your troubles, Bill, and I just want you to know we've been praying for you," she caroled.

"Thank you, Betsy."

"You know, we do all we can for our children, but sometimes they just cannot be helped."

Nicole ducked against the warm protection of the car. She listened to her father's steady murmur, informing Betsy that Nicole was back now, that everything was going to be all right.

"Lord be praised! And just in time for Christmas," Betsy said. Finally her voice faded, along with the crunch of her heels in the snow. Nicole straightened and returned to the tangle of twine, but something was blurring her vision. She blinked hard, trying to clear her eyes.

"I think we need a bowline," her father said. Then his hand was covering hers, his skilled fingers moving. That was what you could count on fathers to do, wasn't it. To tie knots, and hammer nails, and open jars; to settle disputes and wipe tears. All with an air of friendly remove. And in return, you had to promise not to disappoint them.

Her father's shoulders went up, and for a moment he held on to her hands. "You *are* back, right?" he asked.

"Yes."

"Really? Really back?"

She pulled away, angry now. "Yes. Yes, I'm back."

"Good." Slowly his shoulders fell. He was shaking. Not as removed as she'd thought.

It scared her, this love. So much around her, so thick. Whether she deserved it or not.

· · ·

She walked the neighborhood with crutches and then a plastic cane, passing the places where she and Jules had pressed up against each other with a sense of purpose: park benches, children's playgrounds, even under the overpass to the highway once—had that been her? Now in the afternoons the underpass was full of sleeping homeless men, bundled in garbage bags. Had they been there when she and Jules snuck down one windy night? Had they watched?

She took the T downtown and walked the streets she knew near her school, then headed farther afield, to the dark pubs that didn't card, the karaoke clubs where she and Eddie and Jules had rambled and wailed far past last call. She wandered by the fens and along the damp sides of the Muddy River, remembering school trips to study the pond life. Plastic bags tugged on branches in the wind; a lone child's sneaker rested on the bridge. She walked on toward the MFA, hoping for a private moment with the Buddha statue. If she could sit in that dark, church-like space again, maybe she'd remember why she'd left in the first place.

When she got to the museum, the crowds in the Asian wing were heavy; she had to move in a zigzag around people in the last hall, her head low. The Zen temple was closed for restoration, a sign informed her at the end. No one was allowed to enter. On the sign, a cartoon samurai wagged a finger.

That evening, Paul found her on her bed, staring at Jules's notebooks. "Dinner's ready."

"Thanks." She turned a page of one notebook. Eight-point boxes drawn to look three-dimensional, filling the crinkled paper. Maybe it was some kind of code.

He hovered in the doorway. "I don't know if I'm hungry tonight," she said.

Paul sidled in. He was wearing a suit and tie. After the family dinner, he was taking Marion out for drinks and dancing. "Listen— there's a reason that we're here tonight. I want you to know first. I'm asking Marion to marry me."

She looked up; something caught in her chest, trapping the air. The look on Paul's face was wide-eyed and solemn. She thought she might cry. "Thanks for telling me," she said. "That's wonderful."

He sat down on the bed beside her. "The reason I'm telling you first," he said, "is that I want to know what you think. I've always thought—well, that you had high standards for what's important in life. And that you knew what it takes to be happy. I've always thought you were very wise."

She laughed; now she really was crying. "You're kidding, right? I'm the screwup, remember?"

He shrugged. "You can be both."

"Ha." She loved him very much then. "I think—you have to risk everything. I think in a marriage, every day you have to tell the other person, 'I'll risk everything I've got for you.'" That was what had made Jules so easy to love, what no one else had understood about him. Every day he would have risked something terrible for her.

She reached up and touched Paul's head. A Buddhist blessing.

He hugged her hard. "Okay. Okay, I'll try." He drew himself up. It was like he was growing up right in front of her. "I'll take care of you, you know."

She nodded. It was sweet, really. And now, telling Jocelyn, she could see: she'd signed some kind of contract, of what shape their love would take.

He stood up and held out her cane. "Come on, nerd."

. . .

For a few years after the accident, she had little time for prayer or meditation. She studied for her GED and took classes at a local college; she attended Paul and Marion's wedding; she helped with Sunday dinners. First an apartment of her own, then a job with benefits, a car loan, good credit. You checked these accomplishments off a list and kept going. At first her mother tried to bring her back to church. Before she rented her own place, she'd find a silver cross on her pillow each night. Her mother tried getting her to come to church for Christmas, or to say a Hail Mary before bed. A succession of priests were invited for coffee and sandwiches and earnest talks about the faith in which one was raised. This was during the Catholic Church's "Catholics Come Home" campaign. You could see the slogan on signs in churchyards and on flyers tucked under cars' windshield wipers all over town. One hip young priest looked at her over his sunglasses and said, "You know, Catholics have the best tunes. If we get you when you're young, we've got you for life."

But Nicole flatly refused. She couldn't be re-graced.

She read, cleaned houses, sold shoes, all in this state of disgrace. She was twenty-two, when all the people she'd gone to school with were just graduating from college, getting real jobs. And then her father was ill, and there was no time for the counseling her family had urged, no time for weeping, no time for prayer of any kind. Liver cancer was her life now. The life she had begun to see yawning before her—a stunted life, but a stable one—was slamming shut.

Her father was stoic through that year. His father had died young of liver disease, and he began to tell them that this had already set the clock ticking. They protested. He smiled, grimly. But Nicole knew the real reason for the insidious arithmetic happening in his body, the growth of something black and evil in someone so good. Every now and then, when they were playing checkers or Nicole was reading to him in bed, she'd pause and look at him. *I'm the one who's made you sick,* she tried to say. *It's me. It's the anguish I've caused, the time away, all your worrying and searching. That's what's killing you now. Won't you admit it?*

He'd just look back. "Today's a good day, isn't it?"

"Yes. Yes, it's a good day, Dad."

Sometimes he did seem worried. "You'd tell me if you were using drugs again, wouldn't you?"

"Yes. I mean, I haven't used anything since—I came back." For her, the pill taking hadn't progressed to the point of need. Her sensitive stomach and fear of damaging herself, her kidneys, her teeth, had kept her walking a shaky line of control.

"And you'd tell me, if you did?"

"I promise. Please—don't worry about me." *Don't waste your energy on me. Please.*

He looked pained. "Of course I will. About Paul, too, and your mother. You worry about the people you love. That's not a bad thing."

They got used to the wan lighting of hospital rooms, the calming swaths of beige and gray, the language of narcotics, anti-nausea meds, laxatives. They got to know the smells that clung to their clothing, stubborn as cigarette smoke: saline, urine, thin, watery vomit. Through it all her mother remained calm, surprisingly calm. There was work to do. She brought knitting with her to waiting rooms, sent Nicole for meals, let Paul handle the paperwork. At night, when it was time to leave for the day, she sat on the edge of the bed, looking at their father, and she'd smile at him, and stroke his hair back from his face. This was what she'd always done when they were young and sick, when Nicole had her bronchitis and was frightened that she'd never get well. Her hand on his forehead, gentle and sure, and his eyes closing with relief under her touch. Nicole always had to look away.

On some afternoons they left early and went to church. There they could pretend that it was old times and sit together quietly in prayer and then each light a candle and go home. To throw a tantrum about this seemed petty, un-Buddhist, so she sat with Paul; but she would not take Communion. "They wouldn't let me anyway," she told him.

And at night she walked down by the river, listening for the whistles and cries of the feral kids that every city could hide. She watched the tall trays of day-old doughnuts being loaded into white vans, bound for homeless shelters. She stood under streetlights in parking lots, listening to the older men talk and pass bottles back and forth. She lined up at the back doors of churches instead of at the front. She drove the late-night streets of her tiny bounded city, daring herself to take the exit for the interstate. She kept road maps in stacks on the floor of her apartment and pored over escape routes, the next path she'd take. Most of her was still out there, still digging through dumpsters and sleeping on the hard, cold ground. Jules was still alive; he had just gone away for a while, and she had to wait, quietly, her entire self in abeyance, for his return.

She had to keep saying to herself, "This is real, this is real." She meditated, telling herself that she was not dreaming. She was here; her father was dying. *Awake, I breathe in. Awake, I breathe out.*

At the hospital, there was a bulletin board in the hall facing her father's room. She found herself staring at it, examining the offers for therapeutic massage, for grief counseling. One day, a new flyer appeared in the center of the board:

PEACEFUL HEALING ZEN CENTER

Specializing in meditation and
authentic Japanese Zen ceremony.

For Zen Buddhists or recreational
meditators of all skill levels. Find

healing with the ancient spiritual
art of meditation.

Accredited *roshi* Zen master with
years of experience in Rinzai Zen. If
you or a loved one is suffering, find
hope and healing in Zen.

Sit and discover yourself. Walk-ins
welcome.

She tore off one of the address slips at the bottom and put it in her
jacket pocket. In the next weeks, as her father weakened, she'd thumb
the slip into a velvety leather.

· · ·

When her father was released from the hospital and at home, he started
having trouble finding words for things. His brow would furrow and
he'd say a word that was clearly the wrong one, not what he meant.
They played checkers in silence, moving the pieces slowly across the
board. Sometimes his hand on a piece would pause, and he'd seem to
be lost in thought, frozen, until she gently nudged his hand to move
again. Like with a clock that's winding down, sometimes a shake could
get him moving for a little longer. Then he was too weak to play at all,
and her mother simply knelt by the bed, holding his hand and speaking
quietly of favorite memories—the time he'd picked her up for their first
date in a car with a missing fender, the trip to France, the snowy cathe-
drals, games of tennis in late afternoon sun. He didn't move, but his eyes
nodded along with her, grew with sympathy, crinkled with laughter.

When Nicole left her parents' house at night, she couldn't bring herself to go home. She'd circle her apartment complex on foot, peering into the ground-floor windows. She watched families watching television, kids fighting, old people puttering around kitchens. She leaned close to a windowsill. You could live on just the dregs of another person's life, she thought. Then a flashlight swept over her and someone yelled and she ran, becoming feral with the cats and the rats.

She stayed away from her apartment that night, afraid of being caught by her neighbors. She walked the wet, wintry streets instead, hood up, homeless again. She knew the secret places of any city where a person could disappear. She knew the bridge overpasses, the sewer systems, the library ventilation grates. Every bundle of blankets looked like a friend. That one could be Jules, with the lighter illuminating his face as he smoked, telling ghost stories to other runaways. Or that one, asleep and tucked protectively around his lover. She walked for hours through the underbelly of the city.

When she finally returned to her apartment, it was past midnight and there was a message on her machine: her father had fallen unconscious. By the time she got to the house, he had stopped breathing. Her mother sat on the bed beside him, very still, looking away. Paul had called the hospice, and a nurse from the night shift, a large, bustling, cheery woman, arrived to take his pulse and to clear away his box of painkillers. Before she arrived Nicole had already pocketed an orange bottle of the stuff she and Jules used to take; she turned it in her pocket now, just thinking. Just thinking.

The nurse felt for a pulse for a long quiet moment, then said, "He's with Jesus now."

"How do you know—how do you know he's with Jesus?" Nicole bristled.

"Nicole," said Paul quietly. Their mother didn't move or speak; she was far away.

"No—I want to know." The anger she'd wanted to feel all this time was suddenly here, suddenly free. "How dare you? A nurse, telling us about, about medicine—how dare you?"

The nurse held up her hands. "I'm sorry," she said. "Your family checked 'Catholic' on the form. I presumed—" She bowed her head. "I'm sorry. The funeral home will come pick him up in the morning."

Nicole and Paul went to their childhood bedrooms. A while later, Nicole's mother appeared in her doorway. Nicole inched over, and the two of them curled up together, sleeping deep and motionless until the undertaker knocked on the door.

The three of them drove home from the funeral parlor in silence; here they were, exhausted, and the thing they had dreaded was now over. But any relief vanished when they walked through the door: the house full of his things, his reading glasses, paperweights, clocks.

They ate. What else do you do? And sat in the dim kitchen, half-smiling at each other. Paul got up to make a phone call, presumably to tell Marion he wouldn't be home tonight. "I have to know," said Nicole to her mother, "what he thought about my running away."

"I wish you hadn't gone," her mother said. Tears rimmed her eyes. "He knew that it wasn't spiteful. But I wish you hadn't gone."

"It was something I needed to do."

Her mother pressed her hand. "But don't you understand? What makes you think you had the right? My daughter. My only daughter."

That was the only time they spoke of her running away. Paul returned and stood in the doorway; they both looked at him, glad for his constancy, glad for the way he took care of things. "Come here," said their mother. She got up; she was still taller than both of them, slim as a reed, elegant and finely dressed. She put out her hands, pulling them close. "I'm glad for both of you," she said. "I'm truly thankful. Lord, thank you." They bowed their heads before her, waiting for a blessing, something that would protect them when they left the safe afternoon light of the kitchen.

But she had no blessing for them, and eventually they released one another and retreated to their own secret corners of the house.

Here. Here was the place where the funeral sat in her mind, inert as stone, the details exact. Here, her mother struggling to select a tie. This one. No, this one. I gave him this one. Suddenly frantic. This one for winter. This one for summer.

Here was the service, the final Mass. Here was the Office of the Dead, the cry: *God, come to my assistance. Lord, make haste to help me.* Here was the priest in his white vestments, assuring them of the life that goes on beyond life.

Here, Paul talking to relatives in low, tasteful tones. Later, though, there he was out back in the yard, muddying his nice pants, staring at the neighbor's dog barking through the fence. Nicole could see him from the kitchen window. She'd always be able to see him like this. Was he talking to their father? Was he praying? The memory was somehow dear.

And here she was, walking in the woods the night of the ceremony, farther than she'd ever gone, all the way to the train tracks. It was hard to climb the fence with her bad ankle, but she made it over. The cold air was quicksilver sliding through her dress and down her body. Here the tracks receded into the darkness. Here she finally knew why she had come: she was waiting for a train to come and hit her. She was sick: deeply sick, spiritually sick. Jules was gone and her father was gone and she was to blame. Far away was the light of an approaching train. A growing rush of sound. Here is the Office of the Dead.

But her hand, jammed in her jacket pocket, was still turning the slip of paper, the one for the Zen center.

Awake, I breathe in.

. . .

In the little glass storefront of the Peaceful Healing Zen Center, the Master spoke fluently of the Lotus Sutra, which she had read but never understood. It was a puzzle, like all Zen was a puzzle. That was why it was frustrating to outsiders, he said. But the riddles were a way of arriving at intuitive truths. At forcing our minds to think upside down.

"The teaching of Buddhism is that suffering is not only endemic to the world, it is unavoidable," he said. "At first, we want to reject this. There is joy, there is beauty, we want to say. Buddhism does not deny this. But for anyone who has loved, we know that the people and things we love will pass away. This is a source of suffering. The more beauty we see, the more love we feel, the greater the pain."

He put his hands behind his back and walked a few powerful steps, like a sea captain surveying his crew. "Many of you here have experienced skillful means in your own lives. You have seen death and illness and suffering. You know, or you are beginning to realize, deep in some part of your most essential self, that you will die. That anything you thought was certain and unchanging is actually fragile. That the delicate web of people you love is made of the most brittle strands, and when one strand breaks, the rest of the web will disintegrate. You're beginning to know this. But you have to feel it in your bones, or you will never see beyond the abstraction. When you lose someone you love, you will cry, and you will be filled with rage, and then you will scuttle busily away into your half-awake lives."

How startling it was, to hear those words then. How devastating. In the meditation that followed, she felt warm tears on her cheeks. The Master passed and touched her shoulder—the sign to sit up straighter. She gulped back a sob.

After the session, she asked for a private meeting. They sat in the bare meeting room and she told her story sparingly: her conversion, running away, her father. It was like providing a case history for a doctor, listing the most relevant symptoms. He spotted this immediately and stopped her. "Zen is not psychotherapy," he said. "If you are looking for a therapist, a doctor, I won't be that for you. If you are looking for a teacher, I can teach."

She nodded, embarrassed into silence. "I—I'd like to learn."

"Good. Then I will be your Master. I'll start you at the very beginning. You have to trust me and obey me. In Japan, Zen students swear vows of fealty to their masters. Will you take a vow?"

She was quiet. Thinking. "I don't know," she said.

He stopped her from rising with a hand on her knee. "I understand what you've been through. I've lost people, I did enough drugs to drive my family away. I screwed up my life." This was the only time she would hear him speak so frankly. "I didn't know who I was, beyond this creature of craving and need. Then I discovered Zen, and something happened to me. I could see my life was one effect of many causes. And I realized I could shed my addictions because they were meaningless. But I had to break away from my old life. I had to risk everything. I need you to take that risk for me."

That was the thing she'd been waiting to hear. It was like a sign; it sounded almost like love. "I've already lost so much," she said. "I'm afraid to lose any more." *I'm afraid of never being free of sadness. Now Jules is gone, my father is gone, there will never be another day when I hear their voices, I must persist alone.*

He nodded. "Naturally. It's natural to be afraid, especially when we are grieving. Let me give you a Buddhist prayer for the dead. You can say it for your father."

He is passing from this world to the next.
He is taking a great leap.
The light of this world has faded for him.
He has entered solitude with his karmic forces.
He has gone into a vast silence.
He is borne away by the great ocean of birth and death.

She murmured the words after him, and knew she was saying them for Jules, too. His eyes were clear, red-rimmed, direct. She struggled to avoid his gaze, but it seemed to be everywhere her eyes moved.

"Your father is dead," he said. "And your mother will die, and your brother. This is only the beginning of the deaths you'll see in your lifetime. You have to understand this now. I need you to understand."

The air in the room shimmered. She could smell the faint trace of incense on his robes, and beneath that, a clean vegetable smell like green tea. She could smell herself as well—the sourness from the unwashed hospice days, the lingering bite of antiseptic, the bitter dirt on her boots. The candy-chalk pills in her pocket, waiting for her to use them. For a moment she thought she could smell and see and feel everything in the room. She could smell the inside of her nose and see the backs of her eyes. The Master's hand on her knee burned. In the days to come, she'd bow worshipfully at his feet and take the vow to all the innumerable beings and all the measureless infinities. She'd be his first, his best, his only. Soon the hard training would begin. And once she proved herself, her excellence, her devotion, he would grant her everything. This was the thing she had to explain to Jocelyn. He was going to re-grace her. He was going to show her how to awake, how to melt away.

Dear Sean,

Siddhartha and his monks are walking alongside the road to their retreat in Dharamsala. The rainy season is coming and they have to spend the time meditating; travel is impossible when the roads become mud and disease spreads from house to house.

A naked man runs up to them, his hair long and wild, his beard holding burrs and dead insects. He kneels for a blessing. "Save me, give me sanctuary, I take refuge with you," he begs.

We can't take this man, says one of the monks. I know him. He's a murderer. Now he's gone mad. The monks try to come between him and their leader. The murderer clutches at them, bowing and scraping in the dirt.

Give him a robe, says Siddhartha, and the murderer is allowed to join them.

An old man stops them on the road and bows deeply but will not touch anyone in the ragged group. He keeps his eyes on the ground and does not reach for the hands the way others do for blessings. Take me, please. Take me.

We can't take this man, says one of the monks. He is an untouchable. He can't share our robes or our bowls or our tents.

Oh, just give him a robe, says Siddhartha, and the untouchable is allowed to join them.

The group of the devoted continues to grow. It passes by villages scarred with poverty, places where mudslides have destroyed homes. Madmen are living in the woods, refusing to wash, refusing to speak, letting small animals live in their beards. By petrifying the body, you conquer it, the teaching goes.

A young woman comes running out of a house and kneels

*before them. Please, take me, Blessed One. I take refuge with
you.*

*We can't take her, says one of the monks. She is the only
daughter of that old couple that lives there. She takes care of
them.*

I'm sorry, says Siddhartha.

*Why can't I go, when all of these monks have renounced their
families? I heard you left your wife and son.*

*I'm sorry, says the Thus Come One. You are their daughter.
You have to take care of them.*

Why can't I leave everything behind?

*Karma. Be a good daughter; in your next life, maybe you'll
be born luckier.*

And maybe she will. There are prayers you can say, to be
born as a man. I never went that far, never hated being a girl
that much. But I knew that my leaving was an unforgivable sin.
You know the Irish saying: A son is a son till he gets him a wife; a
daughter's a daughter the rest of her life.

No getting reborn in Catholicism; just one shot at the life
you're given. No way out but to weep.

EASTER

Her Master had been giving her more assignments on the phone, now that he had her well in hand again. Chants and poses and koans. She was back to her prostrations; her hands were blistered and raw. Kukai watched her while she bowed and rose, bowed and rose, sitting by the window late at night while she labored, and then they'd both stretch and moan and watch the sun rise together. The clank and roar of the garbage trucks always arrived like a thunderbolt, one of those things decent people were not supposed to hear.

"You have to atone," her Master told her. "If you were a student in a monastery and you had committed such a wrong, you would have to announce it before the entire community and beg for their forgiveness. For months to come you would be the lowest of the low. You would have to crawl on your knees for your daily bowl of rice. But I am merciful. Take off your clothes. Send me a picture of yourself on your knees."

"I'm not going to do that!"

He made a small hiss of impatience. "This is why they put you in the beginners' class with that other *roshi*," he said. "You're afraid to be truly transgressive."

The words rang painfully in her ears. "How did you even know that?" she demanded. And when he refused to answer she said, "I'm not afraid. I've transgressed. I've done hard things in my life. I converted, didn't I? And ran away?"

"And came crawling back, a failure. 'No Buddhas ever attained the Path by continuing their family lives: nor have there been patriarchs in any time who did not assume the form of homeless ones.'" He was silent for a while, and then delivered his pronouncement: "You're terrified of the very idea of doing something that would make you unlovable. Isn't that right? Tell me."

She listened, hollowly, but couldn't speak.

"You have only to whisper, and your Master is there. Isn't that what you always wanted?"

Was that what she wanted? How did he know, how did he always know?

After a moment, her Master laughed his thick, dark laugh. "That's all right. You can always shelter under my wing. I'll always have a place for you, little chick."

• • •

The traffic had a Sunday feel: fewer delivery bicycles tilting madly in the corner of your eye. Nicole was squeezed into the back seat, with Charlie heavy and squirming on her lap, June and her mother wedged in beside her. It was Easter. Her mother had flown in from

North Carolina for the weekend; she had already shopped and lunched with her friends, and now there remained only the family trip to church.

Paul and Marion's heads in the front seemed like those of her own parents. She wondered if Paul felt the warmth of the moment, too. He was resting an elbow on the windowsill, the lines of golden arm hair they shared slanting under an expensive-looking watch. She looked over at her mother, straight-backed and elegant. She was remarkably unchanged, as if age and sickness could no longer touch her.

"Your hair," her mother said to her. "You need a cut."

"You'll love this church, Nicole," said Marion. "Beautiful, a miniature St. John the Divine. I've always found churches to be such inspiring spaces. They have something that secular spaces never will. Don't you think?"

Nicole groped for the right response. "The place you grew up in teaches you what is holy."

"I should say so," her mother said.

The kids—pink-scrubbed, smelling of shampoo, twitched and struggled over a chocolate rabbit they were sharing. "I don't want that on your good clothes," said Marion. June was slippery beside Nicole in a pale blue satin dress with a white sash, done up like a Tiffany's box with a matching white headband for her hair. "We got you some Easter candy," June said, and handed Nicole a crinkling cellophane bag of marshmallow Peeps and tin-foiled chocolate eggs.

"You'd better keep that away from her," Nicole's mother said. "Remember, Nicole, when you left a chocolate bunny in your pocket during church and it melted all over your beautiful dress? Oh, it was ruined."

That morning Paul had come to pick her up, straddling the arm of her couch while she searched in boxes for stockings, jewelry, anything grown-up. "Why didn't you tell me you went to Boston?" she asked. "I could have gotten a ride, seen some friends."

"Oh, they don't give me much notice. All those hospitals, I'm always running over there."

"Marion doesn't mind?"

"She's flexible with her job; we work it out." Paul raked a hand through his thin, colorless hair. With that innocent face, he still looked like a young boy, trying on a man's coat and tie and shoes. "You know, over time, you learn how to coexist with someone, you develop a rhythm. Give it long enough and even the things you hate about another person lose their edge. You make your peace." He looked out the window as if scanning for storm clouds. Then he reached out his hand, and she took it, and they ran down to the car.

"You should have your furniture moved here soon," her mother said. "If we got it out of there and fixed the roof, maybe we could finally sell."

Half of the family's furniture was still waiting for her in the old house in Waban under white sheets, the plan to sell in an unending limbo. "I leave it all to you and Paul," her mother had told them after their father's death. She had recently moved to North Carolina, near her cousins. Widows, she said, need a chance to start anew. She wanted her house, her life, emptied out. She wanted light wicker beach furniture, not dusty old New England dressers and armoires and their itinerant memories. In some ways, Nicole thought with admiration, her mother was very Zen. The space inside her must be cool and dark and derelict, like a house abandoned to the weather.

"I don't want the furniture," Nicole said, though she knew her mother would never stop pressing her to take it all.

"I figured out the riddle you gave me," June said loudly. "I mean, the koan."

"Oh really?" She'd last left them with a haiku by Basho. "The cry of the cicada / Gives us no sign / That presently it will die." It was an old favorite.

"It means that everything's going to die, but they don't know it. All the things you think will last forever—they won't."

Paul's and Marion's backs stiffened in the front seat. "Goodness," said her mother. "Did Nicole teach you that?"

Where did you come from? Nicole thought, staring at her niece. *And what should I say? Kids shouldn't be thinking such things.*

"They're still good, even if they can't last forever," she said. *Careful, careful.* "The cicada sings without the knowledge of its own death. There's something beautiful about that. It goes on anyway. It's the ephemerality that makes things precious."

"There's no need to think about it that way, Junie," Marion said briskly. She'd given Nicole her chance, and now she was sweeping in for cleanup. "It's just describing things in a pretty way." Then she changed the subject: "Who's going to want waffles after church?"

Everyone raised their hands. Nicole turned her face to the window, rubbed the raw, tender blisters on her palms. Really, why *did* she have to make things so difficult? There were, as always, at least two selves rattling around inside her: one wanted to grab Marion by the shoulders and shake her, wanted to ask her Master what it was about and demand a straight answer, was terrified, nauseated by what she had just said, that things were only beautiful because they would die. And one wanted waffles.

The church was a grand old cathedral in the Financial District, with buttresses and a soaring spire. The priest greeted churchgoers at the door in his white-and-purple Easter vestments, snowy fringes of hair flapping. The sight made Nicole sway as she stepped out of the car: she hadn't been to church since her father's funeral.

"Come on, June," her mother said, stepping out of the car. She hugged her close. "Don't you know you're my absolute favorite granddaughter? Do you promise not to grow anymore?"

June smiled tolerantly and tripped on ahead. Paul grinned at Nicole through the window. They both watched their mother striding forward. "She really is glad you're here, you know."

"All right, Paul," Nicole said. "Don't oversell it. I'm here, okay?"

"Right." He rolled his eyes and smiled. "I'm going to park."

To get to the entrance of the church they passed by an old graveyard, with tiny gravestones erupting from the earth. As the kids ran ahead, her mother followed with warnings not to step on the graves, because it was bad luck.

Marion slid up beside Nicole. "I'd appreciate it if you kept the riddles to a minimum with the children," she said.

"What?"

"The Buddhist stories. The pictures, the statues. I'd just really appreciate it if you toned down the Buddhism thing. I don't want to confuse the children."

"Confuse them?"

"Yes. I think the stories you tell are sometimes confusing for their age. The one about the prince who gives his children away, for example. June was troubled by that. Those kinds of stories are really not appropriate."

"If that's what you want," Nicole said. "You're their mother." This was the closest they'd ever stood together, and it was all Nicole could do to keep from rearing back in alarm. Marion seemed to notice her distress; she reached out an arm. "I don't mind that you are," she said. "Buddhist, I mean. Really. It's none of my business, what you do with your life. I'd just rather avoid—confusing the children. It's a difficult age." Then she smiled. *We're in this together, right? This tricky busi-*

ness of child-rearing. Then she moved on, picking her way delicately through the tombstones.

At that moment the church bells began to ring, heavy and soft. The sound was solid, insistent. It was a beautiful call, an undeniable one. Four, five, six rings. Christ is risen. Let joy ring in Christendom.

The inside was just as Marion had promised: cool and shadowed, giant with interior space. The family shuffled into a pew halfway down the nave, and she had to crane her head back and stare into the high ceiling the way she did when she was young. She admired the way Christian architects had figured it out, this formula, the proper effects to make you feel both larger and smaller than yourself. Like you were a great house too, small on the outside, vast on the inside. As the swell of the organ filled the air, Nicole remembered the words. The hymn sprang easily from her lips.

Make me Jesus wholly thine,
Take this wayward heart of mine,
Guide me through this world so drear,
Heart of Jesus, hear!

Beside her was Paul's fine dark baritone and Marion's hardworking soprano. The kids were singing, and she heard her mother's sweet voice, the singing voice she had not heard in a decade. An altar boy swung by with thurible, intent on his task, smiling seriously, and then the white-crested priest took his place in the high pulpit.

"Joy to us on this day!" he said, beaming. Today was Easter, more sacred than Ash Wednesday, more ecclesiastical than Christmas Eve. Today's sermon was the most important part of his job. "I want to talk about abandonment today," he said. "I want to talk about the long absence of the Lord from Good Friday to Easter Sunday. I want to talk about the lonely times when people found themselves in places God seemed not to be. We've all been there. Doubt is part of the human condition. Doubt is when we look through all the corners of our lives and can't seem to find the Lord's presence. That's a scary thought." He paused, allowed himself a patrician look over his glasses. The audience stirred with laughter. It was a moment before Nicole realized that she was laughing, too. The easy, familiar cadence of his words! The relief of English, of the stories she'd grown up with, the words she knew how to pronounce! She leaned forward in the pew.

"We can see the evidence of the Lord's love all around us," the priest said. "We see the mother who loves the child. We see the brothers and the sisters, the husbands and the wives. We see people held together by the sacred bonds of love. But sometimes we forget to look at these things. We see only our own questions staring us in the face. We wonder, 'Who could love me?' Doubt is a potent force, but it is a childish one. We are like children, forever asking, 'Why? Why?' Parents, this must sound familiar." Another benign gaze over the rim of his glasses, another ripple of laughter. "But the Bible tells us there is a time when we must put aside childish things. All our questioning shrinks before the enormous, immutable fact of God's existence."

The priest paused to let this sink in. The church was rich with quiet. "Today we rejoice," he said. "Because Christ is risen again. Because the promise of our God—that death is only a temporary condition—has been fulfilled. Today the doors of heaven are thrown open wide. Today we break the iron chains of doubt. But this promise is only fulfilled when we believe, when we accept the gift of love that is given. When we take body and blood inside us."

Nicole sat straighter. She cast a look behind herself: she could see a mosaic of human faces, all of them familiar in their still poses. Of course they wanted the same things she did. Of course they wanted the promise that sadness was not the inherent state of their lives, that the axle of the world turned on secret wells of joy. When you looked into the night sky, in the gaps between the stars, you needed something to be there. They had to believe it, the same way she did. She closed her eyes and let the words flood her, thick and sweet as syrup, oozing snug and airtight into all the hollow grooves of herself. "This is the day the Lord has made, alleluia," said the priest.

And she and the congregation answered, "Let us be glad and rejoice in it, alleluia."

"Let us pray," said the priest.

Then it was time for Communion. They moved to the front pew by pew, shuffling past the altar and the five priests who now stood there, hustling with packages of crackers and wine. When it was her turn, Nicole found herself in front of the white-crested priest. He smiled—*You're new,* he seemed to say with a waggle of eyebrows—and reached for her. She felt the old push and clasp of her head. The wafer was at her lips. For a moment panic seized hold of her. The priest's hand on her head pressed harder. Almost against her will, she opened her mouth and took the wafer onto her tongue, swallowing it in a rough gulp.

She got back to the pew before anyone else did. There on the wooden seat was Paul's phone; she figured it must have slipped out of his pocket. And there was a new message blinking on the screen. It said:

My pussy misses you.

She froze, closed the phone, placed it back on the pew with infinite care. Then the family was back, pressing in around her for the final prayer, the last song. Paul slipped the phone into his pants pocket. She looked at him quickly, then fixed her eyes forward for the rest of the service.

. . .

On the lawn, a brisk wind played with the priests' surplices. Charlie and June drank orange juice from paper cups and picked the cookies they wanted. They were getting whiny, hanging on Marion's arm, their small window of good behavior closing with waffles on the horizon. Nicole's mother promised egg hunts in the park. She and Marion had been up late last night, dyeing eggs. "Come on, Nicole, I want you to meet our pastor," Paul said, pulling her through the crowd. She stared at his pocket as he walked. The phone seemed to glow inside it.

The pastor was shaking hands amid a circle of churchgoers; Paul shouldered himself into the ring. "Father, I'd like you to meet my sister, Nicole," he said. "She's just moved to New York."

"Of course, I saw many new faces today. That's Easter for you. It brings all the Catholics out of the woodwork." The father clasped her hand with both of his. "Welcome, Nicole, welcome. Did you enjoy the service? I know Paul was raised in the church, so I assume you were as well."

"Yes, that's correct. It was a lovely sermon," she said honestly. The pastor was something out of a children's book, with a kind-wizard twinkle in his eyes. She groped for the right words, the right tactful appreciation. "I haven't been to church in a long time, but I'm glad I did today."

The pastor smiled. "Tell me, do you still get a shiver when you hear Latin?"

"Yes."

He nodded. "The first language that God speaks to us with is the most powerful. It never leaves us. The Protestants got it wrong when they put the prayers in English. There must be a pure language of prayer in our lives. And Catholic magic is very strong."

"You're very wise, Father," she said.

"And didn't you miss spirituality in your life?"

Then Paul was shaking the pastor's hand. "She's been away far too long, Father."

The priest leaned in now, squeezing her arm. "Have you confessed, my dear? It's important, you know, before you take Communion. Start with a clean slate."

The circle of churchgoers pressed in close, ringing her with their noxious goodwill. She tore herself free. "I'm sorry, I can't," she said.

There was a frozen silence. "There's no sin too great—" the pastor said. Beside her, Paul glared. A ferocious silent message in his eyes: *You're embarrassing us.*

She shook her head. "I left the church a long time ago. I'm a *Buddhist.*"

It was astonishing how a group of happy, welcoming people could become so cold so quickly. Now on their faces she saw the whole spectrum of emotion her family had shown: disappointment, smiling indulgence, disgust. Her mother was shaking her head. "You always have to make a scene. Why do you always have to make a scene about it?"

She stepped backward, bumping into someone. "Excuse me—I'm sorry—" She was trapped again. She elbowed and shoved. "Please— I'd better go." She set off fast for the gate.

Paul cut her off while she was still passing the gravestones. "Come on, Nicole!"

She stopped, wiped her damp forehead in the chilly spring air. "What do you want me to do, Paul? Just tell me once and for all what you really wanted me to do when you had me move here. *Tell me what I'm doing here.*"

He hesitated. "You know what I want you to do? You want to do me a big favor, Nicole? Just shut the fuck up about Buddhism and channeling your New Age energy and good and bad karma and all that bullshit. Because I'm sick of it. Everyone's had enough of all the bullshit."

"Everyone?"

"Me, Marion, Mom, everyone. We're all just waiting for you to figure out that leading an *adult* life is about making compromises and then living with them for the sake of the people around you." Paul was no longer angry, just tired. "You can't pretend that you're still some seventeen-year-old who's going to drop off the grid or be the next maharishi. We all figured that out eventually, but you can't seem to understand." Now his hands were on her shoulders; he was shaking her urgently. "You lied to me once, remember? You promised you were coming home, but you weren't. I didn't tell Mom and Dad because I thought you'd walk in the door and be okay. Please. Just find some guy you halfway like, have a couple of kids and go to yoga on the weekends, and stop turning everything into your own personal spiritual quest."

She trembled. "You think you're perfect, you've got life all figured out? I saw your phone, Paul. The text from—whoever. You act awfully self-righteous for someone cheating on his wife. You confess to that today?"

"It's none of your business." He ran his hand through his hair. "Mom's given up on you, you know. She's never going to forget how you threw us all away."

They both looked toward the knot of churchgoers. Her mother

was talking to the priest, her hand gestures expansive, apologetic. She wasn't going to come over now.

Paul turned back toward Nicole, his face haggard. "I'm the one who wanted you to move. It was me, not Mom. I still think you can settle down and live a normal life."

Nicole stared at her mother. Looked at her neatening June's bow, encouraging her to stand up straight with the little gesture Nicole had grown up seeing her make. Paul was right. The realization sank in slowly: her mother hadn't cared whether she came to New York or not. She didn't care whether she had a job or found a man; she'd given up on her only daughter.

"But I still give a damn," Paul said raggedly. "So just do me a favor and *let this go.*"

She tried to breathe, to stay calm. And then she couldn't. "Fuck. You," she said.

This was the part where he reached for her, sorry now, exasperated but contrite. "Come on, Nic." This was where he'd hold her close and she'd weep and apologize. She'd return to the family, to the white fluttering lace and the purple banners, to the waffles. She'd stroll with them through the green park, hunting for eggs that Marion and her mother had stayed up dunking in cups of hot colored dye. And then she'd come back to the townhouse, with its creaking furniture, and eat lamb with mint jelly. And the day would march safely on into the unremarkable story of her life.

But no. She was not going to do that.

Instead, this was where he got hold of her arm, gripping with surprising force, until she had to thrash free, hissing, "Fuck you! Fuck you!" like some mental patient. This was where the churchgoers looked over uneasily and her mother simply looked away, done with her. At last she was free, running for the gates, hailing a cab, not looking back, except briefly, once, to see Paul at the curb with one hand raised. Either trying to stop her. Or trying to wave good-bye.

. . .

Jocelyn had invited her out for Easter dinner with friends, but she'd declined since she had to be with her family. Leaving the church, she'd called breathlessly. "Is it too late to come?" They were meeting in one of Manhattan's giant ballroom dim sum restaurants.

As she'd crossed Canal Street, the sleek marble and glass of the Financial District had given way to low-slung apartment buildings, girded with crates of fish and knotted ginger, bubble tea and bodhi tree seeds. Buddhas were in the windows, fat, laughing, womanly, mysterious. Here, Buddhism was big business. Souvenir shops offered paper lanterns with prayers on them, fake jade, rosary beads, and sandalwood candles. Quan Yin statues thronged together on card tables on the street.

Their group filled up a round table; they were all talking in the loud, vehement voices of New Yorkers, making themselves heard in the general clamor. Around Nicole waiters in crisp red and black swept by with carts of stacked bamboo boxes, red lacquered bowls holding pale flesh-colored dumplings, chicken feet in glistening orange sauce. She was sitting next to Elliot, rubbing elbows with him while she cracked hot, brittle egg rolls. She remembered his fiery little red ears under the edges of his too-small fedora, the taste of him (beer and Altoids and ash). "Are you as bad with chopsticks as I am?" he asked. "I'm going to apologize for my table manners in advance."

"All right, I'll accept." She was good with chopsticks, but her hands were still shaking.

"How's the meditation going?" Elliot asked. "Reach a higher plane yet?"

"It's going."

Jocelyn had grabbed her elbow at the door. "Don't let Elliot suck you into the vortex."

"What do you mean? He seemed nice."

"Elliot's been dealing with a divorce for the past few months. He can be very moody. All of a sudden he starts spinning into a death spiral and he takes whoever's nearby with him."

But Elliot seemed sunny and sardonic today as he had before, eating the shrimp cakes two-handed, grinning and winking at his friends. Jocelyn smiled tolerantly when he reached over her to grab the last pork bun. The giant room was packed; theirs were among the few non-Asian tables, the language around them a flurry of Mandarin or Cantonese.

"This is good timing, coming here now," said Elliot. "Or on second thought, maybe especially bad timing." He was wrestling with a shrimp patty, trying to cut it with his chopsticks. "Wonder how many of these people are having their Easter brunch here. Lots of Chinese are Christian now, aren't they?"

"I suppose," said Jocelyn.

"You can tell by looking at them," said Elliot's friend Drake. Another hipster in red sneakers fond of cocaine.

Nicole raised her head. "How can you tell if someone's been to church just by looking?"

"Like you, for example," said Drake. "The stockings are a dead giveaway. And the shoes. Too fancy to be comfortable. You can always tell when a woman's been to church."

"I bet you're nipping off to a temple right after," said Elliot. "Cheating on Jesus with the Buddha. Or is it the other way around?"

She chewed a ball of rice in silence.

"You *are* cheating," he said. "I see how it is. Got to keep the family harmony, right? Did you ever even leave the church? After the shit you gave me?" He laughed. "When the going gets tough—" He stabbed a dumpling with one chopstick and brought it to his mouth. "Where do you go? Running back to the fold."

She wanted to tell him he was ridiculously wrong, simpleminded, judgmental, hopelessly reductive. But no words came.

"Excuse me," she said, and hurried for the bathroom, leaving him smirking at the table.

In line in the narrow, dark hallway, she found herself behind the mother and daughter from the next table over. They spoke quickly to each other. (Or was it, she wondered, just that unknown languages always seem faster than our own?) The mother pressed her hand to the girl's neck, smoothing her hair. Nicole stared at them and remembered her own mother touching her hair in the same way, the casual gesture of everyday love. She wanted to say a prayer for them, to protect them.

Jocelyn's hand was on her shoulder; she had followed Nicole to the ladies' room. "What an asshole," she said. "I told you."

Nicole nodded.

"Are you still teaching the meditation class?" Jocelyn asked.

Nicole looked into Jocelyn's wide, thoughtful eyes, eyes that could pull the story of your life out of you. Jocelyn shook out her arm, and a bracelet slipped out of her sleeve and down to her wrist. Polished dark wooden beads, with one of glass. A red tassel. Then she knew.

"How did you meet the Master?" she asked.

Jocelyn stared.

"Was it in Boston?" Nicole asked. "Was it when you stopped doing drugs? Was he your Master then?"

Jocelyn looked at her, smiling in feigned confusion.

"Did he ask you to keep tabs on me, or did you do it on your own? Did you give him a weekly report on my activities?" There were so many questions to ask, but only one answer that mattered: It was Jocelyn. Jocelyn had told the Master everything. All her secrets. All her stories. Everything, everything she had been, everything she'd done, had been given to Jocelyn, and Jocelyn had given it obediently away. She could feel the Master's hands on her again, his breath in her ear. When the Master had discovered that she was gone, he must have made the mental calculations: she'd gone and done what he thought he'd dissuaded her from doing. He must have called his old student Jocelyn, told her to mention Buffy, given her the right in. Why else would this stranger have befriended her? He was consuming her again; it was a kind of sex act, a brutal, stolen intimacy.

"Yes, he was my Master first," Jocelyn said, so quietly that Nicole almost couldn't hear above the cheerful restaurant din. "He asked. I'm sorry." She sighed, shaking her head, and reached out to touch Nicole's arm. "I wanted to hear. I wanted to be your friend. But I'm an old student of his. Did you think just by moving to a new city, you can get away from him? He's here. He's with you right now. You don't ever break that bond."

Nicole said, "I will."

Jocelyn smiled, sharp and sad. "He has only to give the command, and you'll come to him. He's getting impatient. It won't do any good to run."

. . .

She ran in her rain-splashed stockings to the bus stop. She had left her coat behind, but it didn't matter, she had to move now, had to get somewhere that Jocelyn, that her Master wouldn't know. She rode the bus uptown, watching it gradually empty, the remaining riders blank-faced, either tired or shut up somewhere inside themselves. She watched her phone ring. A call from her Master. She let it buzz and buzz in her lap.

The bus took her in loops around the city. It was night now. Her body bumped and lurched around the corners. As long as she was in motion, she was all right, she was free. She couldn't go to her apartment; her Master knew the address. She couldn't go to Paul; her Master knew that place, too. She watched the rain drumming on the black armadas of umbrellas, people hunched and hurrying home.

The bus stopped, and the conductor made his way down the aisle. "Last stop, ma'am. Got to get off." His voice was not unkind. She got up and followed him off the bus, into the dark Hopper painting of a street corner. They were in Brooklyn, she realized. There was Manhattan on the horizon, the brother of the skyline she'd seen from the water. She was back downtown again, close to Dumbo. She thanked the driver and started walking.

The rain had stopped, and the streets were shiny and black. Each street she turned down was empty; streetlights winked at their own reflections in the mirrored windows. Something about this industrial silence felt ominous.

She was walking back to the bus stop, hoping for another line to take, when a man peeled himself from the dark to her right, hand out and catching a streetlight's sodium gleam, his face in the shadows.

"Hey, you're looking nice tonight."

The voice, low and intimate, as though they were already friends. She felt herself smile politely. She didn't slow down. But the voice followed her. "Where you going tonight in such a hurry? Where you going? Got a date with your girlfriends?"

She could feel him now, riding just beyond her right shoulder.

"You sure are looking nice tonight, Miss In a Hurry."

She had a nickname. She was named; she belonged to him now. And still she was smiling. Politeness. The need to be liked.

She ducked her head and took the first turn she found, a hard right onto another narrow, high-walled road, and by this time she knew he was following her, not just throwing out a few catcalls for fun but matching her step for step. "What's your hurry? You late for something? What's your rush?"

She stopped walking. She was so terribly tired. She couldn't run anymore. She turned, took a step forward.

The man approached cautiously, his jaw jutting into the circle of the streetlight's gleam. "You want to get some coffee? You lonely?"

"Yeah," she said. The beginnings of an expanding feeling in her chest. "Yeah, I'm lonely. What do you want to do? Want to get some coffee? Want to go back to your place and get a blow job? Or would you rather do it standing up, in this alley, say? Does that turn you on? Want to push me down on my knees? Or does just following me around do it for you? Maybe you just like to watch. Tell me your best-case scenario. Tell me what you've already done to me in your head."

He put up his hands. "Whoa. Whoa."

She tilted her head. "Tell me. Tell me what you've already done. Tell me how you've fucked me."

He took a step back, his hands still up. "Okay," he said. "Okay. Have a good night, lady." She could see only his red sneakers for a while, beating along the road. Then he turned a corner and raised his hand. He was giving her the finger. It was a strange little salute.

She listened to her heart's steady pounding. She was half-wild. Not much further to go the rest of the way.

In another block she was under the first great struts of the bridge.

There was a small gated park here, the kind of place that transformed at night. She could see bodies moving in the children's jungle gym, people settling with their blankets and shopping carts, thin, ghostly figures smoking and laughing near the water. Her people.

One of the users by the water had spotted her. "Hey, you want a light?" he asked.

She nodded, coming over. She didn't have any cigarettes on her, but he gave her one and they leaned on the iron railing, gazing at the dazzling buildings across the river. "It used to be beautiful here," he said bitterly. "Rotten old buildings and collapsing wharfs and vacant lots. Now look." With a jerk of his chin, he indicated the manicured park, the bright plastic jungle gym, the bag dispensers for picking up waste.

"The New Yorker's Lament," she said.

He laughed. "You got that right. It's like, we're too good at transforming ourselves."

"Did you grow up here?" she asked.

He shook his head. "Naw, man. I got here ten years ago. I was gonna be somebody."

"And?"

He shook his head again, but now he was smiling. "Hey, I was here. I *lived*."

It was easy to fall back into the old way of speaking. "You're full of shit."

"Yeah." They smoked in silence, and she pulled out the bag of Easter candy and shared it. The sun was coming up behind them. She knew she had to disappear, but she didn't know how or where. Jocelyn had said that running away would not work. And she could see that; wherever she went, eventually he would find her.

She wondered: What would Paul do, when she was gone? In that way she had of occasionally looking into his life, she could picture him searching for her.

Her friend offered her another cigarette, but she refused. "I'd better go."

He smiled. "It's five in the morning. Where have you got to go?"

She shrugged. "Home." And as she said it, she knew it was true.

Dear Sean,

It is the 1950s. Tibetan monks, lamas, teachers are fleeing to the United States; China's takeover of Tibet, the war and devastation, marches behind them. They are coming to the American West. There, in the high, dry mountains and deserts not so different from their homeland, they are finding the kinds of followers Buddhism has never seen.

The followers keep their shoes, their jeans, their hair. They have crew cuts. They play guitars. They have come from little white houses and mothers with aprons and towns with bowling alleys. The congregations swell with outcasts, losers, refugees from other lives.

Some of the monks from the old country do not know what to do with all the women. The tradition of nuns has all but died out. In Tibet, Chinese soldiers raped the nuns. Now you are not chaste, now you cannot keep your vows, they said.

The women wear their Sunday best to meetings. They are young, desperate for worship. It surprises no one when the monks and the priests begin to see not students but girls. You can picture the scene. The girl pushes a sliding door aside and bows deeply. She does not wear the red robe of a monk. She has taken refuge here, from a world that is oppressive and strange. She is trusting in the sanctuary her master will provide. In the silence of their shared meditation is a fine, high quivering. The breeze of power and authority is heady.

Her master can tell her, "You want enlightenment? Then kneel. Give me your mouth. Bend to your work." And she will.

And I did.

What happened to all those women, when the scandals

finally broke? When the disgraced monks packed up their wares and moved sheepishly on? When the Zen roshis and Tibetan rinpoches refused to comment, when they claimed the same private privilege of the confessional? Did they change religions? Did they fumble their way back home in humiliation? Did they disappear? Was that moment after the command—the surprise, doubt, betrayal—itself its own revelation?

I had been selected for a special honor. Wasn't that what I'd always wanted? I'd said, Dear Lord, please show me the living light. Even if it hurts. But I didn't know it would demand everything I could give. My Master told me, I will require your life. This was the shock: he meant it.

Girl, where are you? Where did you go?

PART THREE

One day, I'll be ready, she says to the Master, in her ninth year of training. Won't I? One day won't I not be your student anymore?

That's not the way it works, he says. You'll always be my student. Like a mother is always a mother, and a child a child. You made a promise.

In the dim light of the meeting room, he watches her complete her prostrations. It's been long enough that he knows her every gesture, he hears the pop of her bad ankle and feels it like it's his. Neither of them are young anymore. Is it really enlightenment that she wants?

Recently he has sensed that she is close to being lost. Something different in the restless way she sits on her heels when he's giving a sermon and gazes out the window. When she pours tea, she drinks before him in thirsty gulps. She's getting impatient. He knows what the beginning of anger looks like before she does.

And he realizes he's terrified.

He has to find a way to make her his again. "Tell me about what happened when you were young," he demands, but she won't.

He tells her the koan about the master who is able to transform lead into gold. An impatient young monk demands the secret, and the master shares the incantation with him. "But it only works if you do not think of a black cat," he says.

The Master tells her he can turn her from lead into gold, if she won't think the things she's thinking. If she stays patient and disciplined. If she lets the questions she has melt on her tongue, if she swallows them down.

PAUL

Nicole wasn't answering calls, but Paul expected that, after the way they'd parted. He'd seen his mother to the airport, saying he'd make Nicole come around, the way he always did. He gave her all the usual assurances. Then he went to Nicole's apartment and found that she'd left: laundry pawed through on the bed, no toothbrush in the cup in the bathroom. The cat was missing, too. He slouched sheepishly through the apartment, feeling like a thief. Remembering her childhood hiding places, he even dug into her underwear drawer, looking for cash. A crumpled five was all he could find; whatever else she had was gone.

More than that, though, was the feeling of the place. Something like waiting about it, in the watchful squares of light in the windows, the drying flower pot on the sill. On the kitchen table were her key to the apartment and her phone, sitting prominently where he would find them.

The phone was locked, and he couldn't guess her code with a few tries. But buried in a box, he found her previous year's datebook, with two phone numbers written on the inside cover, both Massachusetts area codes. He thought one might be the old teacher, the Zen place she'd mentioned. The other he didn't know, but he'd try those first.

On the way home from his sleuthing at the apartment, he bought a bus ticket at Port Authority, then stood under the giant ugly steel overhang as a quick rainstorm passed, eating a pretzel. The tourists coming out often stopped in the flow of traffic here, looking around and pointing, while the businesspeople dodged around them. A couple in matching tie-dyed T-shirts asked him which way to the Empire State building. He was tempted to say, "Fuck off." But he didn't. He politely gave directions.

Marion and the kids dropped him at the station on their way to school, the way they always did when he left for a business trip and didn't want the aggravation of renting a car. Charlie left intricate lip prints on the windows, boisterous in his good-byes, while June sulked. Only Marion knew that this trip was different from the others. She looked up at him from the driver's seat and offered a single raised eyebrow. He matched it with a "who knows" lift of one shoulder, surprised, as always, at how marriage had made them able to communicate in these tiny ways. Why didn't it help them speak in the more important ones?

On the bus he pressed his cheek to the cold glass and watched the city roll back around him, felt the bus begin its familiar shudder and sway on the highway north. He liked taking the bus to Boston instead of the train because it reminded him of being a college kid again, heading home. And it usually meant he was coming back to Jennifer.

He liked the light shifting down into late afternoon, and one lake he always passed with a round wooded island in the center, the sort of thing he and Nicole might swim to on a summer day and come home damp and coated in pine needles. He liked it when the sun set and he knew he was close and the little seat lights came on and he could look at the other passengers, who were mostly young and snared in headphone cables, wondering what lives, what jobs, what Jennifers they were heading to. On Sunday in the line for the bus back, he would see the same people clinging to the lovers they'd been visiting, the kisses good-bye, the longing tugs on backpack straps, and he would feel very old among them.

Nicole wasn't crazy. She'd taken a bag, her winter coat, some clothes, her toothbrush. She was going somewhere.

He wasn't going to tell their mother, not yet, not ever if he could. He'd fix this himself.

It was getting dark now on the bus and the laptops were coming out, everyone's faces washed in their aquarium glow. He read off the screen of the young woman next to him: *I know you're never going to forgive me, but it has to be this way.* He watched her delete and retype: *I know I'm never going to forgive myself but.* She paused, pressing a hand to her forehead, and he looked away.

Soon they'd reach the toll for the Mass Pike, and later they'd all stumble out into the bright fluorescence of the station, sleepwalking as they fumbled for their bags in the freezing belly of the bus, and they'd shuffle gratefully into the arms of the people waiting for them.

The business conventions and sales appointments he told Marion about were usually real. So were the times he had told her he was visiting Nicole, checking up on her, making sure she wasn't in a ditch somewhere. It was just that when he went to Boston, he stayed with Jennifer. That was the only lie.

She picked him up from the station and they went out for pizza in the North End, near her apartment. They always went out for dinner on the night when he arrived because they knew they'd be pulling each other's clothes off the minute they got inside her door; there was no helping it. So they sat in a near-empty restaurant looking each other over first, prolonging the pleasure.

This time, though, they were both distracted. He kept glancing at his watch, planning the use of his hours the following morning. Jennifer kept spinning the trifold beer menu in her fingers. "Have you called the police?"

"No. I don't think that's necessary. She's just—she's got some plan of her own."

"So it's some sort of walkabout. A vision quest."

"I don't know. There was this thing she did when she was eighteen. Maybe it's connected. Whatever it is, I have to find her."

"So you don't trust her to take care of herself."

"No, it's not that—"

"Isn't it?" Her dark eyes were wide and patient. They were sitting by the window with their parkas on because of the cold radiating from the glass. She kept her shoulders tucked neatly into the large shoulders of her coat. It was remarkable to realize that she, like he, was nearly forty now, with lines around her mouth, two miscarriages and a divorce behind her.

She sighed and shook her head. "I'm sorry. You take good care of her." She ran a hand through her hair. It was long and glossy brown and went behind her ears and down her back. As long as he'd known her, since high school, she'd worn it this way. He wanted to reach out for it, but this was the game they always played, pretending they were polite strangers.

"Does it ever occur to you that you spend a lot of time trying to fix your sister's life when there are a few things in your own life you need to get in order?" she asked.

He sat back. "You're making fun of me."

She spun the menu. "What shall we have? Blue Moon? House draft? What goes with pizza?"

"Red wine goes with pizza."

Then they were at her apartment. He had no memory of how they had gotten there, and as always they were pulling each other's clothes off slowly, concentrating with intensity on each button and hook. For Paul, nearsighted sex was what he preferred, zeroing in on one part of the body, attending to it with care. He was systematic. Nicole had often told him how compartmentalized his mind was. Did he ever try to think large things? she'd asked. Had he thought about the universe, life? Never. Almost never. It was better to think small, to see one thing at a time, to see it very well.

Jennifer's breasts were always a good place to start. They did not have Marion's consumptive pink and white but were a healthy brown on brown. Everything about her was practical and wise, from the way she entered her apartment, hanging her key, scarf, umbrella on their hooks, to when she chose to close her eyes and look away, to save them both embarrassment.

. . .

Later they sat at her kitchen counter drinking coffee, as though it were morning, not the middle of the night. "What's the plan?" Jennifer asked. "Where do we look first?"

Paul placed the datebook on the counter and smoothed the pages. "Two people she knows in Boston. I think one is her guru or something. The other I don't know. But they might be able to tell us."

"Here's how it will go," she said. "I'll go along tomorrow, see if I can help. And then I'll see you off, and you'll go home to your wife, and this will be the last time we'll meet like this."

"What?"

"Yes—I've decided. I decided before you arrived."

He got up and came around the corner, tried to put his arms around her. She accepted the embrace; her body was still warm and soft. She was not angry at him, just—decided. "Jenn, why—? What's changed?"

"Nothing's changed. I've just done some thinking, and I've made a decision. This is what grown-up people do, you know—they realize when they're hurting people. I'm too old to go on hurting people."

He tried to speak, but she put her hand on his mouth. "No—that's all we're going to say about it. Your sister is missing. We're going to find her, and then we're going to say good-bye, and everything will be all right."

He didn't sleep. He lay beside her, staring wide-eyed into the dark the way he used to do when he was a kid, wondering what it felt like to be dead. He would wonder how many stars were in the sky and whether they were really holes punched through the wall of night to heaven on the other side. That was the thought circling his head when the birds began to sing.

• • •

By nine, Paul was up and making scrambled eggs, sipping the stale coffee from the night before. Jennifer's apartment was a small, brick-walled space that looked out on tiny twisting streets and signs for gelato and cannoli. Jennifer put the frying pan in the sink and he went to the window, trying to imagine what she was doing behind his back. He ran his hands through his hair. It was sparse and fragile, and he usually tried not to touch it.

Using Nicole's cell phone, he called the first number. A rich Boston accent quickly responded: "Hello? Hello?" Paul waited in silence. Then the voice said, "Nicole, is that you?"

So Nicole wasn't with him. "This is Paul Hennessy. Nicole's brother. Who is this?"

"Paul?" The voice faltered. "Oh right, Paul—she's told me about you. This is Sean. I'm—Sean."

"Can I ask how you know Nicole?"

"Is she all right? Has something happened to her?"

"Well—we don't exactly know. She hasn't been answering her phone for a day or two. And I'm in town, trying to find her." He added with the old exasperation, "She's done this before."

"Well, we were, ya know, seeing each other. Not anymore, I guess. I haven't heard from her recently, either, and I couldn't get her on the phone. I was about to head down to New York myself."

"Can we talk? I'll drive over. Where do you live?"

In an hour they were rattling over the old plank bridge, into the outer rim of Weston. "Do you think he knows where she is?" asked Jennifer.

"Maybe." Paul stayed hunched over the wheel, searching for numbers on the houses hidden among the trees. He was finding it hard to look at Jennifer this morning. He'd gone over a few different strategies for what he'd say to her, but they all seemed to lead to the same inevitable conclusions. The fact was, he'd long been grateful for her goodness, her simple acceptance of the situation. He'd known it was rare. Well, now all his good karma had been used up.

They spotted the house, tall and skinny, too close to the marsh. Paul could tell it was a piece of crap before they reached the muddy driveway. With the cracked and flaking shingles, it looked like it was molting. Rotting planks everywhere. A gaping hole in the roof of the garage, probably snow damage. He gripped the wheel. "Pretty much what we expected."

Jennifer gave him a sad, amused look. "Take it easy, okay?"

At their knock, the door cracked open and a whiskery sideburned face poked out. "You're Paul?"

"Nice to meet you. This is my friend Jennifer." Paul didn't stumble over what term to use this time. Sean came out onto the deck, closing the door carefully behind himself, and they shook hands. "I'm really worried, you know," Sean said. The accent was rich, friendly to Paul's ear. "I don't know what happened. She stopped calling."

"Did you—have an argument?"

"No. Not really. We were okay. I thought we were okay. She seemed afraid of something, but I don't know what. I tried to get her to tell me, but she wouldn't." He rubbed his eyes. There was something Paul hadn't expected in them: anguish.

"We're pretty sure she's not in danger. She's done this before," Jennifer said.

Sean kept his eyes on Paul. "That so?"

Paul turned away. Suddenly the impatient speech he'd prepared, the story of Nicole's case history, didn't seem right. "Yes, well, it was only the one time. When she was eighteen. And there was a reason." He looked restlessly about himself, unsure of how much to say. How do you gauge the intimacy of another? He remembered meeting Jules a few times before the accident. He could tell from the look on the boy's face that he'd had his hands all over his sister. Sean was not so easy to read.

"I hope your father's doing all right," Sean said.

"My father?"

"Nicole said she was helping take care of him."

"My father's been dead for over ten years." It was embarrassing, to be caught up in someone else's lie. "Can we come inside?"

Sean hesitated. "I live alone here, and without Nicole—" He was stammering as he pushed against the door, trying to get it open. "I've been rearranging things—"

They had to slide in sideways past the jammed door. It was a large space, a classic Victorian high-ceilinged living room, but antiques filled most of it. Old dark sea-captain furniture, blue satin uphol-stered couches, teak wardrobes, vintage lime-green fridges—at least two that Paul could see—crowded one another in the room. On top of various surfaces were vintage toys, Matchbox cars, Superman comics, and baseball gloves; robot penny banks and plaster statues of Saint Francis; signed baseballs, antique barometers, ratchet sets. Tools and toys and precious old things. The sound of clocks ticking all around them.

"Jesus," said Paul. "Jesus, Mary, and Joseph."

"I know. I had this furniture from my parents and my ex-wife and it was all in the basement, but that started to flood. I'm still figuring it all out. Look at this," he said quickly, pointing to an antique chest of drawers. "That's beautiful old wood there, good unadulterated cherry. You can tell by the joinings that it's old. There's a maker's mark some-where. And these—" He held up some baseball cards. "Really rare. And there's a real market for religious iconography—" He touched the herd of plaster saints, then stopped, and the frantic air dissipated, leaving only weariness. "I know."

Paul could see, distantly, that this kind of clutter could be com-forting to people. Even now Sean was touching pieces of furniture and telling stories about them: this vase, his mother's. That swishing-tail cat clock, his grandmother's. "What do you think's happened to her?" Sean said. "The last time we spoke, I thought something was wrong. We have to find her."

A heavy rain had started to fall. It was whipping the windows steadily. Paul imagined the creaking house slowly beginning to flood, its artifacts, its family history going under. This man had his own baggage to sort out. "Let me know if you hear from her," Paul said. "I'll do the same."

. . .

Safe in the car, Paul and Jennifer sat for a while in silence. "Jesus," Paul said finally. "Nicole sure knows how to pick 'em."

"She does," said Jennifer softly.

She meant it differently than he did. "Oh, come on," he said. "What?"

"You can't honestly think *that guy* is good for—"

"I don't know, Paul." Jennifer shook her bracelets down her wrist, a sharp, irritated move. "I believe he loves her."

Paul swung the gearshift into reverse. He wanted to argue with her more, but he sensed that it wouldn't do much good. As he drove, he dialed the other Boston number, and a solemn-voiced man picked up. Paul told him they were looking for Nicole. "I think we should speak in person," the man said.

When they entered the little café in Waltham, Paul knew immediately who he was. The man was by the window, sipping tea, his large frame swallowed in navy robes.

As their glances met, he rose. "Honored to meet you," he said. Paul offered his hand. The man clasped and then bowed over it, a strange hybrid greeting. His shaved head was ruddy and freckled with sun. His hands were smooth and very dry. His gaze was direct to the point of discomfort. "Nicole has told me much about you," he said, and they all sat down.

"You're the—spiritual leader," said Paul finally.

He paused with his cup halfway to his mouth. "I have been Nicole's teacher for many years. The word, if you please, is *roshi*."

"Yes—er, *roshi*. As I said on the phone, we haven't heard from Nicole for a few days, and we're getting worried."

"I am also concerned. She has made troubling choices on her journey."

Paul inched forward in his seat. "Am I to understand that you have sent her on some kind of journey?"

"Perhaps."

Careful, careful, Paul thought. They were speaking in codes, dancing some kind of dance whose steps he could only guess. "Where did you send her?"

"A journey can be an excursion in either a mental or a physical space. It can even be a journey of memory. Nicole could have gone on all three."

"Do you know where she is right now?"

"If I did, do you think I would tell you? Am I sure I could trust you not to interfere, not to swoop in and snatch her away?"

"It's not like her to leave without giving me some sort of message."

"Maybe she did, but you weren't listening."

Paul sat back in his chair and laced his fingers together, pressing until the knuckles were white. Riddles. Abstractions. He wanted something so simple, so direct. He wanted his sister here, safe. Even with the crazy dragon skirts and the hippie hair. And this insufferable man—sipping his tea, pretending to be the omniscient narrator of his sister's life—had the answer but wouldn't give it.

He wondered what to ask next. He had to outwit this man, trap him in his own verbal cul-de-sacs. He had to be plainspoken and direct. "It seems that you're deliberately obfuscating," he said. "Nicole talks to me. Nicole would tell me if she was leaving. We talk to each other."

"It may be difficult for a nonpractitioner to understand," the *roshi* said. "But Zen students are always looking for the place that is human experience without words, without talk. It takes hard work to find this place. You must break ties with anyone who prevents you from reaching it. And when the conditions are right, it comes upon you suddenly. Suddenly you get a lightning bolt." He tapped his forehead, smiling scornfully. "Only some people ever experience it. Maybe if you pray, you might feel it. I wouldn't expect you to understand."

Under the table, Jennifer gripped his knee. "What do you teach her?" Paul asked. "What are you telling her?"

"I'm afraid I can't divulge that sort of information. The training my students undertake is confidential."

"You're not a doctor."

"The Buddha called himself a physician of the soul. I take my role no less seriously."

Paul had felt sadness less than an hour ago in Sean's crowded living room; now he could feel the beginnings of rage. "I need to know where she is, and I think you know more about that than you're telling us. Now, are you going to keep fucking with me?"

To his surprise, the man did not blink. "No, I am not fucking with you, Mr. Hennessy. I am Nicole's master, and that relationship is for life. My loyalty is to her, as hers is to me."

"What is all this master and student B.S.? What the hell does that mean? Are you some sort of—creep?" His voice was growing louder. "What have you done to her?"

The man turned his head to the side as if preparing for a blow. "You wouldn't understand."

"You call yourself a holy man? How about not lying to us and try-ing to help one of your followers?"

"I am not lying to you any more than you are lying to yourself."

Paul half-rose in his seat. "I don't have time for Zen mind games right now."

"It's no game. Nicole has mentioned you to me; I know you are married. This woman is not your wife, though; you introduced her as your friend. Yet she has had her hand on your knee under the table. You call my relationship with Nicole bullshit. But you are the one who is lying." The man rose, pulling his robes about himself with a final, satisfied tug. "I know what is best for Nicole. You'd be wise not to interfere." And he left the café, Paul mute in his wake.

He was still for only a moment. He got up silently and followed the man out of the shop and around the corner to the parking lot. It was still raining lightly, and the *roshi* was fumbling with an umbrella. Paul wanted to grab the umbrella and hurl it to the ground. He wanted to smack him across the face, see blood in his little tea-stained teeth. But there was still the choirboy in him somewhere, the boy who bowed his head to priests and holy men. He watched the *roshi* get into his ancient rust-colored car and struggle to back out of his narrow space, adjusting and correcting. Then he drove away.

Jennifer had caught up to him behind the coffee shop. "What's going on?"

"Nothing."

She stopped. "What an asshole."

"I don't know," he said. He took her hand, and they walked quickly away in the rain. Maybe he needed to go home. Maybe he needed to let Nicole lead her own strange life.

. . .

Paul lay on the bed. He could hear Jennifer putting things in his bag. "Where will you look next?" she asked.

"I've got to get back to work." He sighed.

"Maybe she doesn't want to be found. Maybe it's time to just—let her go."

She was at the foot of the bed, folding a sweater and jamming it into the bottom of his suitcase. "Sometimes people don't want to be found. My uncle was like that. My father's brother. He was an addict, a drifter. My family did everything they could. They sent him to rehab, to the family priest, you name it. He disappeared when he was in his twenties. Twenty years later, my father stumbled over his feet. He was sleeping on a grate in Copley Square. My father begged him to come home. My uncle smiled, shook his hand, and walked away."

Paul sat up. He felt cold, but he wasn't sure if he was angry or afraid.

He remembered the warm rush of Nicole's little-girl voice in his ear, when they were both young and staring at the stars, when she whispered to him what it must be like to be in space: it had to be cold, and dark, but darker than any darkness you knew, and quiet, but quieter than the deepest silence. He remembered her questions when he was a little older and she thought he knew everything: what's it like to be tall, and what's it like to fall in love, and what happens to us when we die? And then a little older, impatient with his advice, his hectoring: I know there's a part of you that understands me.

"This isn't like that," he said. "Nicole is not like that. Something has frightened her. I don't know what it is, but I know her." And he said suddenly, fiercely knowing it to be true, "Nicole doesn't want me to let her go."

Jennifer paused; his hands were on her hands. "All right," she said softly.

"Jenn," he said. "Aren't we good together? Can't we just keep going the way we have for now?"

She bit her lip. "How can this be our lives?" she asked.

She went to her desk and pulled out a piece of paper. An e-mail printout. He struggled to read the chain of messages. First an e-mail from himself to Jennifer. Confirming the time of some previous visit, asking her to wear the blue dress and chill the beer. Something more risqué below that, some pillow talk. And at the top of the e-mail chain, another e-mail from his account, sent to Jennifer:

> *Dear person,*
> *Whoever you are, please leave my Dad alone. Leave ALL*
> *OF US alone.*
> *Sincerely,*
> *June*

. . .

It was Sunday and Paul was supposed to be on a two o'clock bus to New York, but instead he and Jennifer sat in her car outside the Peaceful Healing Zen Center. "I don't think he knows anything, Paul," Jennifer said.

He didn't think the guy knew much, either. But he wasn't completely sure. He had to be sure.

"You'll miss the last bus."

"I can go tomorrow."

"You just don't want to go."

"Wait." The *roshi* came out. He was still wearing his navy robes, but he had a Red Sox jacket over them and a newsie cap covered his shaved head. He was carrying a cloth laundry hamper.

They watched him slip the key under a loose brick by the door, then head down the street. "Come on, he might come back," Paul said. They retrieved the key and entered the building, quickly checking rooms. A front studio, with a stack of floor cushions, a back room, a janitor's closet, another back room. He hurried down the narrow halls.

"Where are we going, Paul?" Jennifer said.

There wasn't much to see. No basement, no people hiding, no devotees in chains. Just a converted storefront, a collection of nearly empty rooms. Here was the back exit, which opened onto a gravel parking lot shared with the neighboring stores. Beyond that, a wall of chicken wire and an unexpectedly lush proliferation of bushes and trees.

"That's the community garden," Jennifer said. "You can rent plots there." She pointed: little fenced-off territories, with early spring buds of onion shoots and daffodils.

"Come on." Paul lifted the latch on the chicken-wire door. Here was a narrow pathway through the plots, winding its way on through the damp green. They could see fresh footprints in the damp earth. He'd been here.

"I don't like this, Paul." The air moved loudly through the branches. Just a few steps down the path, they were violently surrounded by green, isolated from the street.

"I don't like it, either," he said. "But I have to see." He started walking quickly down the path. It was too wet for gardeners to be out; he was alone in the sylvan quiet. The wild bushes were tall around him, but the plots themselves were mostly stark black soil, nothing sprouting yet. He followed the muddy footprints down one grassy path, then another. Here must be the man's little plot: inside a roofed enclosure, on tables was a circle of bonsai trees. Paul paused for a moment, admiring the precise proportions of a tiny pine, a minute spruce. He could appreciate the aesthetic pleasure of these delicate things. Beside them was spread an array of tools—wire cutters, snub-nosed pliers. And now he could see the technique behind the artistry: black wires spiraled tightly about the slender fingerling trunks, embracing them cruelly.

He looked around himself in silence.

Down one narrow turn stood a long shed with a hole in its roof, presumably damaged by storms and snow. When he got to the shed, he saw a flimsy bicycle lock on the door. His pulse quickened.

A rotting hoe was leaning up against the side of the shed. He used it like a crowbar, leveraging the door open. And then he was swinging at it, tearing chunks out of the old wood, sending the lock flying.

He had to wait for the dust and splinters to settle before he could see inside. He craned his head through the darkness: a collapsing gardener's shed, full of rusting tools. A hand mower and a rake, another hoe and trowels and a spade. Nothing else.

In the parking lot, Jennifer was waiting for him. They stood wondering what to do. Paul looked around at the rear walls of the familiar dusty stores, their loading docks and dumpsters. The smell of dollar slices and laundromat in the air. Cold rain slipping down his collar.

And then the back door was opening and the *roshi* was coming out with a trash bag, heading for the dumpsters. And Paul was running toward him. He grabbed the shoulders of the *roshi*'s robes and shook him. Under the robes, he wasn't large; he was light, and seemed to rattle inside like a dry seedpod. Not much to him, after all.

"I swear, I don't know where she is," he gasped. "I went looking for her the same way you did. Two days ago, I went to New York to bring her back. But she was gone."

Paul imagined what he might do. He could see, as he had just a few other times in his life, how violence could happen between two people, how it could be simple and easy. He could imagine his fist connecting with the man's mouth, how the little bones might break in his own hand. The smell of blood filling the air. Bright clean splash of pain.

"You're wrong," Paul said finally. The *roshi* seemed to be shrinking by the moment, disappearing into his voluminous robes. "You don't know a thing about me. Or her."

He knew that this puffy-robed bastard had no idea where she was. Somehow this holy fool had lost his hold on her, the same way Paul had.

"Do you?" the *roshi* panted.

Paul released him slowly. He and Jennifer returned to her car and sat in the ticking silence for a long time. Jennifer's hand on his arm was trembling.

"I think I can still make the late train," he said.

His knees were shaking beneath him. There were things he needed to tell someone, things that only Nicole might understand. He wanted to pray, but it was hard when you weren't used to doing it. *Let the brothers and the sisters find each other, and deliver us—* He did not finish the thought.

NICOLE

I t was just in time for the evening rush at South Station. Nicole watched warmed-over food glow red under the heat lamps like coals in a dozen home fires. She walked quickly, looking all around herself for faces she knew, for her Master snapping at her heels.

Here, everyone was waiting, like her. The parents with kids, letting them eat pizza because their train was delayed; the businessmen rapt with their phones; the grandparents with their carpetbags; the college students visiting home. The smell of salt, coffee, doughnuts, socks. In the corners, people sat on the floor with their hands out. Here, Nicole could press herself into the crush before the giant black flipboard, the board of God, the board of missed or kept appointments, of dinners sitting cold or still warm, of husbands and wives looking at their watches and then out the window. She could jostle among the others and be wrapped in people, surrounded by the warmth and pressure of their worries.

But a public place like this wasn't safe. She waited tensely for her commuter rail connection, watching a chess grandmaster sweep a circle of tables, claiming pawns and rooks from the boards of hopeful players. He did not even look up to see whom he was defeating.

She could picture her Master striding through the crowds, hands hidden in his wide-sleeved robes. The people would part for him. He would not need to be violent; he need not even take her hand. He need only wait, and she would come to him, because he had her, he had her always. And if she paused to think about it, remember that all of her secrets and private shames were now his—she might lose her strength entirely.

. . .

In Waban, the key to her childhood house wasn't hiding under a flower pot or a stray brick. Of course, why would it still be there? Did she think that no time had passed since they'd pulled all those white sheets over the furniture, locked up and driven away with the promise to sell?

She told herself, You have to be smart. You have to be wily. You have to survive, the way you used to know how to do.

She stood on the old brick stoop for a little while, considering, while clouds gathered over her head.

It took her until the rain started to gather the nerve to smash a window. Drenched instantly in the downpour, she chose one in the living room, hammered a pane out with a rock, then unlatched it and hefted it open. *These damn warped windows.* She had to use almost all her strength to heave and wrench it open, marshaling the last of it to crawl inside.

She stayed on all fours on the floor for a long moment, listening warily to the sounds of the empty house, of rain drumming on the roof, pattering through the broken windowpane. She stayed still, dripping on the dusty hardwood floor.

Besides a cleaner or real-estate agent or two, and occasional visits from Paul, she doubted anyone had been here in years. The house was perfectly preserved, still and empty except for its ghostly sheeted chairs and tables. She swept one sheet off the couch and wrapped it around herself to still her shivering.

When she was a little drier and braver, she walked through the house, trailing the sheet behind her. Paul had taken some furniture, but you could fit only so much into a New York townhouse. She went through each room, trailing her fingers across the covered walnut backs of chairs. Here was the dark, empty dining room, the den with its white shelves bare of books, the kitchen with its dated pink tile. She crept upstairs, listening for the ghosts of sneakers pounding, the hair dryer going in the bathroom, her mother humming *Que sera, sera* . . .

Her room was untouched. Here was the narrow little bed she had grown up in, with its headboard of dark glossy spindles; here was the Monet poster still stuck with art gum to the wall, the aging mirror going spotty in places. She looked at herself, wet and ragged and with sharp ravines carved beneath her eyes. What was that corner of something tucked behind the frame? She pulled gently, extracting a photograph of herself and Paul in bathing suits, standing by the shore of a lake she didn't remember, squinting lazily into the sun.

The house would keep her safe for a while.

The power had been disconnected, and as night drew on she sat in the blackness, bundled in sheets. She had to make her plan. Perhaps she could get away on a technicality, some forgotten rule in the master-student handbook; or maybe bolder action was required.

If the neighbors saw someone squatting in the house, they'd call Paul; then the jig would be up. So she lay low that night, sneaking out only once, near dawn, to get a burrito from the all-night place at the bottom of the hill. She saw that St. Augustine's had finally been demolished; caution tape and a chain-link fence announced the future home of Evergreen Apartments. She remembered the priest at the Communion on the Common who'd said that sacred ground could not be unconsecrated. So what was it now?

In her closet, behind the loose board, she found her trove of books on Buddhism stolen from the library. She spread them out on the carpet and flipped through the pages, reading her scribbled notes in the margins. She read urgently, looking for clues. What had she said to herself when she was young and enlightenment was just around the next block in the neighborhood? Here was her notebook of collected sayings of Western sages like Gary Snyder and Bertrand Russell, all those writers lusting after Shangri-La. She read a copied-out quotation from Peter Matthiessen: *Soon the child's clear eye is clouded over by ideas and opinions, preconceptions and abstractions. . . . The sun glints through the pines, and the heart is pierced in a moment of beauty and strange pain, like a memory of paradise. After that day . . . we become seekers.*

Next to it, she had written *the living light!!!*

And here she had copied down a Thich Nhat Hanh quotation in her little girl's handwriting as carefully as a catechism: *Our own life is the instrument with which we experiment with truth.* She could see the budding runaway here, the hunger to make her life a testament to that daring search. How had she possibly found the courage to walk out of this bedroom, out that front door, get into a car, and drive away?

In her parents' room, an abandoned bed frame still leaned up on the wall. She opened the drawers of the built-in vanity one by one, finding a stack of old *Cuisine* magazines. This was the magazine that had run her mother's food column. She flipped through the pages, startled to find a photo of herself sneaking a faded strawberry out of a bowl even with her eyes. Far above, her father lowered a steaming plate. His eyes glowed blue, the only vibrant color remaining. She closed the magazine and shoved it back into its drawer.

For a moment she thought, Sean could come. He could protect me. He could get me out of this. She imagined it briefly: how nice it would be to stand behind him while he delivered a stern, threatening pronouncement, pounding a fist into a palm, saying the things men could say to each other. *If you ever come near her again . . .*

But she rejected the thought. What could he possibly do? He was not Jules, not her strongman for hire. Besides, her Master could not be intimidated by tough talk. He held her on a different leash. She listened to rain lashing the windows through the afternoon while she planned and fretted.

She didn't know how to arm herself.

But she knew whom she needed to ask.

• • •

In the fall of their last year together, she padded into the back hall for her private meeting with the Master, and the door to his meeting room was closed. It hadn't been closed in years. She pressed her ear to the door and heard her Master speaking, delivering a lecture on emptiness. Who was in there, receiving his lesson? She couldn't interrupt. She waited while the afternoon shadows crept across the floor, listening to the familiar hum of his voice, the beginning of the Heart Sutra chant. The body is emptiness and emptiness is the body. *She chanted along, working her prayer beads in her fingers.*

The chant broke, and a girl's high, bubbling laugh spilled under the door. Her Master answered it with a wry chuckle. There was someone in there who knew how to make him laugh. She worked the beads faster and faster. Her pulse, throbbing in her ears, set the time. It felt like she was a kid again, listening in dark hallways while her parents fought about things she didn't understand.

The door opened and Helen, one of the newer girls, stepped out. "Oh. It's Nicole, right? Sorry to keep you waiting."

She scrambled up; her foot was asleep, and she almost fell over. "No problem, I was just passing—" They both knew how long the private meeting had gone on. Whatever she planned to say was foolish.

"He's all yours," Helen said, and smiled a narrow cat's-eye smile, and tripped off down the hall, her skinny legs knocking together in their ankle boots, every detail of her walk, the float of her hair, the young slump of her posture suddenly exact in Nicole's vision.

"Ah, Nicole." Her Master was in the doorframe, a private amusement still on his lips. "We'll have to be brief today."

· · ·

That was when she first recognized that all the patience in the world might not be enough to keep his attention. That all the spiritual purity of their relationship might just boil down to desire and need.

Her escape plans might have begun then. But he wasn't about to let her go so easily, she saw now. Love was about possession. What a man really wanted was to know that you were his, and for you to surrender, gladly, to that ownership. He'd shaped her like clay, and she'd let him; there was so little left that wasn't his.

· · ·

In the afternoon, she walked to the station and caught a train into the city. She got off near Boston University and walked down the quiet back streets of student housing. Each house looked the same, in equal states of neglect. She wasn't sure if she would remember which was the right one. But no—there was the house with the sagging deck, a ribbon of caution tape strung haphazardly across the railing. She stilled a deep trembling in her legs and picked her way up the muddy lawn, knocking on the door.

A young man answered. She didn't remember his face; students moved through these houses so swiftly. Could he have been at the Christmas party? "I'm looking for Helen," she said firmly.

He turned his head to yell, but she was already coming down the stairs. Helen. She was in a hoodie and jeans, her face unwashed and sleepy, her hair drawn into an oily ponytail. But still sharp-featured and lovely. Deadly. "This is a surprise," she said.

Nicole drew a deep breath. "I need your help."

Helen belted a coat and they walked slowly around the block, hands in their pockets. "I thought you'd left," Helen said.

"I did."

"Our *zazen* isn't the same without you," Helen said. She worked at the sash of her coat. "I hope you haven't stopped practicing. If you started your own Zendo, I know people would come."

"I need to know what happened after I left. I need to know what *he* thinks."

"After you left? Things got weird."

"Weird how?"

She tucked a long ribbon of hair behind her ear. "He's crazy about you. He doesn't really have any interest in anything else. He was asking everyone if they had a number for you. I think he finally got it from Buffy. Then he started telling me things."

"What kind of things?"

"About his former lives, he claimed. He said that in another life, he had been a warrior and killed people. And now he had a karmic debt he had to repay in this life, and he had to save lives and protect them from harm. He got very angry and said, Am I not tending to the sick? All of you, you're all sick. You'd die without me." Helen shivered. "He really thinks that. He thinks that losing you would—well, he thinks you'd die. But he also said that without you, his teaching was meaningless. You were the one he was going to perfect. Listen, the only secret I can give you is, don't go see him, Nicole. Just don't. Walk away."

Nicole stiffened, trying to hide the cold that had slid through her body, seemed to lie right next to her bones. "What are you afraid will happen?" She didn't know if Helen could be trusted.

The girl took her hand. Helen, she saw, did not want to be cruel, had only been trying it on as something that grown-up women did, and this small thing, this hand in hers, this urgent rush of her voice in Nicole's ear, was unexpectedly touching. "I'm afraid that if you see him, you won't be able to control yourself. I don't know. I'm afraid he'll say one word and you'll fall in line."

She swallowed. "Maybe you're right. Maybe I will."

"Stay the night here and you'll be safe."

Helen was asking her not to go, trying to protect her the same way Paul would if she let him. Boston traffic fled by. College students were waking up in the late afternoon, planning their nightly bar crawls, their frattish parties. Nicole remembered stepping out her door at this time as a teenager, the sun going, all the danger, the excitement, the promise in the air. She knew she was going to go to him. Nothing could prevent it now.

Helen could see that, too. "Nicole, if you're walking down the road and you see the Buddha—"

"Kill the Buddha. I know." She pressed Helen's small white hands in her own. Then she walked away without looking back. One more Irish good-bye, for luck.

Dear Sean,

When the Buddha is at the end of his life, he lies down in a wooded grove and rests his head on his hand. He is surrounded by an army of grief-stricken monks. Closest of all is Ananda, the monk with the eidetic memory, the one who knows all the stories and will recite them for others. That is why all the Buddhist Scripture begins with the phrase "Thus have I heard." Ananda has been with the Buddha for his entire adult life. He has followed him on every journey, has faithfully soaked up every word. And now he weeps.

"It's okay, Ananda," the Buddha tells him. "It's okay. Don't cry." Even he cannot prevent the journey that happens next. But for all their teaching, the parting doesn't get any easier. Ananda knows all of the stories, and when you know them all, you can't help but fall in love.

I know you aren't reading this letter because I'm not sending it. I haven't sent any of them. But I write you anyway, telling you the story. I tell and tell and tell.

Do you remember when you held me in your arms and asked me to stay? And I couldn't?

Will you forgive me for needing to go?

Will you think about the way my hand fits inside your hand like two seashells? Or maybe you'll think about how afraid I was when we were walking on that steep, rocky jetty by the ocean. I wasn't afraid of falling. I was afraid when I looked at you with the wind whipping your hair. I saw how easily my happiness could become wrapped up in yours. You knew I was afraid and held my arm but you didn't know why.

HOME

Through the window of the Peaceful Healing Zen Center, Nicole could see the afternoon class wrapping up; the students were coming out of their meditation as from ether, blinking and dreamy. She could see Buffy, lean and fit in her tracksuit, checking her pulse; George and Frances, yawning in sync.

Amy with the heavy black mascara and the dry, amused smile, Amy with cancer, was no longer there.

At the front of the room, the Master raised his hands and spoke. Nicole watched his lips move without sound. At any moment he could glance out the window and see her staring in. The danger thrilled her.

She stepped away before anyone recognized her, but turned back at the corner to watch them leave. They moved in a block along the sidewalk at first, laughing and talking animatedly. The first feeling after *zazen* was elation: you were liberated, giddy, overflowing with words. Then you got quiet. She watched the group break apart, students heading for their cars. If the session was bad, you walked with your face blank, you pawed restlessly at your phone as you sat in traffic. At home you picked a fight with your lover, couldn't bear folding laundry, stared at TV without seeing until bed. You were a failure, Buddhism was nonsense, you had better ways to waste your time.

But if the session was good—

Then you kept blinking in the late afternoon light and stumbling a bit, like you'd just come out of a movie theater. Colors hurt and sounds stroked your skin. You smelled onions frying at the restaurant next door and felt hungry for them as though you had discovered hunger. Crossing the bridge, you paused and watched the river glitter in the sunset and the little boats scudding near the horizon, and you kept having to pull yourself back in, because you seemed to be diffusing outward, ready to join up with the jumping atoms all around you, bleeding out into the bay.

Nicole watched the students get into their cars. And then the Master was walking down the sidewalk, his sash loose and his robe flapping, his arms wide in welcome. "Nicole. So very glad to have you back. I knew you'd return." He took her hand in both of his own and pulled her gently down the street, talking all the time. "We'll have to make up for lost time. You've endangered our mission, but we can refind the path together. We have so many things to discuss."

"We do," she said.

"Sometimes we must enter a great silence," he said. "I understand. But we must then learn again to speak."

That voice! Her body responded to it, like church bells, like the smell of incense or Jules's leather jacket. It was imprinted on her, had worked its way deeply inside. He was leading her back into the

Zen center, back through the meditation room, passing through the smoke of candles just snuffed. She couldn't quite free herself from his tugging hand. Now they were in the narrow back hall. He was trying to lead her into the private meeting room. There she'd kneel and accept her punishment for her disappearance; there he'd take her head in his lap and slowly, slowly forgive her. He'd take his time, forgiving her.

She planted her feet. "No. I won't go in there."

"Nicole," he said, full of tenderness. "You're confused. You're upset. Come with me. Tell me everything."

"Not in there."

"Fine." He led her past the meeting room. Now they were going down another narrow hallway, one she'd never been down before, and he was opening a door into a tiny private apartment. Here was where the Master lived.

It was suitably austere: a sofa bed pulled out, the bed neatly made; a kitchenette with tiles of ivory and beige; a television in the corner, a dresser with a small cabinet shrine. A calendar on the wall with pictures of a Japanese rock garden. A cigar tin overflowing with receipts. It was not the velvet-rimmed den of a corrupt bishop, nor the barren cell of a monk. More like the garret of an aging pensioner: unmistakably humble, unspeakably sad.

The Master sat and patted the pulled-out sofa bed, the tidy hospital tuck of its worn blanket. "Come here. Come and tell me where you've been."

She didn't move.

His eyes narrowed. At last he seemed to understand that something had shifted between them that could not be rolled back into place. "It doesn't matter if you won't talk to me," he said. "I already know everything. I know why you ran away, all those years ago. I know about Jules. There's nothing you can hide from me; I know it all. I know what you're ashamed of. And I know what you need."

"That's not true." It came out breathlessly, not at all what she'd intended. "I have to leave. I know you think you have to save me. But nobody can save me. We can't do this anymore."

He rose, grasping her wrists. "I know what you were looking for, and I'm the only one who can give it to you. If you leave, I can take it away. I can take the living light. All the people you've loved, everything good you've ever thought or felt or done. Your silly little dreams and needs. They all come through me."

"Why?" She was seventeen again, querulous and terrified.

"Because you gave it to me. That's what you have to do, to achieve enlightenment. You have to give away everything. You have to offer yourself up." He stroked her cheek, tucking her loose hair tenderly behind her ears. "And you have been very good. You have given me everything, and now I can do what I want with it." He was kissing her brow gently, his voice soft. "Little *theri*. Little chick. I love you. Isn't that what you want?"

His voice filled her, low but everywhere, like distant thunder. She looked at the cracker crumbs on the table, the veneer of dust on the Buddha statue, the scummy little window through which he saw his world. Then she pushed him away. "You're full of shit," she said, saying each word slowly, so he would understand.

He watched her, his eyes narrowing cunningly. "Don't you want to learn? Don't you want enlightenment?" And after a pause: "Don't you love me?"

She thought about it. *"Mu,"* she said finally, and made for the door.

He knew what she meant, and that he was losing her, maybe that she was already lost. He lunged up at her, his arms around her. He was too strong, he was bearing her back to the bed, whispering sweet things in her ear, kissing her neck, making promises that he never would have made before. *I love you, you will be my only, we will live together, I'll be loyal.* She reached out wildly, flailing for anything solid. Against the dresser leaned the *keisaku*, the teaching stick. She grabbed it and cracked it against the side of his face. He cried out and she whipped it again, saw blood running down his forehead. He fell to his knees, clutching his face. She stood swaying over him, a position she had never held in all the years of their intimacy.

· · ·

Paul was in the front yard of the old house when she returned. He was standing by the FOR SALE sign, wearing jeans and an old sweatshirt, his hands jammed in the kangaroo pouch. She hadn't seen him in such casual clothes since he was a teenager.

And Jennifer was with him. Of course, Jennifer: the girl he always seemed to refind. She was leaning on the sign in a belted trench coat, gazing stoically at the smashed windowpane. Her hair was long and straight and dark like it had been in high school, but it was a shock to see her with the lined, measured face of an adult. She'd had her own growing up to do, her own sadnesses to bear. She and Paul stood together but not touching, shy and distant.

Paul moved quickly, wrapping Nicole up in a long embrace. "You're safe," he said. "Dear Lord, you're safe."

"I'm safe," she agreed.

They kicked at the mud, out of talk. "Where's the cat?" he asked.

"Oh, Kukai! So you did go by my apartment."

"Of course I did. I was looking for you, idiot."

"I left him with a friend." She'd given Jocelyn the spare key to her apartment and asked her to take him. She knew the cat was safe in her hands; the same qualities that had won Nicole's trust would win over her stray, too.

"I thought you might have let him go," said Paul. "You know, liberated him."

"You would think that."

"Well? Why didn't you?"

She sighed. "Too much rabies out there."

"I looked everywhere for you," Paul said. "Where were you?"

"Around." She didn't tell him that the broken window was her responsibility, or that she'd been hiding right under his nose.

"I even thought you were with that old teacher of yours," said Paul.

"Who?"

"He said he was your master." Paul pointed to the object still clenched in her hand: a long, whiplike length of wood, like a yardstick, with Japanese kanji written on one side "What's that?"

She'd almost forgotten about the *keisaku*.

"It's my walking stick," she said.

"Did you tell him you were leaving?" he asked.

"I told him—*mu*."

"What does that mean?"

She could have explained that in the first koan of a Zen student, there was a question and *mu* was the answer, and all of Zen life is a struggle to figure out why *mu* was the answer. *Mu* was "no." It was "nothing." And it was "no more."

But there were things he wasn't about to understand. "It's a joke. A Zen joke," she said.

He was quiet for a while. "Listen, there's something else. Marion and I—we're going to separate. Marion wants a divorce."

"Oh, Paul. I'm sorry."

"I know." She heard the cost of every word in his voice. "No one to blame but—you know," he said, and took Jennifer's hand.

"We talked to someone else," said Jennifer. It was the first time she'd spoken. "He's waiting for you to come back."

"His name's Sean," said Paul.

Nicole nodded. "That's where I have to go now. I'm going, okay?"

"Hey, don't need my permission," he said.

. . .

At Sean's door she hesitated, watching her cab retreat. The curtains all were drawn; the house seemed to have slipped a little more into the mud. Spring snows had stained the walls.

She knocked, and Sean cracked the door open. Then he stepped outside and pulled her to him, squeezing her right through her puffy jacket. "You're back," he said.

"Of course I'm back." Tears were coming down her cheeks.

"But listen." She pushed him gently back. "Listen, I want to tell the truth. I want you to understand."

He nodded, cleared his throat. "I want the same thing."

"So, I—" She fumbled inside her jacket. "I haven't told you much about where I've been or what I am. And you deserve to know." She brought out a sheaf of papers. Letters she'd been writing since she'd met Sean. Scraps she'd been writing and adding to since she was a teenager. The fables and notes and stories. This one on the Fire Sermon; this one about the Buddha's enlightenment. This one about the followers, this one about leaving home. Her life story. They were a diary of sorts, these stories she liked to tell. They were the things she'd wondered when she was afraid or joyful or lonely. "I want you to read these. All of them. It'll explain—hopefully it'll explain things. And I'll fill in any gaps."

He took the sheaf of papers, flipping through them. "Okay." He blew out his cheeks. "Okay." He pressed the papers to his chest. She loved how he wrinkled the papers that she'd kept so carefully. "And if fair's fair, then I have to show you something, too. Can't really put it off much longer."

"What's that?"

He gestured behind himself, to the waiting house. She'd wondered why they weren't going in. "You've got to know—look, you've got to know what I'm about, too. I don't let go of things that easy. I'm sorting through it. I'm still figuring it out. I want you to go in without me and take a good look around. And if it's too much, then—you can go."

She started to protest, then fell silent. She could tell by his eyes, by the way he wouldn't look at her or the house, the way he gazed into the distance, that she would have to do this.

"All right," she said. And with a heave she opened the door.

The house had become a rabbit warren, den upon den of antiques. She tried to get her bearings, figure out what all the stuff was. She floundered on the back of a sofa, slipping down. She craned her head back to see the tops of his skyscrapers, a miniature Manhattan of things: dark walnut card tables and French armoires. Nantucket baskets piled with vintage toys. Enamel beer mugs with wild geese etched on the sides. Whaling paintings and whale-oil lamps. Family Bibles. Handfuls of wartime Bazooka gum and old-timey cigarette ads. City blocks of Archie comics. Scattered everywhere, she saw as she began to climb and probe, were things that a child would like. Lead soldiers and blushing Kewpie dolls. G.I. Joes and cowboy sets. Threadbare Steiff animals. Halloween masks. Jars of colored marbles, the cat's eyes and tiger's eyes, the shimmering blue aggies and red devils.

She wondered, After the churches closed, where did men like Sean go? And where were the boys who had been abused? You couldn't see it on their faces; you couldn't know. Some of them had taken their own lives. Some of them were alcoholics. Some of them hadn't told their wives and children and never would. Some of them, maybe, collected things. There was this Catholic way of thinking that you locked whatever sadness was yours away. But she had to reach out anyway. She'd love more.

Through the house's narrow tunnels and dark labyrinths, she found a small corner of the living room that hadn't been filled, under a rolltop desk. It was just big enough for her. She pulled herself into the little cavern and sat in a half-lotus, breathing in the dust.

"Sean," she called. She was ready now. "Sean, come find me."

EPILOGUE

The meditation space is a barn in a forgotten orchard that she's renting, and Sean's helping her to fix it up, insulate it, get the little families of mice out of the rafters. It still smells sweetly of years of apple stores. Her students come by word of mouth—friends of Buffy's and, increasingly, college students that Helen sends her way. For a modest donation they'll come for a class or a private session with her, a taste of ritual they miss from a former religious life, or a completely new exploration.

You take a breath. You turn something you love over and over in your hands, studying it. It could be your lover or your child or your-self, your mother or the way your mother makes you feel. You take a breath. You feel the fear of the thing's loss; let it pass over you. Then you let it go. It doesn't always work.

She remembers, most days, to be patient. With her students, she's amazed at how much flustered anxiety, how much complaining she can bear. Now that she's at the front of the room, leading the chant and lighting the candles, she can see how funny she must have looked in the early days, meditating with her eyes squeezed shut, the effort nakedly on her face. They're both earnest and cantankerous sometimes, her students: they come to her with questions that they've looked up on the Internet; they challenge every point of doctrine that doesn't make sense to them. And they try so hard not to glance at their phones or out the window. They want the secret knowledge at the heart of all things. They want science and mystery together, ritual and magic and cold, hard answers.

They're here for her help, after all, even though she doesn't tell them she's just as hungry as they are. They demand excellence from her. But how can they possibly take her seriously, as she struggles to keep her sleeves away from the candle flame, as she trips over the pronunciation of "Tripitaka"? And she's supposed to be some kind of master.

All she can do is tell her story. So she does, in fragments. She's working on a book—*Letters to the Buddha* she's calling it—and there's the letter to her mother she finally sent, not asking for forgiveness or apology but saying *I need you to not worry about me.* And her mother's surprising reply, in fragments too, offering details she never had before about her childhood in Boston, her secret dream of being a nun. But falling in love intrudes with the best-laid plans, she said. And then you have a family, and when things fall apart, you have someone to pray for. You want them to be safe and you want them to be happy, but safe more than happy if you must choose.

She can see, in what's written and unwritten, that her mother's faith has kept her alive. In that, they are very similar.

And every day there's the challenge of the house, of helping Sean sort and let go of things. He's selling his family's pieces one by one so that they'll have room for their own lives; every day is a difficult decision. They'll fight bitterly over a rolltop desk or a rosewood chair until she hears herself, the threats and ultimatums she's this close to delivering. Then she laughs. Sean does, too. They touch, sheepishly, and move on.

Sean has cleared a room for her, and she keeps nothing in it. It lets her breathe. Every now and then, she goes in and closes the door and thinks for a while about the rooms of her memory, places she's left that she can't reenter. When the Buddha attained enlightenment, it is said, he saw all his past lives, and relived them simultaneously. How painful that must have been, to live and die again and again. When her own meditation is right, she glides into some kind of no-time, when she is seventeen and thirty-two at once. She's standing outside her childhood home. Her mother is in there; and her father, too, and Paul. She can hear the sound of their lives: dishes clinking in the sink, voices muted and friendly, rich with sorrow, reproach, all the textures and tones of love. She could join them or she could leave, but always she stands there for a while, feeling the cold earth under her boots.

Sean is reroofing the barn on weekends. When she's sweeping the corners of their apple-scented dust, and he's on a ladder somewhere, she stops and says to herself: There. There it is. There's this moment, and then the next, happiness within it; and then it's gone, and she is too, busy with the broom, preparing for their first winter.

ACKNOWLEDGMENTS

Thank you to my terrific agent Chris Clemans, my deeply insightful editor Jill Bialosky, and the rest of the wonderful team at Norton, for making this book a reality.

Thank you to Dad and Margot, for your unflagging love and support.

Thank you to Suze, for the gift of your friendship, and the inspiration of your life. The universe is energy dancing.

Thank you to my writing groupmates: Olivia Tandon, Sash Bischoff, and Daria Lavelle. You saw the earliest seeds of this story and told me to keep going.

Thank you to my teachers: Jeffrey Eugenides, Edmund White, Sheila Kohler, Darin Strauss, Zadie Smith, David Lipsky, and many others.

ACKNOWLEDGMENTS

Thank you to other readers and supporters along the way: John Meyer, Olivia Cerrone, and the many amazing writers at NYU.

Thank you to the *Worcester Review* and *A Bad Penny Review*, in which early excerpts of this book were published.

Thank you to the residencies that allowed me time to write: Ragdale, Vermont Studio Center, and Byrdcliffe. And thank you to the workshops that gave me the gumption to keep writing: Tin House, Bread Loaf, and Sewanee.

And thank you to Kamil, who knows all the many reasons.

———

Thank you to the authors and translators of the wonderful Buddhist literature I devoured, consulted, and cited.

The haiku:

Aston, William George, and Matsuo Basho. *A History of Japanese Literature.* Heinemann, 1899.

Basho, Matsuo. *Basho and His Interpreters: Selected Hokku with Commentary.* Translated by Makoto Ueda. Copyright © 1992 by the Board of Trustees of the Leland Stanford Jr. University. All rights reserved. Used by the permission of the publisher, Stanford University Press, sup.org.

Basho, Matsuo. *Japanese Haiku: Two Hundred Twenty Examples of Seventeen-Syllable Poems.* Translated by Peter Beilenson, published in *Japanese Haiku* © 1955 by Peter Pauper Press, Inc. www.peterpauper.com.

The parables, poems, and stories:

Burlingame, Eugene Watson, translator. *The Grateful Elephant: and Other Stories Translated from the Pali.* Yale University Press, 1923.

Dogen, and Kazuaki Tanahashi. *Enlightenment Unfolds: The Essential Teachings of Zen Master Dogen*. Shambhala, 2000.

Murcott, Susan, translator. Reprinted from *The First Buddhist Women: Translations and Commentary on the Therigatha* (1991) by Susan Murcott with permission of Parallax Press, Berkeley, California. www.parallax.com.

Nanámoli, Bhikkhu, translator. *The Life of the Buddha*. Buddhist Publication Society, 1992. Reprinted with permission.

Rogers, T. *Buddhaghosha's Parables Translated from Burmese by Captain T. Rogers*. With an Introduction, Containing Buddha's Dhammapada, or "Path of Virtue." Translated from Pali by F. Max Mueller. Trubner & Co., 1870.

Santideva. *A Guide to the Bodhisattva's Way of Life*. Translated by Stephen Batchelor. Library of Tibetan Works and Archives, 2011. Reprinted with permission.

Warren, Henry Clarke, translator. *Buddhism in Translations*. Harvard University, 1900.

Woodward, F. L., translator. *The Book of Kindred Sayings*. Pali Text Society, 1930. Reprinted with permission.

Zen funeral prayer from *The Zen of Living and Dying: A Practical and Spiritual Guide* by Philip Kapleau. Copyright © 1989, 1998 by the Rochester Zen Center. Reprinted by arrangement with The Permissions Company, Inc., on behalf of Shambhala Publications, Inc., Boulder, Colorado, www.shambhala.com.

The koans:

Koans and koan commentary from:
Secrets of the Blue Cliff Record: Zen Comments by Hakuin and Tenkei, translated by Thomas Cleary. Copyright © 2000 by Thomas Cleary. Reprinted by arrangement with The Permissions Company, Inc., on

behalf of Shambhala Publications Inc., Boulder, Colorado, www. shambhala.com.

Senzaki, Nyogen, and Paul Reps, translators. *101 Zen Stories*. David McKay Company, 1940.

The writings of contemporary Buddhist thinkers:

Aitken, Robert. *Original Dwelling Place: Zen Buddhist Essays*. Copyright © 1997 by Robert Aitken. Reprinted by permission of Counterpoint Press.

Cook, Francis H. *Hua-Yen Buddhism: The Jewel Net of Indra*. Pennsylvania State University Press, 1977.

Peter Matthiessen quotation from *Nine-Headed Dragon River: Zen Journals 1969–1982*, by Peter Matthiessen. Copyright © 1985 by Zen Community of New York. Reprinted by arrangement with The Permissions Company, Inc., on behalf of Shambhala Publications, Inc., Boulder, Colorado, www.shambhala.com.

An informative perspective I consulted on the closing of Boston's Catholic churches:

Seitz, John Chapin. *No Closure: Catholic Practice and Boston's Parish Shutdowns*. 2008. Harvard University, PhD dissertation.